RIDING WITH FORREST

RIDING *with* FORREST

The Memoir of
John Barrett, Escort Company,
Forrest's Cavalry, CSA, during the
War Between the States

(A NOVEL)

BY

L. E. DENTON

to

Stephanie and Christian

CHAPTER ONE

People have often asked me what it was like to fight under that great cavalry leader, Nathan Bedford Forrest, during our recent conflict. I have always replied that those were the most devastating, awe-inspiring, terrible yet wonderful years of my life. Hardships and fear were our constant companions, but faith and trust in our leader guided us to the end.

He was a strange man, Forrest. He could be gentle, kind and thoughtful to those who fought with him, yet turn into a raging demon when faced with the enemy. His rules were obeyed instantly by those of us who knew him, having witnessed severe punishments imposed for seemingly insignificant infractions. Although he lacked any military training, he knew almost by instinct that the men of a successful army must be ready to obey all orders. Common sense was his guide, and without it I fear we would have failed more times than we did.

Through hard fighting, bad weather, poor rations, endless marching and riding, we were always aware of his objectives. He wanted to win. His purpose was to drive the Yankees from our soil, no matter the cost. Because we knew his goals, and believed in them ourselves, we trusted his instincts. His air of confidence and optimism inspired us to continue on, even when the odds were against us. Somehow, we knew he could turn almost certain defeat into glorious victory!

Having recently heard of his passing away in Memphis, and growing weary of the incessant questions asked by my neighbors and friends, I have decided to put on paper, in my own modest way, a full account of my adventures with Forrest and his cavalry. Perhaps I can help clear up some of the misconceptions concerning his military career, and in this way repay some of the kindnesses shown me in the past.

My name is John Barrett. Born and raised in Athens, Tennessee, I am the only child of the late Dr. Robert Barrett and his wife, my mother Emily Barrett. It was expected of me to follow in my father's footsteps, and I resigned myself at an early age to enter into the medical profession.

My father had been born and raised in Athens, but orphaned at an early age. Raised by distant relatives, he had worked hard and long to fulfill what he believed to be his destiny – to become a doctor. He trained in his 20's with old Dr. Reynolds before he passed away, and learned the rudiments of his trade from him.

Driven by his desire to minister to the sick, he spent his early youth entirely ensconced in his future life's work. He met my mother late in life, in Athens, where she had come from North Carolina to visit cousins. They shared a warm and happy relationship, even though it had come in their later years.

Although a sole offspring, I had a happy childhood. My mother – short and on the plump side, with wispy, graying hair and a fondness for keeping a tidy house despite a rambunctious son and a physician husband who used the front room for his office – was a gentle and kind influence. She saw to it that I took my studies at the day school seriously, and that I understood the niceties of civilized society. She wasn't above rapping my knuckles when I tried to sneak a slice of pie before it was time to eat. A quick smile after the punishment let me know I wouldn't be going to hell for it.

She saw to it that I attended church on Sundays. My father often missed services due to his profession, but she and I could be found every Sunday, sitting at our place near the middle of the congregation. She wasn't above pinching me when I became restless, and saw to it that I knew the basic tenets of our faith.

When I was 12 she became ill. Father said it was consumption, for which there was no cure. She slowly lost her plumpness and her joy in life. When I was 14 she passed away.

We had always hired old Ned, owned by Mrs. Willis down the street, to come by every morning to take care of our two horses, feed and tend to the chickens, split firewood and do other necessary chores. Mrs. Willis needed the extra income, since she was a widow and had the upkeep of old Ned and her own home on her hands. So father gladly paid her weekly for the use of her slave.

We called Ned old, but it wasn't because of his age, although I do believe he was in his early 40's when we first hired him. He was tall and gaunt, dark black, with a sadness in his eyes that belayed his always-quick “yes sir, no sir.” Where he had come from he had no idea. He had been sold several times through the years. He once told me he believed he had come from somewhere in Virginia, but he wasn't sure. He had a wife and two children at one time, but they had also been sold off. Where they were, he did not know. The sadness and loneliness in his eyes were there for a reason.

With mother's passing, father decided to hire Miss Mattie from another neighbor, Hiram Odom. He, too, needed the extra cash, as his penchant for gambling always kept him in financial difficulties.

Miss Mattie came in twice a week, on Tuesdays and Thursdays, to tidy the house, do the laundry, and cook for us. We called her "Miss" for a reason. She was not to be crossed. Although a slave, she knew that two lone men had no idea how to run and maintain a household, and she expected us to do our part in keeping up with the necessities of running the house. She didn't have the plumpness or kind eyes of my mother, but she knew the rules, and enforced them. No muddy shoes in the house. Do not sit on the furniture with dirty clothes. The small parlor in the front of the house, next to father's office, was for company, not carousing. Washing up before meals was expected and enforced. We both followed the rules while she was there. In all honesty, we sorely missed the feminine aspect of home life after my mother's passing.

The railroad had come through Athens in the early 1850's, and with it more prosperity for our little town. It also brought new people and new ideas, neither of which were always welcomed by the staid old-timers.

Secession became a hot topic down at the town square, and among the political speakers brought in to berate the townsfolk, either for or against. We even had Senator Andrew Johnson, past governor of the state, come and say his piece. He argued for staying with the Union, and coming to some sort of agreement with our Northern neighbors. Booed and cheered at the same time, his appearance highlighted the deep divide over the issue in our part of the state.

Unlike many parts of the South, slavery wasn't as common here in the eastern portion of Tennessee. The land was hilly, rocky and heavily wooded, making large plantations impractical. Small dirt farms were the general rule, and most of those could be worked easily by owners and their families. Other than house slaves, owned by the more well-to-do who lived in town, few people could afford to buy or maintain slaves.

As the war drew closer, tensions among the townspeople of Athens increased. Friends of long standing distanced themselves, and even family members cut ties.

Father, busy with his practice, began to see a drop in business. He was not a political person. However, he always maintained that slavery had its uses, and he didn't see how chucking the whole institution without plans to replace it was a good idea. He had no animosity for those who sided either way. He wanted to grieve for his wife and continue to minister to those who needed his services. If some refused his services over politics, in his mind they were free to do so.

At the outbreak of the war in the spring of 1861, I was a first year student, barely 17, at Cumberland College in Knoxville. Lukewarm in my studies, the chance to fight seemed a perfect escape from the dull routine of academic life. Young, foolish and spirited, war was a romantic adventure to me, a chance to show my bravery and courage, to win medals and perhaps ride in parades, to be kissed by pretty girls and to become a man in the eyes of the world. Everyone I knew believed the Yankees could never beat us.

I was not alone. Many other young men were afraid the war would be over before they could strike a blow against the foe, so they rushed home to join up with neighbors and friends in local companies. My father instructed me to stay put until the end of the school term. But luckily, in my eyes anyway, the school closed a week after the news of war. Feverishly, I straightened out my affairs and returned home as quickly as possible.

I soon realized, however, that my military career would have to be delayed.

My father's age was beginning to tell, and he was having trouble keeping up with both his medical practice and running the household without my assistance. I stayed put for the time being, helping him the best I could with his patients. I helped bandage wounds, administer concoctions to the sick, and helped Old Ned and Miss Mattie around the house. By the time my 18th birthday arrived in March of 1862, the war was in full swing.

My service in the war could be put off no longer. I was now of legal fighting age, and there was little to be done to keep me from doing my part. The South was now beginning to enforce conscription, and my father knew there was nothing more he could do to keep me from fighting for the Cause. I had my heart set on joining the cavalry, but the companies that had formed around Athens were long gone, off defending the South from the Yankee invaders in Virginia.

In May, I set off for Chattanooga with David Knox, a friend since childhood. Quiet and well mannered, David had been an important part of my early life. We both loved to hunt and ride, and had spent many happy hours following those pursuits in the thickly wooded hills around Athens. Because of our close friendship, we decided to join up together, and David had waited with patience while my father made up his mind for me to go.

We found Chattanooga bustling with all kinds of military activity. The streets were clogged with horses, ambulances, marching troops and a cacophony of sounds that went along with it. We wandered the busy streets until dark, then found a neatly run boarding house on the edge of town.

The next morning, bright and early, we started our search for a cavalry troop in need of new recruits. Diligently, we stopped at every headquarters we came upon, but all had reached their quotas. We were beginning to give up hope when we were directed to a dilapidated tent set up in a vacant lot between two buildings near the downtown section of Chattanooga.

Inside, we found Colonel Payton, commander of the Tennessee Fighting Grays. An old Mexican War veteran, he was very willing to accept our enlistments, and we gleefully signed up. Within two weeks we found ourselves heading west into Middle

Tennessee. Despite the forlorn appearance of our regiment as a whole, David and I were satisfied we would soon be thick into some real action. Low rations and no pay seemed a small price to pay to us. We were on the greatest adventure of our lives!

Within the coming months, the Yankees slowly gained a foothold in our state, and then took control over most of Tennessee. Our unit, the Fighting Grays, did little to impede their progress. Because we were an independent unit, we were unable to muster up enough men to accomplish anything of consequence. An occasional raid on a small outpost was all the action we saw in six months. We lost a few horses, and had a handful of men wounded, none seriously.

After about six months, Colonel Payton told us that he was going to transfer to the Quartermasters Department in Atlanta, so that we could either go home and wait for conscription or feel free to enlist in another unit. David and I decided to strike out on our own, hoping to find an outfit with a little more gumption. We headed north, in the direction of Murfreesboro.

It had turned bitter cold, even though November had only begun. The trees had lost their leaves, and they lay crumpled brown, yellow and orange across the landscape. Our horse's hooves crunched the half-frozen ground on the roads. We passed small cabins and houses along the way, most with a small, thin plume of smoke emitting from their single chimneys, but saw no one. After two days' ride, we reached our destination. Our spirits rose as we sighted a large encampment on the edge of town. We looked at each other and grinned.

"Ho, David, I think we've hit it! There must be hundreds of men here!" I laughed and goaded Goldie, my horse, into a trot, as we drew close. At that moment, a tall, grizzled man with a long beard and an unmistakable limp jumped into the road, not five feet in front of me. As Goldie shied and then stopped, I jumped down and started a vigorous protest, only to be halted in mid-sentence.

"Hold on now, boy. I wouldn't start sompthin' I couldn't stop if'n I was you. If'n ya wasn't in such a dang fool hurry . . ."

"Listen, old man, my friend and I have got more important things to do than stand around and listen to you. Now, get out of the way before I'm forced to remove you myself."

Cackling, he replied, "A real hothead, ain't ya? Don't worry, boy, I'm movin'."

Remounting, I asked arrogantly, "By the way, we want to enlist. Can you direct us to the proper channels?"

"Maybe, maybe not." Squinting, he continued, "Ya lookin' for infantry, cavalry, er what?"

"We've got horses, so we want cavalry."

"Had some experience, have ya?"

"A little. My friend and I have been riding with Colonel Payton of the Tennessee Fighting Grays for the past six months. We're interested in joining a real fighting unit, though. No more wandering around looking for action for us."

He grinned and said, "Well, now, that's mighty interestin'." He looked us over. "Ya'll been real lucky today, boys. I think I done figgered out the perfec' place fer ya."

As he motioned for us to follow we dismounted, and leading our horses we obeyed. We made our way through and around the scattered tents and campfires, and after some minutes found ourselves facing a large tent slightly separated from the others. The old man stopped.

"Well, fellas, here it is." Loudly clearing his throat, he spoke up, "Sir, some fellas out here to see ya."

The flap of the tent opened. Out stepped a tall, lanky man who looked to be in his early 40's, with salt and pepper hair paired with a short, black beard and mustache. He had twinkly gray eyes and was meticulously dressed in a plain gray uniform. No insignia of any kind adorned it, but he had an air about him that bespoke a man used to having his orders followed. He looked us over sharply, then welcomed us into his tent with a wave of his hand.

"What have we got here, Josh?" His voice was soft and resonant, with a twang that told of backwoods origins.

"Sir, I found these two younguns on the edge of town. Say they want ta jine up. They look ta be in good health, and seein's how the escort company's a mite short, and they have their own horses, I thought I'd bring um here."

Turning to us, the tall man said, "What makes you think you can qualify for a cavalry unit?"

Speaking for us both I replied, "We can ride and shoot, sir, and are not unfamiliar with military matters. Our enlistments with the Tennessee Fighting Grays recently expired, and we came to Murfreesboro hoping to associate with a more, um, a more spirited unit."

Laughing, the man said, "Well, you've come to the right place." He paused, looked from one to the other of us, and continued.

"Your names?"

"I'm John Barrett. This is my friend, David Knox, both of Athens, Tennessee."

"Yes, I think you'll do. I reckon you have what we're looking for."

He turned and said, "Josh, take 'em over to the quartermaster and get them some rations. Set 'em up in camp and fill them in on our rules and regulations. Someone'll be over later with the paperwork."

David and I saluted and followed Josh back through the tent flaps. We untethered our horses, then asked our guide about the rather handsome man in the tent.

"Boys, you jist jined up with the best cavalryman in the whole gol'durned war!"

"Oh, and who is that?"

"Why, Bedford Forrest, ya dang fool. What's wrong, ain'tcha never heerd of him?"

"Of course we have! Wasn't he at Ft. Donelson?"

"Yup. Him and me too."

Josh took us to his own mess and introduced us around. After taking us to the quartermaster's, he drew us aside.

"The Genrul asked me ta fill ya in, so I guess I better. The Genrul knows ya both got good horses, or I wouldn't a brung ya. An ya' got yer own guns and purty good clothes. That's what he meant when he said ya had what we wuz lookin' fer.

"Things round here are run purty tight, I don't mind tellin' ya. Number one rule – take care of yer horse. The Genrul don't look kindly on anyone found mistreatin' his critter. Number two – don't never disobey orders, leastwise on purpose. If ya kin foller these two rules, you got this war licked." Squatting down, he continued: "You boys is now part of

Forrest's escort. Meanin' you ain't in a reg'lar outfit. We ride and fight with the Genrul, and no one else. There's ’bout seventy of us now, but don't let numbers fool ya – we kind do anythin' we have ta.

“By rights I ain't really nothin'. I don't hold no rank er nothin'. But I been with Forrest since the beginnin' – jined up with the Kelly Troopers back in '61, an' been with the escort nigh on that long.” Proudly, he stood up. “I ain't as young as you boys, but I got a big chunk a' fightin' behind me, an' I aim ta keep on as long as I'm able. Now, if you got any questions, I'll help if I kin.”

“I gather you have a high opinion of General Forrest.”

“High opinion? By God, where you been?” His face reddened as he turned his head and spat. His voice rose as he sputtered, “Boy, if it hadn't a been fer the Genrul, my ol' bones woulda been rottin' in a prison camp up North, after Donelson. Since, he's got us outta more snake pits than I kin count.” Waving his arm behind him he said, “You think these tents are Confedrut issue? We took ’em from the Yanks at this here town, along with 1,200 prisoners. And don’t dare get me on Shiloh. High opinion? You bet! He's the bravest, smartest, orneriest man this side a' Virginia!” Indignantly, he turned on his heel and left us.

By nightfall, we had settled our belongings into camp, and decided to take a look around. We wandered through many groups of men huddled around their campfires, and heard many astounding stories about the man who was now our leader. Midnight dashes against a surprised enemy, unknowing Yankees easily bluffed out of safe and secure positions, and wild charges led by a man waving a sword and hollering in excitement.

Contented, we returned to our tent and slept.

We learned that Forrest and his cavalry were in the middle of a well deserved rest, mainly devoted to training new recruits, but it was rumored we would be moving out soon. In anticipation, David and I spent the morning writing to our families, letting them know our circumstances.

We also spent time furtively eyeing our messmates, knowing they would soon share a large part of our daily lives. There were six of us – Josh, of course, and a short sturdy fellow from northern Alabama named Monroe Simpson; Bill Anderson from McMinnville, apparently of a good family; and Jim Wright, a rather quiet, nondescript fellow from Chattanooga.

We readied our mounts for the action we were sure would soon follow. Although kept in a common corral, our horses and their upkeep were our own responsibility.

As I brushed and tended to Goldie, I recalled the day father had given him to me – my 16th birthday. He was a roan, coated in a mixture of brown and gray, with a dark brown tail and mane. I named him Goldie, because when the sun shone just right you could see some golden flecks in his coat. He was a beautiful animal, I must say. Only a year and a half when I got him, I had spent many hours getting him broken into my way of doing things. He had a stubborn streak, no doubt, but he was smart and strong, and had been a benefit to me already while we were with Colonel Drayton.

Our supper that evening was interrupted by the news that we were being moved to Lavergne, a small town southeast of Nashville. Josh told us General Breckinridge had arrived in Murfreesboro and assumed command, and had ordered Forrest to watch Nashville from Lavergne and harass the Yankees stationed there whenever possible.

As Forrest's escort company, we were assigned space near the General's own tent when we set up our new camp. During the next few days, couriers and staff members visited his tent at all hours of the day and night. Privately, David and I wondered what was afoot. We finally approached Josh one evening after supper.

"Say, old man, we have a question for you."

Josh settled himself against the trunk of a small tree near the fire, spat, and said, "Yeah?"

"We couldn't help but notice all the activity around the General's tent these last few days, and we were hoping you could enlighten us."

"Well, boy, that's simple. We been sendin' out scouts 'n whatnot to keep an eye on them damn Yankees in Nashville." Grinning, he added, "An' been foraging fer the food that's been fillin' yer bellies, too."

"Oh."

"An' if you wasn't so dad-blamed green, you'd a know'd it. I'm beginnin' to wonder if I was wrong in recommendin' you to the Genrul."

Throwing my chest out in indignation I said, "I resent that."

Squinting up at me, "Guess we'll find out soon 'nough."

"Do you know something?"

Turning scornful eyes at me, he said, "Course I do."

"What?"

Don't git all riled up now, son," he replied calmly. "I jist know the Genrul's been itchin' to get on with it. An' since there's lots a Confedruts in these parts, round six thousand I heerd, countin' infantry, he's got a notion to clean them Yanks outta Nashville. Fact is, he's done asked Genrul Breckinridge for the go-ahead."

"How do you know all this, Josh?" I asked.

"It ain't hard ta figger these things out." He scratched his head under his forage cap and continued, "Besides, me and the Genrul's old friends."

We left Josh at the tree and moved closer to the fire. As the evening darkness got blacker and the moon came out, we quietly discussed our hopes of success, and of adventure.

Josh woke us up early the next morning and told us to gather our gear and get our mounts. We were to report to the north end of camp ready to ride. In great excitement David and I did as we were told, and arrived to find the rest of the escort gathered in the center of a milling mass of horses and men. Forcing our way through to Josh's side, our eyes fell upon the General himself.

The bugler was ordered to blow assembly. While the troops mounted and got into position, Josh motioned us to our places behind the General, where the escort company formed itself into three uniform lines. Riding forward a few paces, Forrest turned and addressed us.

Proudly, in lofty tones, he explained the purpose of the coming operation and its importance to the Confederacy. Recapturing Nashville would strike a severe blow to the Yankees, and uplift the spirits of the Southern people. He expressed his hopes for our success, and asked that all bow their heads while the chaplain offered a prayer.

I bowed my head as the chaplain rode to the General's side. After a short prayer for victory over the invaders of our homeland, the bugler blew advance, and in orderly fashion we headed north on the road to Nashville, the escort company with Forrest at its head in the lead.

We had not gone very far before we met up with General Hanson and his infantry, about 3,000 strong. Joining together for a brief conference, the generals ordered us to separate and advance up the four main turnpikes to the capital.

Our spirits high, the noise and orderly confusion of the march seemed amplified to us. This was war, and David and I were enjoying ourselves to the fullest. Josh and the others in our company seemed quiet and taciturn, but we could hardly contain our excitement. Our scouts drove the Yankee pickets back in the direction of Nashville, and by nightfall we were within six miles of our objective.

We bivouacked, and as we were finishing up our skimpy meal of beans and hardtack, we received a visit from the General. As he approached, David and I jumped up and saluted. Smiling, he said, “Don't be so formal, boys. You'll have to get used to me snooping around. I don't expect a salute every time you see me.” He hunched down near the fire, rubbing his hands over it.

“Starting to get cold, boys.”

“Yeah, Genrul, but we're expectin' to warm things up some tomorrow.”

Laughing, he said, “I expect you will, Josh. I just thought I would come by to tell you we plan to launch our attack at sunrise.” David and I exchanged grinning glances as he continued. “I know we can whip these Yankees, men. According to our scouts, they're in a weak position and have only half our men and guns. If we strike hard and fast, we can run them out with nary a loss to our own selves. I need your all in the fight tomorrow.”

“You have that, General, just like always,” spoke up Bill Anderson.

“Good.” Rising, Forrest said, “Get a good nights' sleep. You'll need it.” We watched him as he made his way to the next campfire.

“Well, I don't know about the rest of you, but tomorrow is going to be a big day for me,” I said confidently.

"Spoken like a true greenhorn, Barrett." Yawning, Monroe Simpson added, "Tomorrow is just another day and another fight."

"Maybe to you. But to me, it's a chance to prove myself."

"Ha!" spoke up Josh. "Stayin' at home, raisin' a fam'ly, workin' yer land – that's the only way to prove yerself. This here's jist a way to get kilt."

For a moment, the only sounds were the crackling fire and the wind whistling through the hardwoods. Six thoughtful faces, eerie in the flickering campfire light, each belonging to a man thinking of home and family and what lay ahead for him. One by one, without further conversation, we made our way to our tents.

I was awakened before daybreak by a familiar voice bellowing and cussing outside my tent. Hurriedly getting dressed, I rushed outside in time to see Josh heaving our mess kettle into the woods nearby.

"Next to Abe Lincoln, I b'lieve Braxton Bragg is the most ign'rant sonuvabitch east a' the Mississippi!" he screamed at me.

"Calm down, Josh, and tell us what's happened," I said as the others appeared, disheveled and as sleepy as I.

"I'll tell ya what's happened! That dang fool Bragg's called off the whole shebang, that's what's happened!"

Almost in unison we shouted, "What!?"

"You heerd me! Called it off! After me 'n the Genrul's got the whole thing worked out, an' everythin' runnin' so smooth. We coulda' had Nashville in our hip pockets come noon today!" With that, he stomped off in the direction of the other tents, apparently with the intention of spreading the news.

We returned to ours, but instead of sleeping, I spent the next two hours deep in thought. It seemed to me that the operation planned against Nashville had every chance of succeeding. Superior forces against an inadequate defense seemed a golden opportunity to strike a successful blow at the Yanks. The recapture of Nashville would be a huge victory, and not just in the military sense. It could help to lift the morale of the entire Confederacy. Why were we in this war, if not to drive the Yankees out of our country and keep their meddling hands out of our affairs?

As I rose from my pallet at daybreak, I shrugged off my questions. After all, I wasn't a general. If Bragg had called off the strike, he must have had a good reason to do so. He was the commanding general of all the forces in our area, and he hadn't reached such a position without knowing what he was doing. Or so I thought at the time.

Smelling coffee on the brew, I went outside. Josh was sitting at the fire, a cup in his hand. As I poured myself some from the mess kettle, he remarked, "Shore is nice a' them Yanks to pervide us with this here coffee. Better drink up – can't never tell when you'll taste it agin."

Morning reveille sounded, and we were soon joined by our other messmates. Before long, Lieutenant Nathan Boone of the escort company came by and told us to saddle up and get ready to move out. Grumpily, Josh asked him what for. Boone told him to keep his mouth shut and do as he was told.

Within 30 minutes we had broken camp and joined the rest of the escort. We were told that we would head west and meet with Colonel Dibrell and the Eighth Tennessee Cavalry, who had run into a scrap with the enemy.

"Well, perhaps today won't be a total loss. We may get a chance to face the Yanks yet!" I said brightly. My only reply was a look of scornful disapproval from Josh.

Riding hard, we arrived just as the Eighth Tennessee had finished chasing off a small Yankee cavalry force. While Forrest, Dibrell and their staffs held a conference, Josh, David and I held one of our own.

"I really don't understand why we're heading back to Lavergne," David said.

"Simple, boy. Bragg's ordered us back, and the Genrul always follows orders. He's a real soldier, the Genrul is. Jist cuz Bragg's doin' sompthin' stupid don't make it right fer him ta do the same thing by disobeyin'." Leaning over his saddle, Josh spat.

"Seems to me, though, that Bragg is making a mistake," I opined.

"Let me tell ya sompthin', Barrett. Jist cuz a man got hisself made a genrul don't mean he's got good sense. Me and the Genrul's been fightin' lots a folks besides Yankees ever since Fort Donelson. Some a' these high and mighty officers should a jined a ladies sewin' circle 'stead a' the army. They prob'ly know a dang sight more about sewin' than they do fightin."

As we pondered this, the bugler blew to mount up. Orders were passed around. We were to ride west and help out Colonel Starnes and the Fourth Tennessee, who had run into a strong body of Yanks. Riding hard, we reached the Franklin road in a short time, but before we could get more than warmed up, the enemy turned tail and headed back to Nashville.

Cheered by this brief encounter, we confidently followed our General back to Lavergne.

CHAPTER TWO

We were stationed at Lavergne for almost a month. Bored and restless, the General did his best to keep us occupied by alternating forage and picket duties among us. He also kept the scouts busy watching the Yanks in Nashville, monitoring their movements.

The confusion of real army life (our stint with the Fighting Grays didn't really count) began to clear up for us at Lavergne. The command under General Forrest at the time consisted of three cavalry regiments – the Fourth Tennessee under Colonel Starnes, the Eighth Tennessee under Colonel Dibrell, and the Ninth Tennessee under Colonel Biffle. We were ably supported by Freeman's

Battery of artillery. We learned to distinguish one from the other and gained some understanding of the chain of command.

The escort received its orders from several different sources – from the General himself, one of his immediate staff, or Captain Montgomery Little. But we had little doubt that Forrest was in complete control of our every movement.

One thing I can say for the General, he never played favorites. We had been with him some time before we found out one of his aides was his own son. Willie Forrest had joined the Confederate Army with the general at the tender age of fifteen. He was an unassuming, gentle young man who had great respect for his father.

The general's brother Bill was a captain of scouts. His brother Jesse would eventually become a colonel in charge of a regiment, and Jeffrey, his youngest brother, was also a leader of some worth. He had two brothers missing from his command – his eldest, John, had become disabled during the Mexican War, and Aaron, who commanded an independent regiment somewhere in the west. All in all, they were a fiercely competent group of men who fought hard and well.

Our confidence in Forrest grew during this time. He insisted on directing every operation himself, even forage duty – he had a remarkable ability to remember names, and personally picked out the men he wanted for each operation. Every detail fell under his scrutiny. He continually checked the condition of the horses, their harness, the blacksmithing supplies, the forage, the rations, the ammunition, the men, and most of all, the enemy. If he saw a horse in poor condition, he made sure the owner knew of it, and very often suggested a remedy. If he noticed a man in glum spirits, he did his best to pick them up, either by keeping him busy or by a kind word. He spent hours around the campfires of his men, talking about the Confederacy and his hopes and dreams for the future. David and I soon realized why Josh held him in such high regard.

As the month of November progressed and the weather grew colder, the military situation of the South worsened. Bragg had fought a major battle at Perryville, Kentucky, but was forced to withdraw from the state. We heard that out east Lee was forced to retreat likewise from Maryland. Bragg set up his headquarters at Murfreesboro, and one of his first directives was to replace Forrest as chief of cavalry with General Wheeler. He took away our trained regiments and assigned us a passel of new recruits. Then he ordered us to Columbia on the Duck River, to prepare for an expedition into West Tennessee, by then safely in Yankee hands.

"Well, at least the durn fool had enough sense ta give us a whole brigade ta work with," Josh said as we rode toward Columbia. Even if they were green, half-armed and hardly knew which way to mount a horse.

We all were upset at the General's demotion, but Josh took the news harder than the rest of us. Since he had ridden with Forrest for quite some time, and knew his abilities, he was sure his replacement could never match his skill or daring. Wheeler's only quality, he said, was that he had graduated from West Point, same as Bragg, while Forrest had barely any schooling at all.

In those days neither David nor I had any interest in military politics, so we could shrug off the implications of Forrest's demotion without too much trouble. We were in the war to fight and have a good time, not to worry about the vagaries of high command.

Our purpose in West Tennessee was to create a diversion in the rear of U.S. Grant's army, which had gone south into Mississippi, and wreak havoc on his communications. We fought three hard engagements, captured eighteen or twenty stockades, destroyed the Mobile and Ohio Railroad to such a degree that is was useless for the rest of the war, and managed to return to middle Tennessee stronger in numbers. We stayed for almost a month, when we were forced to retire due to the enemy's numerical superiority.

Fear overwhelmed me at the beginning of the campaign. Somehow, I kept myself from turning tail and running. David was there with me during our first big fights, at Lexington and Trenton, and I felt the need to prove myself to Josh. He watched us with contempt as we fumbled with our rifles during our first few engagements, and those cool blue eyes of his prompted me to act with more bravado than I actually possessed. And if I had any doubts as to what was expected of me, I had only to watch our leader.

The General's behavior during battle could only be described as magnificent. Standing tall in his stirrups, he led his dismounted men in charge after charge. His normally soft, resonant voice took on a metallic edge and could be heard above the booming of cannon. His normal complexion turned crimson, and his eyes lost their twinkle and became glaring and bloodshot. Instead of being polite and thoughtful, he was demanding and almost ruthless. The purpose of war drove him, but the pressure never clouded his mind or perceptions. Lightning quick orders were issued whenever necessary, and woe to the man who delayed in carrying them out! In the instant of battle, his personality underwent a total transformation.

While we rampaged through the western part of our state, the somber reality of the destruction wrought by war was reflected in the faces of the men in our midst from that area. At first, there were looks of disbelief, which soon changed to anger and bitterness. Stories of Yankee atrocities, whether true or not, were spreading across the countryside, brought to us by the scouts Forrest sent out and the new recruits we picked up. These stories brought a murderous intensity to our fighting whenever we met the enemy.

Under the General's leadership we were able to trounce every Yankee detachment or garrison we encountered, although there was one close call near the end. Just before we were ready to end our expedition we met an enemy brigade at a place called Parker's Crossroads on the way to the river. We took our time, because by now we had captured some cannon to add to Captain Freeman's battery, so for once we had more artillery

than the Yankees. For a few hours our gunners just blasted away at the them, silencing their own guns and ripping holes through their infantry line. All the bluecoats could do was try to charge our artillery positions, at which point our infantry took part, mowing them down on the slope.

The enemy started showing white flags and were teetering toward surrender when suddenly we heard shots behind us. Another Yankee brigade had snuck up on us from the rear, so we were now caught between two fires.

The General was as cool in a fight as any man who lived. He gathered up the escort and immediately launched an attack on the newcomers, driving back their advance. Then he issued a series of orders in every direction to guide us out of the closing jaws. Not that those jaws were closing very fast, in my view. The first Yankee brigade had been demoralized, while the second seemed wary of us.

We did lose a group of horse-holders and some wagons in the melee, but brought out just as many prisoners and captured wagons from that same day's work.

Soon we were re-crossing the river, which was a spectacular sight to see. Torches and bonfires lit the herds of horses and cattle, boats with men, rafts with wagons, and ferries with guns, all strung or guided with ropes under a threatening sky. Throughout that night the General went back and forth across the river, attending to every detail he could find.

Although our campaign was successful, my image of war was slightly tarnished after our first major campaign with Forrest. Weariness, cold, hunger and fear are integral parts of war, ones I had not been fully aware of. Low rations and lack of sleep had taken their toll on all of us, and we were ready for a rest by the time we made it back to middle Tennessee. Despite the fact that we were physically worn out, however, David and I were more sure than ever that the Cause we fought for was just, after viewing the willful destruction we witnessed in western Tennessee.

Wearily, we turned east and were temporarily stationed at Mt. Pleasant. We had barely arrived when we learned of the Battle of Stones River. It was the usual story, like Shiloh and Perryville, of the Confederates striking first and smashing in the Yankee line, but then the generals didn't know what to do with their initial success. Braxton Bragg and the Army of Tennessee had withdrawn to the south, even though the battle had ended up a draw. Nashville and Murfreesboro were lost to us, along with thousands of young men who had given their lives.

While our army settled into camp, we and half the escort rode with Forrest to Shelbyville to report to General Bragg. Cold and hungry from the long ride, we huddled around campfires while the generals conferred.

“What I wouldn't do for a nice chicken dinner right now.” Shivering, I pulled my now threadbare gray coat tighter around my throat and rubbed my hands together over the fire.

Snickering, Josh spoke up. “That's easy, boy. Jist go out an' find you some Yanks an' ask 'em real nice, an' maybe they'll share theirs with ya.”

“That's not very funny,” David said.

“No, it ain't. But that's 'bout the only way ta find any chicken dinners 'round here.”

When Forrest returned from his conference we rose and gathered up the horses. Four abreast, we moved west out of Shelbyville back to Mt. Pleasant.

As we rode, the General explained the new orders he had received. We were to return to Columbia and provide protection for Bragg's left flank, post pickets along the Harpeth River in the vicinity of Triune and Franklin, and harass the enemy wherever we could.

“If ya don't mind me sayin', sir, seems to me we could be keepin' busy doin' sompthin' a little more important,” spoke up Josh, who rode to the General's right.

Sternly, Forrest replied, “Josh, I don't like that tone of voice. You should know by now that all aspects of war are important. Just because we aren't facing the enemy in a major campaign doesn't mean our job is any less important. War requires the best of everyone involved, and if we expect to win this war we must give everything we have on every occasion."

"Yessir," Josh said humbly.

Riding on the General's left, I spoke up. "Sir, Josh didn't mean any disrespect."

Sighing, he replied, "I know, John. Sometimes it's hard to realize our purpose in this war. The frustration of waiting can get to all of us, if we let it. We have to remember that our independence should be uppermost in our minds."

"Yes sir," I replied.

"We have gone through all we have for two simple words – state's rights. The chance to live our lives as we choose, to make decisions necessary to cultivate our way of life without interference from those who cannot understand us or the things that are important to us. Slavery is an example of that issue."

He continued: "I remember when I was a boy, we had a neighbor who had two vicious dogs. My brothers and I used to ride by on horses, throwing rocks and yelling at those dogs. They would chase us, snapping and barking, but couldn't catch us because we were on horseback. Then one day I was by myself, and I rode by that farm on a horse that wasn't completely broken yet. When the dogs ran out at him, he bounded to one side and threw me off. I have never since felt such overwhelming terror as I did on that day. I was sure those two dogs would tear me to pieces. I jumped up and started to run. I looked behind me for the dogs, but they were nowhere to be found. Apparently, finding a boy right in their midst was too much for them. You see, they were frightened by the unexpected.

"I learned a lot from that incident, son. In a way, we're like the boy on the horse and the Yankees are the dogs. Although they are capable of destroying us, we also have an advantage. If we do what the Yankees least expect, we'll have a chance at victory. And with endurance, luck and the Lord's help, we can surprise them into giving up ground and leaving us be. That is, of course, if we don't turn tail and run without taking every advantage that comes our way."

Straightening, he smiled. "Well men, let's move up! We have a lot of ground to cover!"

We picked up our pace. Although Mt. Pleasant was thirty miles from Shelbyville, we arrived there late that evening, stopping only briefly to rest the horses. The General was very anxious, as Josh put it, "Ta git on with the war."

We spent the next day moving on to Columbia. Cold and damp, we were a scraggly lot. Although we had captured new horses and clothing in West Tennessee, the harsh winter weather had taken it's toll, and the people of Columbia looked at us with dismay. Unperturbed, Forrest directed us to set up camp on the outskirts of town while he re-acquainted himself with the lay of the land.

As we raised our tents, unsaddled and corralled our horses, and started the evening fires, the usual group of townspeople gathered close by. Old men and boys, with a sprinkling of women in patched and worn clothing stood in a group, watching us with curiosity. Trying not to be obvious, David and I couldn't help but notice the pretty young girls in the crowd. We smiled at each other when we noticed two in particular, standing together at the edge of the gathering. As we nonchalantly made our way toward them, they giggled and whispered back and forth.

With a surge of confidence I strode up to the taller of the two, and as I looked down into her large, soft, smiling brown eyes, the thumping of my heart increased. Smiling, I nervously rubbed my sweating hands against my worn jacket, above the navy sixes strapped around my waist.

“Hello, ma'am. Allow me to introduce myself. My name is John Barrett.” I swept off my forage cap and bowed.

Her smile widened as she replied, “Hello. I'm Clara Brown, and this is my sister, Eva.” She nodded in the direction of the young lady standing next to her. I bowed to her sister, but kept my eyes on Clara. As David and Eva began to talk, Clara and I moved a few steps away.

"I couldn't help but notice your interest in our camp, ma'am. I would be happy to answer any questions you may have."

"Well, Mr. Barrett, I would like to know why you are here."

"That's simple, ma'am. As you know, the Yanks have stationed themselves only thirty miles north, and we're here to keep an eye on them."

She started to laugh, and said, "That's amusing. When your army was first seen, we thought the Yankees were descending on us." Coyly blinking her lowered lashes, "Ya'll should trade in those blue coats most of you are wearing for some sturdy gray ones."

Enchanted by her coyness, I replied, "In this war, ma'am, we have to take what we can get. But I agree – we must have caused quite a stir when we first came into sight."

Josh stumped up to us and interrupted by saying, "You fellas best git back over here on the double, 'fore the Genrul sees ya." David and I hastily tipped our caps to the young ladies and followed Josh back to the half-assembled camp.

Forrest set us right to work observing the enemy and their movements. Large scouting parties were in and out of camp at all hours, always reporting to the General himself. David, Josh and I spent several days in close observance of the Yankees stationed in Franklin, along with ten other members of the escort. When we had anything to report, two of us would carry a message to Forrest, then return with instructions from the General.

Near dawn on one particularly cold, gray morning, we tethered our horses in a small but thick grove of trees two miles south of the enemy's main camp. We stealthily moved forward and posted ourselves behind the trees and bushes a few hundred yards from the main entrance and watched without interruption.

Hundreds of enemy tents neatly set in rows, with soldiers lounging about, repairing equipment or napping, didn't offer much to observe. After several hours, our cold limbs demanded movement, so we made our way to the rear. Gathering together, we discussed the situation.

“This shore is borin' work. Any a' you fellas got any ideas?” Josh asked.

“Not me,” said Monroe, as he scratched his unshaven face and leaned his squat body against a tree. The rest of us muttered in agreement.

Captain Little spoke up. “I have an idea. It could be dangerous, though.”

“Okay, Captin, let's hear it,” said Josh.

“It seems to me that we need to get into that Yankee camp over there. That would be the easiest way to hear of their plans.”

“How do we do that, sir?” I asked respectfully.

“Simple. One of us rides in and pretends to be a Yankee. Since quite a few of us are wearing uniforms we stole in West Tennessee, all we need to do is pick out someone who hasn't much of an accent – and who isn't afraid, of course.” Smiling around at us he continued: “Any volunteers?”

David spoke up. “I'll go, sir.”

Captain Little patted him on the shoulder and said gently, “I appreciate your offer, David, but you don't have the proper uniform, and I'm afraid no one else has one small enough to fit you. Besides, we need someone who can string their words together confidently.” Suddenly, he turned his piercing brown eyes to me. “How about you, Barrett? You don't have a blue coat, but you can trade with Josh here – you're both about the same size.”

“Dang it, Captin, I was plannin' on goin'!” whined Josh.

We all burst into quiet laughter as the Captain said, “That accent of yours wouldn’t fool their mules. I think Barrett's the man – he has the looks and the air we need. Now change coats."

Quickly, we made the exchange. I borrowed Monroe Simpson's blue forage cap and was ready to go. Captain Little told me to ride into the camp on the main road until I came to their headquarters. If anyone asked me questions, I was to tell them I'd been out on scouting duty. Once there, I must look busy and try to pick up any information I could. "And for God's sake, Barrett, look like you belong there," he growled.

"Yes, sir," I stammered out.

The others followed me as I went to get Goldie. Quickly mounting, I trotted off in a northerly direction. Coming through the woods, I crossed the clearing immediately in front of the camp and headed for the main entrance.

The town of Franklin is nested inside a u-shaped loop on the south side of the Harpeth River. Quiet, well-shaded streets lined with neat houses characterized the town before the war. Since then the Federal General Granger had built impressive breastworks and a fortification on a bluff at the north end of town. The majority of troops were stationed a short distance south of town, in the camp I was now entering.

I tried desperately to maintain a cool exterior, but my insides were all aquiver. Unable to control my thumping heart, I concentrated on keeping my back straight, my eyes forward, and a ready smile on my face. Casually glancing from left to right, I was greeted only with disinterested looks from the soldiers loitering about their tents and fires.

Breathing easier, I continued along the well-worn road through the camp until I came to a tent larger than the rest, with banners and the flag of the United States flying in front. Since there seemed to be more activity around this tent than any of the others, I quickly decided it must be headquarters. Dismounting, I tied Goldie's reins to one of the hitching posts in front.

Exuding a confidence I did not feel, I walked boldly to the front of the tent and posted myself at its entrance. Hoping to be mistaken for a sentry, I stood at attention. No one noticed me. The officers and men wandering about were wrapped up in their own thoughts and had no time to wonder about my presence there.

My eyes straight ahead, I kept my ears open to the conversations around me. Mostly gossip and small talk, I was beginning to think I was wasting my time. One officer complaining to another about his disappointment in not receiving a promotion was the closest thing to military information I heard the first 30 minutes I was there.

Just as I was about to leave, a conversation being held just inside the tent caught my attention. Apparently an officer had asked for a furlough, and by concentrating I could faintly hear the answer to his question.

"Major Abbot, I see no reason why you can't go home for a few weeks. I know you haven't been home since the war started. We have no major operations planned at present, so I suggest you leave at once." Laughing, the voice continued, "Give the wife and children my regards."

Exuberantly, another voice replied, "Yes, sir!" A tall man with a wide grin came out of the tent and hurried off.

Sighing my relief, I carefully looked around for any observers, and seeing none, I moved toward my horse. I made my way out of camp at a slow trot, then as soon as I reached the woods spurred Goldie to a gallop and soon rejoined my companions.

Jumping up when they saw me approach, my comrades eagerly bombarded me with questions as I dismounted. The Captain quieted them with a word, to give me a chance to catch my breath.

I gulped a few breaths in an effort to calm my shaking nerves. I moved to a fallen log, sat down, and told my story. Captain Little looked me over sharply as I relayed my information, and when I finished he smiled his approval.

"Good job, Barrett. Now tell me, you're sure they didn't mention any time limit?"

"I'm sure they didn't, sir."

"Okay. I guess the thing to do now is to get back to the General." Looking up at the sun, he went on, "It's about noon. If we ride hard we can be back in Columbia by midnight at the latest. Josh and Monroe, stay here. The rest of us will head back."

The long, vigorous ride back to camp had a calming effect on me, and by the time we arrived I was tired but still elated. My comrades threw me looks of respect along the way. They didn't know about the fear and panic that had possessed me while I was in the Yankee camp, which suited me just fine.

We took care of the horses while the Captain made his report. As soon as we had unsaddled and fed them, we went to our tents. "Maybe tomorrow I'll ask permission of the Captain for us to go into town and call on those pretty sisters we met the other day," I said to David. He smiled and said, "That would be great, John!"

The next morning dawned cold but clear, and as I gulped the bitter brew we made out of burnt corn and jokingly called coffee, the Captain appeared and told me the General wanted to see me. Hurriedly rising from my spot by the fire, I brushed and straightened my clothing and headed for his tent. The flaps were open and I could see Forrest inside, seated at his small desk and talking with Captain Anderson, his adjutant. Glancing over, he saw me at the opening and waved me inside.

As I entered his spartan quarters, I pulled off my cap and nervously twisted it in my hands. "You wanted to see me, sir?"

"Yes, I did, John. You know Captain Anderson, don't you?"

"Yes sir. Good morning, Captain."

Smiling, the major replied, "Good morning, Private."

The General reached over and slapped me on the shoulder, and the twinkle in his eye brightened. "No need to be nervous, son. I just wanted to offer my congratulations on your caper yesterday. It took great courage to pull that off, John."

I could feel myself reddening as a smile spread across my face. "Thank you, sir."

"Now, I need some information from you." He turned in his seat to face me directly. He and the Captain watched me closely as he went on. "How many men would you say were in that camp?"

"I can't say for sure, sir. Several thousand, I think."

"Did you notice any unusual activity at all?"

“No, sir,” I replied. “The men seemed very unconcerned and carefree. Most of them were just sitting around, minding their own business.”

“Did you see any cannon or heavy artillery?'

“No, sir.”

“Did you notice their horses or their condition?”

“No, sir. They must have had them in a different area of the camp.”

“How about the men? Did they seem well-dressed and fed?”

Bewildered, I said, “I don't know, sir. I guess so.”

“I see.” Glancing at the Captain, his face took on a sterner look. He stood and continued in a serious tone. “John, I have a favor to ask of you. The next time you have such an opportunity, pay attention to every detail. I don't mean to belittle your accomplishment, but you could have brought me much more information than you did. You are an intelligent young man, and I know next time you'll do better.”

Somewhat crestfallen, I said, “Yes, sir. Sorry, sir.”

“Don't be, John!” Smiling, his eyes lit up. “You're new at the game, that's all. I have every confidence that, in time, you'll make an excellent soldier.”

“Thank you, sir.”

“You may go now, John.”

I saluted and left the tent. I put my cap back on and slowly, thoughtfully returned to the fire in front of my own quarters. The General had been right, of course. I had spent too much time in that camp worrying about my own skin, when I should have spent the time observing as much as I could. Strangely enough, instead of being resentful, the General's criticism only made me vow to do a better job next time, if there was one.

Later that day, I screwed up the courage to ask Captain Little if David and I could go into town that evening. He gave his permission after grinning and asking whether our interest in town had anything to do with the young ladies he had spied us talking to a few days before.

After receiving his permission, I excitedly found David and told him the good news. He said, "Great. But how are we going to find them? We don't know where they live!"

"Don't worry about that. You just leave it up to me."

After our rather lean supper – foraging and finding supplies for our force was getting more difficult – we went into town. The late afternoon sun shone coldly on the peaceful, tree-lined streets.

Columbia was laid out in neat, clearly marked squares. I must say it was more pleasing to the eye than most towns.

When we neared a general store, I decided to go inside to inquire if anyone had heard of Clara or Eva Brown. Once in, I walked straight up to the counter and asked the older gentleman who was straightening the shelves if he knew the young women we were seeking.

Cackling and scratching his head, he answered, "Shore I do. Their Daddy's the best lawyer in this here town. They live over on Elm Street."

I returned to the street, and after asking directions from a young boy dawdling along the roadside, David and I proceeded to Elm Street. Walking briskly, we managed to distinguish the Brown house from its neighbors by a small sign hanging from the porch with "William Brown, Attorney" printed on it. We went to the front door and knocked.

We were greeted by a tall, plainly dressed woman with intelligent brown eyes. Removing our worn caps, I introduced us and related the reason for our visit. Smiling graciously, she showed us into the parlor.

"I am Clara and Eva's mother. They told me about meeting you gentlemen the other day. Won't you please have a seat?"

"Thank you, ma'am. I know we haven't been properly introduced . . ."

"Young man, this is wartime," she said firmly. "In these times, we can't be expected to follow all the proprieties. With most of the young men off fighting the war, my girls don't have many chances to receive gentlemen callers. Besides, my husband is acquainted with General Forrest, and I know the General would not permit you to come calling unless he knew you to be gentlemen. Before I get the girls, please tell me a little about yourselves."

David shyly told her about his father, who was president of the bank back home, and his mother's volunteer work for the Confederacy, helping make bandages and other supplies that were sent to wherever the fighting was. She smiled her approval and turned her eyes to me. I quickly related my family's credentials, and when I finished she rose from her spot on the couch and summoned her daughters.

Nervously, we rose as the girls entered the room. Smiling and blushing, they seemed pleased to see us. The four of us sat down, Clara and I on the sofa, and David and Eva in two comfortable chairs opposite.

She was as pretty as I remembered. Brown, gentle eyes, like her mothers', looked at me innocently. Behind that, though, I could see strength and a strong resolve.

I learned many things about Clara that first evening. She was seventeen and a firm believer in the cause for which we fought. Her father was a major in the cavalry and was presently in Virginia, under the command of General Lee. She told me her father was the bravest, kindest man she had ever known.

"What about me?" I asked in mock dismay.

Giggling, "Now Mr. Barrett, I haven't known you long enough to make any kind of judgment about your character." Trying to be suave, I answered, "We'll have to see what we can do about that. Perhaps David and I will call again soon." Hastily, "That is, if it's okay with you, Miss Brown." When she smiled her assent, the nerves in my neck and face began to tingle.

At that moment, we were interrupted by Mrs. Brown, who entered the parlor and announced the hour. David and I rose from our seats.

"Thank you, ma'am. It's time to return to camp," I said. Clearing my throat, I asked Mrs. Brown if she would agree to our calling again in the near future.

"Yes, that would be fine." She showed us to the door, and warned us, "Keep your collars pulled up – the air has a hard bite to it this evening." Waving goodbye to the two faces peeking over her shoulders, we went down the steps and made our way back to camp. We were content.

CHAPTER THREE

The reality of war intruded before our aura of contentment could become more ingrained. We had been ordered by General Wheeler to proceed to the Cumberland River at once to do what we could to interrupt Yankee navigation on that waterway. Grudgingly, David and I packed our blankets and other necessaries. Leaving as we did, we were unable to send a message to the Brown house. Our next visit would have to be delayed. For how long, we had no idea.

The weather had turned to cold, wet and miserable. We deployed at Palmyra on the river but did nothing but watch the flow of freezing water, with no Union supply ships in sight. The General was astride his horse, a pair of navy sixes strapped to the outside of his rain slicker when Wheeler appeared. After the usual amenities, he told Forrest he believed the Yankees were aware of our plan and had halted all traffic on the river. He decided an attack on the enemy garrison at Dover, alongside the old Fort Donelson, would be more fruitful, and that we would proceed there immediately.

"General, I must advise against such a move. My men don't have enough ammunition for an attack on the fort. Perhaps we should postpone until we're better supplied," Forrest said respectfully but firmly.

"I must disagree, General," spoke Wheeler with equal determination. "We may be low on ammunition, but we have the element of surprise on our side. Mount up your men and let's move."

"Yes, sir." Turning to his staff, Forrest gave the necessary orders.

We moved west, the cold wind in our faces. The rain had turned to sleet and snow.

Josh rode next to me, a glum look on his face. Under normal circumstances I would have left him in peace, but I was in need of a distraction to help keep my mind off the bitter cold. Leaning over, I slapped him on the shoulder and said, "Why so solemn?"

"If that ain't a dang fool question, I don't know what is. Fer one thing, it's cold as hell. Fer another, I got a feelin' that we ain't about to make a very smart move." Grunting, he leaned over and spat.

"What do you mean?"

"In case you fergot, me an' the Genrul's already been in a fight up this way, an' I jist don't think this time's gonna be any different."

"Superstitious?"

" I shore as hell am. I can't fergit how them fools Pillow, Floyd an' Buckner almos' got us all captured at Donelson, an' I jist don't like goin' back there." He stopped talking and put his hands to his mouth to blow on his fingers in an effort to warm them.

"I've heard about that. What exactly happened?"

"It was shameful, that's what it was. We'd a been afightin' them Yanks for two days, an' that evenin' Genrul Floyd pulled us all off the field and back into the fort. The Yanks had been pushed back nearly a mile, an' all that was left was our campfires. By early evenin' the wind picked up an' made those fires start burnin' fierce. Those blockheads Floyd an' Pillow decided the Yanks had come back and taken over the field. Well, Forrest sent out his best scouts, includin' me, an' we see'd that the only Yanks round those fires was wounded from the fightin'. The Genrul, he told 'em they was getting all worked up over nothin', but they wouldn't listen. So to save their own skins, Floyd an' Pillow left poor ol' Genrul Buckner and his men there to surrender fer 'em, an' they hightailed it outta there."

"What happened to you and Forrest?"

"We wasn't about to surrender, not by a dang sight. The Genrul asked permission to fight his way out, an' they said okay. So when it was good and dark, we packed up an' left. There wasn't a Yank anywhere in sight, an' we left without losin' a man."

"Unbelievable."

"Yup, it shore is. And ta' think there's hunderds of Confedruts rottin' in jail jist 'cause them genruls was so blind they couldn't see the noses on their own faces." Shaking his head, he fell silent.

"I see now why you aren't particularly anxious to return. I wonder if Forrest is remembering the same thing you are." I glanced ahead at the tall back, stiff and straight, riding at the head of the column.

"Probly. But he ain't gonna let it get in the way a' his duty." A painful look flitted across his face as he rubbed his knee, and said, "I'll tell ya, this cold ain't doin' my game knee no good. A nice warm bed an' a shot a whiskey shore would make a feller feel better right 'bout now."

By noon, February 3rd, we had arrived in sight of the fort built around the town of Dover. It sat between two small creeks, running more west than south, that branched off the western bank of the Cumberland River. Small hills and gullies interspersed the landscape directly to the southwest, the area we would need to cross to capture the Yankee garrison inside. Although there were no trees or shrubs, we knew these hills and gullies would afford us good protection.

Wheeler ordered us to deploy to the right, with Wharton's Brigade at the center and left. Having heard of enemy reinforcements on the way from Fort Henry, he sent the Eighth Texas of Wharton's Brigade, a wild and woolly outfit of cowboys, on the road to detain them. A flag of truce was sent to the town almost immediately, demanding unconditional surrender. The terms were declined.

Despite the bitter cold, the idea of a forthcoming battle numbed us to the falling sleet and snow. Apparently, the situation had the same effect on the General. In constant motion, he checked his force at every point to make sure all were ready. The now-familiar look of determination was on his face, and no one dared disobey any order he gave.

Our artillery opened up, forcing their skirmishers stationed in the outbuildings to take cover behind the town's breastworks. We waited patiently for a general assault, but before the orders could come, Forrest's sharp eyes spied a movement by three or four enemy companies toward the river behind the town. Thinking they were attempting an escape, he ordered us to mount and charge.

We galloped forward, but as we approached we realized their true purpose. The enemy had no intention of abandoning the fort, but were attempting to reach a deep ravine beyond their position in order to prevent a flanking movement. They opened up on us and retreated back to the fort. Recklessly, we kept after them, hoping to capture them before they reached their breastworks.

As they made it over the embankment, the whole side of the fort opened up on us. Their artillery, loaded with grape and canister, had a devastating effect on us. At one moment we were riding fast and hard, the next we were stopped cold, our comrades' bodies littering the ground.

Mad confusion reigned. Man and beast cried out in anguish and terror. The sound of the enemy guns roared in our ears. The reek of blood, sweat and gunpowder filled our nostrils, and the sight of the battlefield, with the anguished bodies of our dead and dying comrades filled our eyes with horror and shock.

Suddenly, a cry was taken up. The General, our General, had been shot down in the fusillade. Without hesitating, to a man, we retreated.

The power of the enemy's artillery barrage had knocked me out of the saddle. I found Goldie's reigns and remounted, heading back with the others. Dazed and weary, I was gratified to see David had made it through the disastrous charge. As he galloped beside me, I could see my own panic and dismay mirrored in his eyes. What would we do now, without Forrest, and all the other comrades we had lost?

Captain Little was re-forming the escort when we reached our original line of battle. As he calmly passed through us, giving words of encouragement, my sense of stability returned. Josh was there. As I pushed my fear and panic to the back of my mind, a cheer arose from the men stationed in our front. Miraculously, the General had returned from the battlefield on foot. The word was passed around – only his horse had been shot. He soon found another mount and was riding among us again.

Looking exultant, Josh sputtered, “It'll take more than a few rounds a' grapeshot to git the Genrul! Yessirree!” Relief and gratitude swamped his scraggly face as he rode off to see for himself that his general was all right.

The battle was far from over. Forrest had us dismount, and while he rode at our head, the whole Confederate line attacked simultaneously. Despite all our efforts, we were unable to dislodge the enemy. Still dazed from our first encounter of the day, I am unable to recount with any accuracy our storming of the barricades. I do know we lost many good men that day, including Monroe Simpson, who, despite all his roughness was a good soldier.

By late afternoon, it was decided to give up the attack. We were almost out of ammunition, and Yankee reinforcements were fast approaching. Before leaving, we burned the supplies we had captured from the outbuildings but couldn't carry. The wounded were loaded into wagons, and our troops left in good order. David and Josh went with the main body of troops, but I was assigned to a detachment under Captain Anderson and Colonel Woodward, with orders to bring away the ordnance we had taken from the enemy.

As the sun descended, the cold became almost unbearable. Our frostbitten fingers fumbled as we loaded the ordnance into wagons. Rain and sleet fell steadily. We wrapped ourselves in the blankets we had captured that day. They weren't very warm, but they helped keep out the wet.

We left the battlefield with the sounds of bursting artillery shells in our ears. Several gunboats had come up the river and were firing at us, but the distance was too great for them to do any harm. Jeeringly, we made fun of their attempt to scare us away. In our hearts, though, there were feelings of disappointment, even outrage. The attempt to fight again at Fort Donelson had been foolish, and we knew it.

♦ ♦ ♦

I rode next to Captain Anderson on the way back. He was a pleasant sort of fellow, with a finely tuned sense of humor. Short and somewhat stout, his broad face always carried an affable look. I saw why the General usually kept him at his side. He was very orderly and efficient, working quickly and silently on the task at hand. He wasn't afraid of hard work, and pitched in without a word wherever necessary. Once finished, he would carelessly joke about the job just completed, as if war, and the dangers involved, were nothing to worry about.

The main body of troops bivouacked only four miles south of the battlefield. Nearly frozen by the time we arrived, my stiff legs could hardly disengage from the saddle. Limping, aching in every joint, I found David, arranged my pallet by the fire and fell into a deep, dark, dreamless sleep.

We returned to Columbia by a long tortuous march around Centerville, then across the Duck River. The Union cavalry was after us, and even captured our advance detachment, which had taken the wrong road and marched right into the enemy. By long, forced marches in the freezing cold, we finally reached camp on the 17th of February. High-spirited and self-assured when we left, we were quite the opposite on our return.

Forrest's spirit, however, had not wavered. He immediately asked permission to take a force north to Nashville to capture a large number of mules in the suburbs of that city. His scouts reported that the livestock was only guarded by one regiment, and he felt sure we could capture them. His request was denied.

Undaunted, he spent the next few weeks on discipline and drilling. He kept the escort busy on forage and picket duties, and sent scouting parties far and wide. These scouts reported that the Union force stationed at Franklin had received reinforcements. The General, always looking for an opportunity to strike a blow, suggested to Wheeler that an expedition be sent against them.

In between our duties, David and I spent a few idyllic evenings with Clara and Eva. I knew I was developing deep feelings for Clara. Humbly aware that the time was not right, I kept my feelings to myself and enjoyed her company whenever I was able.

We had lost 200 comrades during our attack at Dover. This sobering statistic forced me to accept the finality of war, and to think longingly of my home. I had not seen my father for almost a year, and had received only two letters from him in that time. I was coming to the realization that I might never see him again. During quiet moments in camp, happy memories of childhood would cloud my mind, often bringing tears to my eyes. My political convictions remained the same, but the consequences of those convictions were becoming clear. The thought of my own mortality had a very maturing effect on me.

By early March, it had become apparent the enemy was preparing to make a move south in our direction. Union construction parties were sent out from Franklin to repair bridges, roads and telegraph lines. Major General Van Dorn, who was now commander of our corps, organized a force consisting of five brigades, including ours, and launched it against the enemy.

Red Jackson's brigade had been sent in advance, and by the time we reached Thompson's Station they had already engaged a large Yankee column. After they were forced to retire because of overwhelming numbers, we joined them in camp that evening.

The next morning, Van Dorn formed us into battle line, with our brigade to the right, unmounted. The thought of vengeance was sweet as we waited impatiently for the battle to commence. The General nervously rode back and forth in front of us, checking a rifle here, an artillery piece there.

Excitedly, I rested my rifle on the fence in front of me and said, "I hope those Yanks are ready for a rough time. From the look in his eye, I'd say the General's ready to give them hell."

David smiled. "He didn't take kindly to their treatment of us at Dover."

"You can say that again. He looks ready to eat nails."

As if in slow motion, the Yankees advanced on us. An artillery battle commenced as the Yankee cavalry charged our position on the left. In anticipation of a movement to our front, Forrest sent two regiments at double quick to a cedar-covered knoll on our immediate right, where they drove off a force of dismounted troopers and effectively protected us from any other forward movements. He then ordered a general advance and forced the Union cavalry in our front to take refuge behind the infantry at its back. Seeing an opportunity, Forrest hurried Freeman's battery of artillery far in front, raking the Union flank and forcing their cavalry and artillery to retire.

By this time, we were a full half-mile in front of the main Confederate line. We flanked the Yankee position to cut off their line of retreat as the two lines of battle locked horns. We swiftly gained their rear and countered a Federal charge, their last hope, with one of our own. The enemy gave way, and right after that practically the whole Yankee force surrendered.

Elated, we watched hundreds of bluecoats lay down their arms. Still unsatisfied, Forrest sent a strong detachment up the Pike to catch as many escapers as could be found. But the few who got away had gotten a good head start, and their fear fueled them. The detachment came back empty handed.

Jubilant but weary, we marched south again. The air was tinged with a warmness that told of approaching spring. The hardwood trees were beginning to leaf out, and the rolling hills showed faint hues of green where the grasses gave promises of warmer weather. Breathing deeply, I thought to myself that this must be the most beautiful country in the world, and worth every effort to protect and keep.

We made camp at Spring Hill that evening. As we set up, we learned with shock that Captain Montgomery Little had died of wounds received during our last charge.

That night, David and I shared outpost duty a mile north of the main camp. We placed ourselves next to the main road, behind a fallen log, and decided to take turns sleeping. David took the first watch, stretching out behind the log with the barrel of his rifle resting on its scaly bark. Lying in my bed of dead leaves, with my coat buttoned up to my throat to ward off the chilly evening air, I thoughtfully analyzed the day's accomplishments and the death of Captain Little. He had been a good soldier – intelligent, brave, and a true leader.

I heard a rustling noise behind us. Quickly rising, I grabbed my rifle, and crouching, moved swiftly to our rear. Peering desperately into the darkness, I heard a voice calling to me in a loud whisper.

"Is that you, Barrett? Take care not to shoot me!"

Sighing in relief upon hearing the General's voice, I replied, "Yes sir, it's me. David and I are over here." I led the way to our place at the fallen log.

He sat down next to us. "I was making my rounds and thought I would check on you. Have you heard anything?"

"No, sir. It's been quiet."

"Good. By the way, I wanted to commend you both. I appreciate the way you tore into those Yankees today."

I could almost hear David blushing as he said, "Thank you, sir."

Clearing his throat sternly, he continued. " I also wanted to talk to you about Clara and Eva Brown. I've been a business associate of their father for many years, and since he's off fighting with General Lee, I feel duty bound to make sure your intentions are honorable."

Almost in shock, I replied, "Of course, sir. We're both from good families, and we know how to treat ladies."

"I'm glad to hear that. I know you have good backgrounds, but war can change a man. Remember – I will not tolerate any indiscretions from my men.

Our efforts won't do us much good on the war front if we cower from shame whenever we're around our own people. I'm depending on you two conducting yourselves as gentlemen."

The darkness couldn't hide the tormented look on the General's face as he continued. "We lost a good man today. Captain Little will be sorely missed." After a moment's silence, he said, "Keep your eyes and ears open, boys. Report back to camp at daybreak." He rose and disappeared into the darkness behind us.

We reached Columbia the next day, rejoining the sick and wounded comrades we had left behind. We were met by a delegation of citizens from town, who wished to offer us their congratulations on our victory. Smiling graciously, Forrest gave a short speech in which he gave all the credit of victory to the men in his command. He issued orders for setting up camp and went to town to visit with friends.

Although still weary, David and I asked for and received permission to visit the Brown sisters that evening. The visit was all too short. On our way out the front door, Clara pressed a small packet into my hand. David received one from Eva, too, and when we got back to camp we discovered they were clippings of hair. Seeing that dark, shiny curl brought tears to my eyes, and I kissed it passionately.

I slipped it into the breast pocket of my shirt, where it was to remain for the duration of the war.

By March 15, we were back at Spring Hill, where Forrest's command had been stationed before. On independent outpost duty, our scouts soon learned of an enemy force emplaced around Brentwood, on the Nashville and Decatur Railroad. The General had always been aware that, by destroying the railroads, he could restrict the movement of the enemy and keep them isolated from each other. He promptly asked for and received permission to move against Brentwood from General Van Dorn.

He immediately sent Colonel Starnes, in command of the old Forrest Brigade, toward Brentwood, with orders to cross the Harpeth River six miles east of Franklin, still held by the Yankees. While moving toward his goal, he was to destroy the telegraph lines and tear up as much railroad track as he could, thus isolating the force at Brentwood from the main body of troops in Franklin. There were 500 Yankees in a fortified position near the fork of the Wilson and Franklin turnpikes leading into Nashville. Starnes was to post the Fourth Tennessee so as to prevent their escape to Nashville, and then wait until daybreak, and the arrival of Forrest with the rest of us.

We learned later that Starnes' men had been unable to capture the Yankee pickets. Alarmed, they alerted their comrades in Franklin, who sent out reinforcements. When daylight came, Starnes found himself facing the enemy alone, with no reinforcements in sight. Knowing he was badly outnumbered, he withdrew south, looking for Forrest.

Meanwhile, our crossing of the swollen Harpeth had been delayed. The rushing water, filled with debris, almost swallowed up our artillery, and only by a great effort were we able to save it. When we reached our destination, Starnes had already left. Unperturbed, the General sent two companies of the Tenth Tennessee to guard our rear, and two more to the rear of the enemy to prevent their escape.

Riding hard toward the Franklin turnpike, we came upon a Union courier, who on seeing us, turned his terrified face around and attempted to escape. Fearlessly, the General spurred his horse and caught up with him. Leaning over, he jabbed his pistol into the courier's side, and ordered him to halt. Silently, with trembling hands, he turned over the message he had been carrying just as the rest of us rode up.

The General chuckled and read it aloud. "Well, boys, it seems the Colonel commanding that fort needs reinforcements. Let's see if we can take care of him before he gets them."

Hallooing in loud excitement, we chased after Forrest. Union skirmishers placed in front of the fort fled before us. When we came in sight of the enemy position, Forrest sent Captain Anderson, under a white kerchief tied to his sword, to demand immediate and unconditional surrender. The Union commander, Colonel Bloodgood, refused.

Forrest immediately ordered the six remaining companies of the Tenth Tennessee to dismount and attack the fort from the front, while Armstrong's Brigade and the artillery attacked them on the flank. Forrest himself led the escort in a charge against a wagon train that was attempting to break through and escape to the rear. Our attack was so vigorous and abrupt, they broke and ran back to the safety of the fort.

We had them surrounded, and just as we brought our artillery to bear, the fort surrendered. Before we could enjoy the victory, however, the General sent the captured prisoners and equipment south with General Armstrong and had us destroy what couldn't be carried. He ordered the Sixth Tennessee north toward Nashville, to give the impression of a move in that direction. With as much speed as we could muster, we moved over to the Harpeth River and surrounded the fort that guarded the bridge spanning it's tumultuous waters.

Forrest ordered the artillery to discharge one shot at the fort, and then turned to Captain Anderson, who had been at his side all day. “Major, take a flag of truce to them. Inform them they are completely surrounded, and if they don't surrender I'll blow them to hell with artillery before I'll sacrifice my men in storming their works.”

Anderson hurriedly looked for the white kerchief he had used earlier in the day, but it couldn't be found. Laughing gaily, the General said, “Strip off your shirt!” Chagrined at the less-than-clean condition of it, the Major did as he was told, tied it to his sword, and moved forward.

The Union garrison could see they were greatly outnumbered. They surrendered without a fight. We quickly destroyed all supplies that couldn't be carried, along with the railroad bridge across the river.

By this time, we were very much aware of Union cavalry from Franklin close behind us. As our long train of troops, artillery, and captured men and supplies headed south, the escort, with the General leading, worked its way along the length of the column, seeking its front. Before we reached it, word arrived that our rear had been thrown into confusion by an attack. Forrest turned around and headed us back, determined to take the situation into his own hands.

A scene of wild commotion met our eyes. Panic-stricken, the men had thrown away their gear, had lost most of our captured supplies, and were stampeding those in front of them. Quickly, Forrest threw us across the road directly in the path of the running troops. We drew our pistols and pointed them at the fleeing melee. Shouting and cursing, his eyes red and bulging, Forrest ordered them to halt and fall in, but to little avail. A few stopped their attempts to get past us, but many turned a deaf ear to the General's commands. Furious, Forrest grabbed a double-barreled shotgun from the hand of one of his men, and from his horse shot both barrels into a group of soldiers who continued their mad attempt to escape. Surprised, the men halted, and seeing the source of the shot, they did as ordered and fell into line.

Laughing silently behind his hand, Josh shouted, “Them fellas is dang sure smart. I'd a heap rather face a few damn Yankees than the Genrul when he's mad.”

Calm was quickly restored, and with the arrival of Starnes and his brigade we were able to discourage the Yankees from further pursuit. On down the road, the men were given permission to exchange their old rifles for the new breech-loading ones we had just captured. Joyfully, I rubbed my hands over a smooth, new barrel, and was thankful for it. Because it was easier to load, it was a much more useful weapon than my old one had been.

Returning to the relative quiet of Spring Hill, we rested up for a few weeks and enjoyed the heady feeling of victory that all soldiers experience after a well-fought campaign. Spring had definitely arrived, and the sights and sounds of the new season fit my mood of contentment perfectly.

During this time, I received a letter from my father, worn and creased from the many hands it had passed through. It opened with the usual amenities about the weather, then continued:

> I remain in good health. We have all suffered from the shortages the war has forced upon us, but I am making the best of the situation. I will plant a large garden in the back of the house again this year, and with the Lord's help I will be able to put away enough food for the winter.
>
> I was thankful to receive the letters you have written. We have heard good reports on

General Forrest, and I'm pleased that you're fighting under an able commander. I can't help but worry that you are getting enough to eat and are properly clothed. War is a terrible thing, son, but something that is necessary at times. Please remember you are in my thoughts and prayers daily.

I hope this letter reaches you. I have given it to John Conrad's son, Aaron, who is under General Bragg and is stationed in the vicinity of Tullahoma. He will pass it on from there.

The Yankees sympathizers have turned Knoxille against us. We see their scouting parties occasionally. Although I would give anything to see you, son, I must warn you not to attempt to come home at the present time. I would much rather know you are fighting than biding your time in a Yankee prison.

My hopes and dreams ride with you.

Your Loving Father

P. S. Tell David Knox that I see his parents quite often and they are doing fine.

According to the date on it, the letter was over a month old. Despite the brave front he presented, I could tell by his shaky handwriting that all was not well with my father. Knowing him as I did, he was working himself too hard, spending too much time tending to his patients. I thought back to all the times during my childhood when he had put his own needs aside to help someone else in trouble. Older now, with the aches and pains that always accompany advancing age, he would nevertheless refuse to slow down his pace.

Suddenly, clearly, I could picture him in my mind's eye. Tall and distinguished, with a flowing white beard and an understanding smile, he was a true gentleman who held fiercely to his beliefs, even when they weren't popular. He was always admired by others, even those with opposing political views. I missed the quiet talks we had shared together. I sighed.

"Cheer up, my good man. It can't be as bad as all that." Startled, I looked up from my perch on a stump near the fire to see Captain Anderson looking down at me.

"Yes, sir," I answered glumly.

He crouched down. "I see you've gotten a letter." I looked down and saw I still held my father's letter in my hand. "I hope it's not bad news from home."

"Not really, sir. At least, not on the surface." I cleared my throat and looked down. "I'm just worried. My father is getting older, and I know he's struggling on his own."

"Let me ask you something. Does your father believe in the Cause?"

"Yes he does."

"Well, there you have it. You're doing something here that he cannot. That should be enough. We all have to make sacrifices, even our folks on the home front if we're going to win this thing." Rising, he patted me on the shoulder and left.

I found David and shared with him what I had heard from home. Then I returned to my tent and wrote a long letter to my father. I described our exploits without including any of the dangerous details, figuring my father could guess those on his own. I found a courier heading back to Tullahoma, and he agreed to carry it for me.

Our suppers had become increasingly skimpy. After a meal of stale hardtack that evening, Josh sauntered over where I was relaxing underneath a hickory tree a short distance from the mess fire. Groaning and clutching his stomach, he squatted down and sat next to me.

"I'll tell ya sompthin', if I don't git more real vittles soon, I'm gonna wither away an' die."

I grunted in agreement.

"What's eatin' you, boy? You seem awful disagreeable this evenin'."

I sifted the good Tennessee earth between my fingers and said, "Oh, nothing in particular."

Spitting, Josh said in a half-angry tone. "Come on. I know ya better'n that."

"I just feel kind of useless. My father needs me. I can sense it in my bones. Yet here I am, a hundred miles away, and no way to help."

"So yer startin' to feel sorry for yerself, huh?"

Offended, I sputtered, "That's hardly what I would call it."

"Now, don't git yer feathers ruffled. I ain't tryin' ta git yer dander up. I'm jist tryin' to tell ya you ain't alone."

"What do you mean?"

"I mean all of us, at one time er another, gits ta feelin' the same way. I got a fam'ly dependin' on me too. A wife an' five young'uns. My oldest boy is twelve now, so he can help some, but it ain't a life a luxury, that's fer shore." Absently, he drew figures in the sandy soil with his finger.

"Where is your family?"

"We got a place, ten acres, south a' Fayetteville. My daddy, he left me half of it, an' I bough the rest 10 years ago." A glimmer of pride showed in his eyes. "I always grow a little cotton an' some tobaccy. An' my wife's got a big garden in the summer. But with me gone, Emma can't waste no time on cash crops, seein' as how there ain't no money around anyways. She's been keepin' a cow an' some chickens along with the garden, jist enough to keep body an' soul tagether. Five young'uns take a heap a feedin."

Thoughtfully, I asked him, "So why don't you go home, Josh?"

"Cause I figger I kin do more fer those young'uns by fightin' the Yanks. Shore, I could go home an' work my land, an' see they was fed, but what about later on? I'm jist a dirt farmer, but I love them kids, an' I want to pertect 'em from people who don't know nothin' about 'em or the way we want ta live. That's why I'm fightin'."

Since knowing Josh, I never imagined him to be much of a philosopher, but I could see he had thought this through. I felt a twinge of shame, because his obligations were far greater than mine, yet I was the one whining.

"You've certainly given me something to think about."

"Think nothin' of it." Slowly, creakingly, he rose to his feet and wandered off in the direction of his tent.

As it was, I didn't have much time to dwell on my personal problems. The General kept me busy with picket duty for the next little while.

I had gained a new respect for Josh after our recent talk. Mysteriously, we found ourselves being appointed to the same assignments, and as a result,

David and I spent more and more time with him on as well as off duty.

One bright spring morning, Josh found me at the horse corral. Leaning over, one of Goldie's hooves between my knees, I was busy trimming it, chipped and worn from hard riding, when I was interrupted by his loud, sputtering voice.

"Dang it, Barrett, I jist about had it with these bastards!"

"What are you talking about?"

"I'm talkin' about those lily-livered, no-good asses that run the Quartermaster's Department of this here army." Fuming, he stomped around me a few times before I could calm him down enough to get some sense out of what he was saying. Finally, he continued. "Ya know, we been breakin' our backs, stealin' supplies from them damn Yanks to help out an' do we git any thanks fer it? Hell, no! All we git is snivelin' and complainin'!" In a flippant, sing-song voice, he went on. "Seems the head quartermaster got his little feelin's hurt cause the Genrul let us have new rifles outta the batch we captured at Brentwood."

I sputtered, "What?"

"You heerd me! He didn't think we shoulda got 'em! Thinks we outta risk life 'n limb ta capture supplies an' turn everythin' over ta him!"

“That's outrageous! We've got to have proper equipment if we're to fight!”

“I know'd it, an' you know'd it, but that idiot quartermaster don't!”

“I wonder what Forrest has to say about that.”

“Ho! Ho! Sometimes I think that's why me an' the Genrul git along so good. We both think the same way.” Looking around to see if there was anyone close by, he said, “Don't tell nobody, but I heerd the Genrul let him have it with both barrels!” He giggled. “Yup, if it warn't fer the Genrul, this war would be right dull!”

CHAPTER FOUR

The broad Tennessee River, with its rushing green water and unpredictable behavior, forms a natural barrier that effectively divides the state of Tennessee into three separate parts. Starting near Knoxville, it lazily moves south down to Chattanooga, where twenty miles west, in the southeast corner of the state, it capriciously turns sharply south and makes a broad curve through Alabama, then flows north through western Tennessee. Like a wall, it separates the state into three areas, each with a different geography and culture. The eastern section, rocky and mountainous, ill-suited for large farms, was a hotbed of Yankee sentiment. The middle section, with its rolling, wooded hills, leaned toward the Southern point of view. The western third, with broad plains and flatlands ideally suited to plantation life, embraced the Confederacy wholeheartedly.

During 1863 the river became a focal point of Yankee strategy. Because it was a barrier, the Union decided they would rather see us south of it, defending Georgia and Alabama, and leave the state of Tennessee to them. There was only one nagging problem – the city of Chattanooga. Surrounded by mountains and in a bend of the river, it was a natural stronghold. Two Rebel-held railroad lines, one leading north to Knoxville and one south to Atlanta, connected Chattanooga to the outside world. In turn, the town supplied the Army of Tennessee with food and supplies from the rest of the South. General Rosecrans of the Union Army wanted to break both railroads, making it impossible for Bragg's army to sustain itself. Rosecrans figured that with those railroads cut he could maneuver Bragg, then stationed around Tullahoma, southeast to Chattanooga and out of the state.

Plans were made. A small but able-bodied force, selected especially for the purpose, would be shipped down the Tennessee to Eastport, Mississippi. From there, it would march east through barren country populated by Union sympathizers, across northern Alabama to Rome, Georgia, destroying a Confederate arsenal there, and then on to Dalton, cutting the railroad that ran between Chattanooga and Atlanta. Colonel Abel Streight of the Union Army, who had proposed the plan, was given command of the operation. The Yankees hoped to create enough diversion to draw a large portion of Bragg's army south, leaving the Confederate Army shorthanded in Tennessee, and make their offensive somewhat easier.

Cagily, the Yankees planted a larger force in northern Alabama to disguise the Streight expedition. Headed by General Dodge, it mustered 5,500 men, made up of infantry and cavalry. When Streight joined him at Eastport with 2,000 hand-picked men, their only opposition was a small brigade of Alabama cavalry headed by Colonel Roddey.

Roddey was a determined man with a huge problem on his hands. Faced with an enemy four times his number, and with no idea of their intentions, he decided to delay them until he could alert his superiors. One evening, his men stealthily invaded the Union corral where the enemy had their mules penned, and stampeded the animals. It took two days to replace the ones lost.

Meanwhile, Bragg had learned of the enemy operation, and he speedily selected General Forrest to oppose the invasion. Losing no time, we left

Spring Hill in a hurry, and by forced marches reached and crossed the Tennessee River on April 26 at a place called Brown's Ferry near Courtland, Alabama. Before moving on, the General sent Colonel Dibrell and the Eighth Tennessee Cavalry west, along the northern bank of the river, to create a diversion in the enemy's rear. We were still unaware of the enemy's purpose, but the General was determined to stop whatever plans they had.

By May 28th we were directly in the path of the invaders. Exhausted from our hard march, we camped near Courtland without the benefit of fires so as not to give our exact position away. Forrest set up headquarters a short distance from where our mess gathered, and we watched the activity around his tent with amazement.

"I don't see how he does it! He hasn't slowed down for days!" David said tiredly.

Stretched out on his pallet, Josh ended a yawn with, "That's why he's the Genrul, an' we ain't nothin' but privates."

We fell into an exhausted slumber, only to be awakened by a commotion around Forrest's tent. Slowly rising to his elbows, Josh said, "What the . . .!" Cursing, he stood up, then stomped over to the scene of confusion. It seemed like only seconds before he was back.

"Git up, fellas! Rise n' shine!"

I rubbed the sleep out of my eyes and asked grumpily, “What is it, Josh? What do you want?”

“I said, git up! We gotta git movin'!”

Hastily, we gathered up our gear and headed for the horse corral at a fast trot. On the way, Josh explained: The General had received a visit from a local citizen who had informed him of a large Union detachment, possibly 2,000 strong, moving from Mount Hope in the direction of Moulton. Suspicious of such a large mounted force, the General decided to take out after it. He sent a courier to Dibrell with instructions to draw Dodge out of the area. Colonel Roddey was ordered to place his men between Streight and Dodge and prevent any attempt to reinforce the raiders. With three regiments, the escort and eight pieces of artillery, Forrest set out to stop the invasion.

Mounted, we joined the rest of the escort where the General's tent had been. As a cold, dismal rain began to fall, we were given two days' forage for our horses, three days' cooked rations for ourselves, and were warned to keep our cartridge boxes dry. Heading the column, we rode out of Courtland about 1 a.m. As usual, Forrest stayed behind to review the troops as they passed to make any adjustments he felt were necessary. He joined us after several miles of hard riding.

Despite the damp, uncomfortable weather, we were in high spirits. With Forrest leading us to an enemy far from their own lines, into a country that was rightfully ours, we knew we couldn't lose.

The spring rains had turned the roads into a gummy mess. Rain clouds obscured the heavens, filtering out any light that might have helped us. Doggedly, we kept on, eastward, stopping for an hour to feed and rest our horses about eight in the morning, and again when we reached Moulton in the early afternoon. As we continued the chase, Forrest gave his customary order. “Move up, men!” Enthusiastically, he was answered by 1,200 waving hats and an equal number of rebel yells.

By midnight we were four miles from Day's Gap, a deep gorge that leads to the summit of Sand Mountain. Here, our scouts returned with information that the Yankees were camped at the entrance to the Gap. Forrest ordered us to bivouac while we waited for the rest of the column to catch up. Gratefully, we sheltered ourselves as best we could and slept.

Forrest was up and about when I awakened early the next morning. I wondered aloud if he had even bothered to rest, and was answered by a shake of Josh's tousled head. The sun was just rising as we rolled up our pallets and loaded our horses.

The Yankees had risen long before the sun. The head of their column was already near the summit of Sand Mountain, but it was such slow going, their procession stretched all the way down the mountain.

Forrest sent his brother, Captain Bill Forrest and his band of scouts to nip at their heels while the two regiments under Colonel McLemore were sent to the flank and rear of the fleeing column.

The country into which we were entering was easily defended. Characterized by thinly wooded, sandy ridges interspersed with small streams and gorges, even I could see that once the Yankees dug in, they would be hard to dislodge. Worriedly, I surveyed the countryside. As my glance passed over Josh, he reached out, patted my shoulder, and said, "Don't worry, boy, we'll be okay."

The escort gathered, and then we were ordered to follow and join up with Captain Forrest and his scouts. Although still weary, we complied with as much energy as we could muster. We followed behind Lieutenant Nat Boone, who had replaced Captain Little. A huge man with a long flowing beard and bright blue eyes, he led us at a gallop until we reached Bill Forrest, two miles from the top of the mountain.

The Yankees had formed an ambush along the crest of a ridge bordered by a marshy stretch of country on their right and a deep ravine on their left.

Captain Forrest had just chased their rear guard up and into this position when we came upon the scene. The entire Yankee line had opened up on them and they had been forced to retire from the field. Several scouts had been killed, and the Captain himself, a particularly daring young man with the same quiet manner and dark good looks of his older brother, had received a severe wound through his thigh that had crushed the bone.

We waited out of range for the General to arrive. David and I quietly discussed our position, and we decided the situation was hopeless. The enemy, well placed and with good cover, seemed to outnumber us. “We’re not going to be able to move them,” I said.

Josh sputtered. “So you got this all figgered out, huh? If I was you, boy, I'd let the Genrul finish inspectin' that Yank position 'fore I decided one way or t'other.”

Never one to waste time, Forrest dismounted one regiment and ordered them to advance, placed two mounted companies on the right, the escort and his brothers' scouts on the left, and opened up on the enemy with two guns of Morton's Battery.

We moved forward, slowly. Bullets from the Yankee skirmishers whizzed by our heads. Suddenly we heard a tremendous fire, and looked to our right in time to see our comrades break and run from an enemy charge. We were ordered to fall back, and as we did Josh pointed out our two artillery pieces, entangled with dead and dying horses, stranded in the middle of the field. He said, "The Genrul ain't gonna like that one bit."

Josh was right. When we reached the rear we could hear the General's voice, raised above the almost ear-splitting level of noise common to a retreating army, cursing and storming at the men responsible for leaving the guns. Curiosity got the best of us, so we got closer and saw Lieutenant Gould of Morton's Battery receiving a scolding that he would not soon forget. Abruptly, the General rode off, and the look of hatred thrown at him by Gould made us uneasy.

Ever since our first expedition with Forrest's Cavalry into West Tennessee, I had noticed how the General was particularly fond of his artillery pieces. When the war started, he knew little about handling the big guns, until we faced the Yankees in the fight at Parker's Crossroads. There, as the artillerymen placed their guns to fire, the drivers had moved the horses and caissons out of range, according to the standards set in the manual of artillery drill. Forrest, unfamiliar with the procedure, saw the drivers moving to the rear and thought they were running away. Furiously, he rode over and started beating the man on the lead horse with the flat of his saber. "I'll kill you if you don't turn those horses around and get back to where you belong!" The artilleryman answered that he was only moving according to the drill, but the General yelled back. "No, you're not! You're running away with the ammunition!" Shortly thereafter, a lieutenant of artillery ventured to take a book of tactics to the General and gave him an exhibition drill as set out in the book. Intrigued, Forrest spent a week mastering that manual and became an expert at using artillery. Typically, he was quick to apologize to the artilleryman he had abused.

The fury elicited in the General by the loss of those two guns was awful to behold. He raged among us, shouting for us to hitch our horses to anything we could find so that every man would be available in the coming fight. The lost guns would be retaken, no matter what the cost.

Desperately, we moved forward. The enemy greeted us with only scattered shots this time and without the benefit of artillery. The bugler sounded the charge, we ran forward, and were confronted by the sight of their rear guard mounting their mules and heading off in the direction of Blountsville.

I would be lying if I didn't admit to a feeling of relief as we rushed to the rear to get our horses. Meeting a well dug in enemy across an open field was not my idea of a fair battle. I hoped a more equitable situation would arise further down the road.

By the time we had organized into a column, the Yankees had an hour's head start on us. Riding at our head, Forrest's face had a sulky, determined look that boded ill for anyone who got in his way. We followed him quietly, but with equal determination.

We had barely gone six miles when we were joined by the two regiments under Colonel McLemore that had been sent off on a flank movement. Forrest breathed a sigh of relief when they came into view.

"It's about time you all showed up. I could have used you a few miles back."

"Sorry, sir." Colonel McLemore answered sheepishly. "We tried to come into their rear, but the distance was too great."

"I understand, Colonel." Briskly, Forrest continued, "Let's get on with the matter at hand."

As the staff closed around him, he fired off the following orders: Colonel Roddey with his original force would go back the way we had come, to keep an eye on Dodge. The Eleventh Tennessee, under Major Anderson, was sent north, to move parallel with the Yankees and make sure they didn't try to escape in that direction. He kept two regiments, the escort, and his brother's scouts with him, directly on the enemy's trail.

Shortly after we resumed the march we came upon the enemy's rear guard. Forrest urged us on at top speed and we soon developed a running skirmish. Abruptly, we came upon their full force, placed along a ridge called Hog Mountain. Dusk was falling as we made our first charge.

Some believe the most desperate fighting of the war took place in Virginia. That could not be further from the truth. Both sides fought like demons on that cool spring evening, long after the sun had set. Equally determined, the two sides clashed with such vigor that we were soon fighting hand to hand.

Dismounted, we were placed on the left hand side of the battle. With David and Josh on either side of me, I found myself slowly but steadily moving toward the Yankee line.

As we advanced, Forrest appeared. Red-faced, he bellowed fiercely for a charge. He led us mounted and with his saber raised, directly at the Yankee line. Screaming our fear and recklessness at the top of our lungs, we followed at a dead run, and were soon across their line. My pistol in hand, I fired at a freckle-faced young man who tried to hack at me with his bayonet. He fell at my feet, his life's blood pumping out of the hole in his side.

Shaking, shattered, my hazy eyes saw more men in blue running up. Strength of numbers forced us back, across the space we had just crossed.

Stumbling, I fell, and felt more than saw Josh pull me to my feet and hustle me back to safety.

In shock, I realized that complete darkness was upon us. I could see flashes of light across the way, as the Yanks continued to shoot at us, answered by flashes of our own. Occasionally the boom of their big guns sounded, followed by searing streaks of light across the sky. I was almost hypnotized as I watched.

I was brought out of my trance by Nat Boone, who ordered us to the rear to get our horses. Grinning, Josh shouted, "Git ready, boys! The Genrul's sendin' us off on a midnight ride!"

Exhausted, I mounted Goldie with as much energy as I could. Our orders were explained – the escort would attempt a flanking movement. We galloped off into the darkness.

The brisk ride through the evening air helped me regain my composure. I had killed before, but for some reason I could not shake the image of the freckle-faced Yankee soldier, or the sound his body made as it hit the ground. I can see and hear it still.

With an effort I concentrated on our mission. We rode around the enemy flank until we came upon their mules. The handlers, surprised, raised the alarm. The entire force quickly descended on us, and we withdrew to safety. We circled around to rejoin our main body, and the chase resumed.

The Yankees had been forced to leave behind the two guns they had captured from us earlier because they didn't have enough horses left to drag them. Recapturing them was a hollow victory, however. They had plugged them and burned their carriages, making the General even more determined to destroy the force that had so far eluded us.

The moon was shining brightly, and by its light we were able to make good time. Bone weary, we kept up the agonizing pace until a scout came back and reported a suspected ambush ahead. They had come upon an area of thick brush that was a perfect place to spring a trap.

The General rose in his stirrups, turned around, and called for volunteers. He picked Josh and two others and quickly instructed them to ride forward, keep watch, and retreat as soon as they drew fire. We all moved forward as quietly as possible. The three picked men ventured ahead at a faster pace. They were several hundred yards ahead of us when I saw them wheel around and head back just as the sound of gunfire met our ears. Josh and his companions slipped down over the sides of their saddles, to protect themselves from flying bullets, and rode up to the General, out of breath.

One piece of artillery was brought forward, double-shotted with canister and pushed by hand up the soft, sandy road. When it reached within 200 yards of the thicket hiding the Yankees, the officer in charge opened fire.

Answered at once by small arms fire, the General ordered another gun brought up. Soon both were hard at work. Before any real damage could be done, however, the Yankees were off again.

Relentlessly, the chase resumed. Sometime after midnight another ambush was laid for us, but we managed to smash it like the one that had come before. I was so tired I could hardly keep myself in the saddle. Although we moved at a fast pace, my eyes would close and my body would slip sideways until a sudden jolt would wake me and I would right myself once again.

Forrest ordered a rest at 3 a.m. Too tired to even spread our blankets, we slept wherever we could find a spot. Before we knew it, the General had us up again and back on the road, the escort in the lead.

Late the next morning we galloped into Blountsville, driving the Yankee rear guard before us. Suddenly, we heard a shout of jubilation. The enemy had lightened their load to gain speed, leaving a smoldering pile of supplies and ammunition. Before the fire could consume the pile, we managed to put it out and salvage part of what was left. Gratefully, we passed around the food we had saved before we took to the road again.

The General mostly stayed at the head of his troops. Although he looked tired around the eyes, his back remained as tall and straight as ever. He spoke words of encouragement to those around him, and even went to the rear from time to time to make sure everything was proceeding as it should. Casually, he would pass the time of day with various troopers, always filling them in on what was happening at the front of the column.

Before we had gotten very far out of Blountsville, one of our scouts, dirty and ragged, rode up on a lathered horse and asked to see the General. Josh and I took him to Forrest, who pulled off the road and snapped, “Well?”

Nervously, the scout said, “Sir, I stopped off at a blacksmith's shop a way’s back, and heard there was a big Yank force movin' close by.”

“Did you see them?” With sharp, harsh eyes, Forrest watched him as he replied.

“No, I didn't see 'em myself, but while I was there a man came ridin' up an' he said he had seen 'em, movin' directly across from us about four miles off.”

The General's face became fiery red and his hands shook as he pulled the scout off his horse, and with both hands around his neck, beat the poor trooper's head several times against a nearby tree. He let him go, and hoarsely shouted, “Now, damn you, don't ever come to me with such lies again, or I'll do much worse to you! I don't want to hear rumors! I only want to hear what you see with your own eyes! Now, get along!"

We reached the Black Warrior River, ten miles east of Blountsville. We had been worrying their rear guard all the way, but when we reached the river the Yanks had crossed safely ahead of us. Two howitzers had been placed on the opposite bank and they kept up a continuous fire. Our greater numbers eventually made them give up their positions and follow their comrades.

The swiftly moving stream, swollen from the spring rains, detained us for a short time, but we managed the crossing without any significant loss. Once on the other side, the General ordered a rest, after sending two companies after the Yankees to keep on their trail.

Two of the enemy's mules, loaded with boxes of hardtack, had drowned crossing the river. Several men managed to salvage part of the cargo, and hungrily gulped down the soggy bread before they rested. We were all hungry. The cooked rations we had brought with us were long gone, and we were forced to depend on what we could find for sustenance. Thanks to the scavenging Yankees that marched ahead of us, the countryside had been stripped clean and there was little left for us.

After several hours of rest, we continued our march that evening. Hard traveling had considerably weakened our little army. Every time we stopped we were forced to leave several of our comrades behind, too worn out to go on. Persistently, Forrest would continue on with those who could still travel.

We caught up with our advance guard by eight o'clock the next morning. At nine, we attacked the Yankees' rear guard while they were attempting to cross Black Creek, near Gadsden. The General sent Colonel Biffle, along with two companies that had been hammering at the Yankees all night, to the rear to get some rest. With the escort behind him, he took command.

We raced down a low hill and saw an old, rickety bridge directly in front of us. We could see wisps of smoke rising from the bridge, and several squads of men on the far side, manning two howitzers. A lone Yankee, riding as hard as he could for the bridge, suddenly whirled around and gave himself up. His route of escape was burning briskly, and he realized there was no way to get across.

"Damn it!" The General yelled in frustration. Then he noticed an old dilapidated farmhouse about 200 yards from the bridge. He spurred his horse toward it.

He was met on the side of the road near the farmhouse by a young lady, not more than 16 years old. We came up in time to hear them introduce themselves. She then proceeded to tell him of a ford on her mother's property, unknown to anyone else, by which he could get us safely across. The closest bridge was two miles away, and Forrest knew he would lose valuable time in trying to reach it.

"Sir, if you will have my horse saddled I will gladly show you the way myself."

"There is no time. You'll have to mount behind me."

Without a word, she moved to the edge of the steep bank along the roadside and jumped up behind him. Before they could move off, her widowed mother appeared, out of breath, and panted, "Emma, what are you doing?" Forrest replied, "Don't be afraid, ma'am. She is only going to show me a way across the creek. We must catch those Yankees before they reach Rome. I will bring her back safely."

Our men were already in the field, firing at the enemy on the opposite bank. Emma Sansom directed the General down a steep ravine that led to the stream. Within a short time they were back.

The firing between the two banks continued, and several of our men were wounded. Robert Turner, a respected member of the escort, was killed. Sadly, Josh and I carried him to the farmhouse and laid him out on the floor in a bedroom. The General followed behind us, and we left him alone with Robert, to say a prayer over his body.

We left the house together as the firing ceased. Miss Emma came up, and the General told her he had left a note for her, and about Robert Turner. "He was a very brave man, ma'am, and I would be beholden to you if you would see that he had a proper burial."

"I would be honored, sir."

With that, Forrest said his goodbyes, mounted his horse, and we left. We went briskly to the ford, where we were ordered by the General to clear the opposite bank of all bluecoats. Screaming the rebel yell, we rode across to the opposite bank with little interference. The Yankees continued their habit of retreat.

Impatiently, Forrest directed several companies to clear the ford of all brush and debris. Working hurriedly, the stream was made passable within a few minutes. Forrest paced back and forth along the bank as each trooper carried his share of artillery ammunition across the stream. The guns and empty caissons were rolled to the edge of the stream, connected to the opposite bank by long ropes tied to double teams of horses, and pulled across. As soon as we were all safely over, we galloped east after the advance guard sent ahead by the General.

There was a small amount of commissary supplies captured at Gadsden, after the advance guard had chased the Yankees out of town. But by the time we rode in, all was quiet.

The enemy had been able to confiscate all available livestock, a fact that made the General understandably irate. By this time we had lost a good many of our horses, unable to keep up the rigorous march. Forage was scarce, and without food the horses we had left had taken to stumbling and weaving. Goldie was maintaining, but I knew it would not be for long. We were again forced to leave some of the men behind who were suffering from exhaustion and dysentery. Those whose horses had given out were ordered to follow as best they could.

Doggedly, we moved on. As we rode, Forrest issued an order to his staff – a detail of men was assigned to ride along the lines and keep the others awake. "I will have no more men falling off their horses and being left behind. We need every available man if we're to catch these scoundrels," he said with finality.

Due to death, disease, injury and exhaustion, the escort had dwindled to forty men. Lieutenant Boone kept an eagle eye on those of us who remained, as if he could keep us going with the strength that showed through his sky blue eyes. Somehow, he succeeded.

Leaning over in an attempt to stretch my legs, I spoke up. "Between the lieutenant and the General,

I would feel like the worst sort of coward if I wasn't able to keep my seat."

Chuckling, Josh leaned over and spat. "That's jist how they wantcha ta feel. They figger ta keep us goin' any way they kin."

Smiling, David said, "I guess they know us pretty well."

"They shore do, son. They know that some of us feel like John here. Kinda like we's duty-bound ta keep goin'. Then there's some that jist wants ta backslide first chance they git."

In an effort to keep myself awake, I thought back over the many times Forrest's understanding of human nature had been displayed. One particular incident came to mind. It happened on our first expedition with Forrest into West Tennessee. Still inexperienced in matters pertaining to war, David and I had failed to grasp it's significance until much later.

Several Union sympathizers were arrested and brought into camp. We had come into possession of a few extra marching drums, and the General ordered them to be used liberally at all hours of the day and night. He had troops dismount and march in front of the prisoners' tent. Then, when the men reached a grove of trees, they remounted and rode by, representing themselves as cavalry. "Accidentally" the prisoners learned that Cheatham's Division of infantry had joined with Forrest's cavalry and intended on staying and holding that part of the country. The captives were then permitted to "escape," and immediately went to Union headquarters and reported our great strength. Naturally, they were believed, for hadn't they seen it with their own eyes?

Forrest knew how to feed information, and to whom. As with everything else he did, he could lie so convincingly, and with such daring, that no one could help but believe him. God fearing, religious and respectable, he knew that he had to sacrifice something in order to achieve his objectives.

If those prisoners had been told we possessed as many men as we pretended, they might have believed us. But, then again, they might not. To make sure they would tell the story his way, Forrest had us put on quite a show, so there would be no doubt as to what they'd seen. The results were in our favor. The Yankees didn't press us as hard as they could have, and we made good our escape from their territory.

There was always a lot at stake, but Forrest was willing to gamble. Often, I thought ruefully, with my life and the lives of my comrades. Yet I knew he was right. One has to gamble in order to win.

Here we were, in the middle of a country overrun with Union sympathizers, without proper sleep or rations or enough horses, and little chance of getting them, following an enemy that greatly outnumbered us, and yet our leader was as determined as ever to catch and destroy them. Wearily, I lifted my eyes and looked forward, only to see what I knew I would. A ramrod stiff back, clothed in a familiar duster, crisply giving orders and carrying on conversations with his staff, as if he didn't have a worry in the world. Only a man of solid determination and boundless energy could seem so carefree under these circumstances, I thought to myself.

Fifteen miles east of Gadsden, at Blount's Plantation, we found the enemy in battle formation. We attacked savagely, without mercy. Forrest moved the artillery and troops back and forth, to give the impression of great strength. Darkness soon descended, and as we flanked the Yankee position, they half-heartedly withdrew.

Our spirits rose considerably at the sight of those bluecoats retreating. Instinct told us the Yankees were growing weary of the chase, and they couldn't hold out much longer. A rest was ordered after the General sent a squad of men to keep on their trail.

We set up camp, trying hard not to listen to our growling stomachs. David had saved a piece of hardtack, still soggy from its stay in the Black Warrior River. Very carefully, he broke the sandy-tasting stuff into three pieces and shared with Josh and I. As we ate, my mind drifted back to the soft, fluffy biscuits my mother would bake for me whenever I requested. Sighing heavily, I rolled up in my worn and tattered blanket and slept a deep, dreamless sleep.

I awoke before the others. It was still dark as I added wood to the fire and stirred it until it blazed. Hacking and coughing, Josh rolled out of his blanket and joined me beside the fire.

"Morning, Josh!" I chirped.

"Yer awful spunky this mornin'," he growled in reply.

"I guess because I almost feel rested for a change."

"Yup. There ain't nothin' like a good night's sleep ta make ya feel like a new man."

David joined us. "I wonder what today will bring."

"The end of this expedition, I hope."

"Could be. We got them Yanks worn down to a frazzle. I think we kin take 'em when the time's right. Course, we could use a few more men an' some fresh horses, but we got 'em licked," Josh said contentedly.

We jumped in fright as a voice issued out of the darkness. "That is, if we don't get too overconfident." The General walked closer to the fire and squatted down next to us. "No fight is easy, boys. Remember that."

"Yessir." Josh looked chagrined in the dancing firelight.

Laughing, the General slapped him across the shoulder. "Don't look so down in the mouth. I'm glad to hear you think we can whip them. Your opinion means something."

Swelling slightly with pride, Josh looked him in the eye. "Have ya warned the folks ahead that them varmints is headin' their way?"

His eyes twinkled as he replied. "Yes I have. I sent Colonel Wisdom to Rome. He'll tell the people there to either guard or burn the bridge across the river." Rising, he continued. "Get your horses ready. We'll be moving out soon."

We learned later that the Yankees also had that bridge on their minds. Colonel Streight sent 200 of his best men to secure its crossing. When they reached it, they found it heavily defended by a group of home guards. Unwilling to risk a fight, the officer in charge sent a courier back to his commander, informing him of the situation.

Like bloodhounds after a scent, we kept on. Hungry and ragged, we were nevertheless in high spirits after our ten-hour rest. We could feel victory in the air, as if it were a tangible thing we could reach out and touch.

We clipped along at a fast pace, We passed through a countryside much lusher than the one we had just crossed. Pine and cedar trees grew in thick groves, their fallen needles forming thick, soft mats underneath their boughs, with an occasional spring flower peeking through. The air, still tinged with the morning's coolness, smelled heavily of pine. We saw small farms and large plantations along the way, with the occupants, black as well as white, on the roadside. They all had the same story – the Yankees had passed through during the night and taken all the riding stock and food with them.

The woods were full of runaway slaves, "freed" by the rampaging Yankees. We could hear them scurrying off through the underbrush as they saw us approach. We made no attempt to capture them. We had a much more important job to finish.

"I wonder how those runaways will survive," David said thoughtfully.

"Oh, they'll find a way. After all, the poor devils are probably field hands and not used to much," I said.

"If them damn Yanks wouldn't fill their heads with ideas 'bout freedom an' such, they wouldn't be in the mess they're in," Josh grumbled.

"That's true. But I don't suppose we can blame them for hoping," David said gently.

Before long we reached the Chattooga River, where we were met by a deputation of local citizens. As we approached, a short, stout man in a worn and patched coat stepped forward and asked for General Forrest. The General rode to him and asked him to state his business.

"Well, we just wanted to give you our best wishes, and offer the use of the ferryboat we have on hand, " the man said nervously.

Forrest visibly relaxed in the saddle as he expressed his appreciation. "What have you seen of the Yankees?"

"The main body headed north along the river several hours ago. About 200 of them passed through here yesterday, and used the ferry to cross here. We heard there were more following, so we hid the boat to keep them from crossing."

"Good work! I hope you caused them some delay."

"We did." Chuckling, "They had to detour north through the charcoal fields. It was nighttime, sir, and I'm sure they had a rough time dodging all those tree stumps and keeping off the wagon trails."

In a booming, resonant voice, the General said, "My congratulations to you all. You've performed an invaluable service to your country."

We worked quickly, and were soon safely across the river. There was no time to rest. The General had us on the way immediately.

Shortly, we came upon our prey. They had formed into a crescent-shaped battle line, with the men lying down to afford the greatest amount of protection. Forrest spaced us apart and ordered us to create as much noise as possible. Clinking our field gear together, yelling and hallooing, we did as we were told, forming a line parallel to the Yankees and in the same crescent shape.

As soon as orders were given, we opened fire. The three of us were dismounted and were among a grove of trees some distance away. When we were answered by a suspiciously scattered return fire, I realized we had a problem.

"Hey, Josh, David! These fools are asleep!" I shouted excitedly.

Josh squinted in their direction and happily replied, "By dingy, yer right! I better tell the genrul." He hurried off toward Forrest, who was at the center of our position, surrounded by staff. Before he could reach him, however, the Lieutenant ordered us to cease fire. Silence fell along our line.

A lone Confederate rider, carrying a flag of truce, crossed over to the Yankees. Josh returned to tell us that Captain Henry Pointer was carrying a message to Colonel Streight demanding surrender.

We relaxed at the news, but kept our rifles up anyway.

"Do you think they'll give up?" asked David.

"I don't see they have any choice. I answered with an air of satisfaction. "They may outnumber us, but they can't fight if they can't stay awake."

"Hold on, fellers, the Captin's bringin' the Genrul some comp'ny."

Sure enough, Captain Pointer was re-crossing the field with another rider. They approached at a fast trot, then dismounted when they reached Forrest. As he and the Yankee soldier walked away to speak privately, Josh volunteered to move closer to find out what he could.

Slowly, irrevocably, the minutes ticked by. Sometimes I think the hardest job of a soldier is to wait while decisions that impact his life are made by others. We kept our eyes trained on the Yankees across the way, to make sure they didn't try anything foolish. After awhile, the Yankee soldier mounted his horse and crossed back over to his side of the battlefield.

Josh came back with a smug look on his face. As he approached, I said, "Any news?"

"Yup. The Genrul told that there Yankee colonel to give it up. Said he had fresh troops closer to Rome an' that we had 'em outnumbered. Said we could overrun 'em if we had a mind to."

"Did he believe him?"

"I dunno. He went back over ta talk with the other officers. Looked like he wasn't shore 'bout what ta do."

He barely got through speaking before we got our answer. A group of Yankee officers rode across the field and surrendered. Shouts of jubilation rose all along our lines as the news spread. Chuckling and laughing, David and I slapped each other on the back.

"Well, John, it was hard going, but we made it!"

"Yes, we did. If it hadn't been for the General we couldn't have done it."

"That's right, boys, an' don't you never forgit it!" Josh piped in.

We had started the long march with 1,000 men and ended it with less than 600. With this small force we captured an enemy numbered at 1,600. Healthy and strong when we began, we finished the expedition half-starved and ragged, having left many of our exhausted and sick comrades along the way. Yet our spirits were high, proud of the feat we had accomplished.

The pursuit of Streight's raiders would one day be considered a remarkable accomplishment. The Yankees we pursued had many advantages – a well-prepared, superior force marching through a country filled with Union sympathizers, well-supplied with the necessities for such an expedition, and with the opportunity to glean from the populace anything else they might require. We, on the other hand, had been ordered to the pursuit at the last minute, with little chance to make preparation. When we reached Alabama, the purpose of the Yankee invasion was still unclear. While on the march we were forced to do without food or fresh mounts, as the enemy stripped away anything that could have been of value to us.

To those who rode with Forrest, however, it was just another successful campaign. With only rare exceptions, we always fought with the odds against us. Forrest simply used the same basic principles – be persistent, pragmatic, and above all, be ready to bluff your opponent into believing your power is far greater than it really was.

With sheer determination, reckless bravery and a little luck, Forrest was able to do the impossible. He hounded and badgered the enemy every step of the way. He grasped every opportunity to weaken their force, and closed off every possible avenue of escape, leaving them stranded in enemy territory.

Forrest never expected more from his men than what he was willing to give himself. He pushed us to our limits of endurance on the expedition against Streight's raiders, but no harder than he pushed himself. He kept no special privileges, but shared what he had with those around him. By being our comrade as well as our leader, he gained our utmost respect and admiration.

Some came to call him the "Wizard of the Saddle." Others called him "Old Bedford." But we could never bring ourselves to address him as anything but "the General."

CHAPTER FIVE

We arrived in Rome, Georgia on the morning of May 5, and were treated as conquering heroes. The streets were lined with cheering crowds, the young women throwing flowers and kisses as we passed by. We rode on until we came to the center of town, where we were met by a delegation of leading citizens. The mayor of Rome gave a short, flowery speech, in which he expressed his thanks to us for saving the town from marauding Yankees. He then presented the General with a beautiful young stallion and invited us all to a barbecue set for the next day. The General accepted the invitation on our behalf, and directed us to set up camp on the edge of town.

Our first priority was to tend to the horses. Since the Yankees hadn't reached Rome, there was plenty of forage to be had, and the grateful populace was more than happy to share with us. David and I fed and watered our animals, then brushed them down with a currycomb I kept with my gear. By the time we joined our messmates, Josh had already been to the quartermaster's station and gotten our rations for the day.

Our mouths watered when we saw the wonderful feast we had been supplied. There was a bag of fresh peas, two chickens and two pans of cornbread. We all pitched in, gutting and plucking the birds, then hungrily watched them cook with the peas in our kettle.

As we waited for the agonizingly slow process to be completed, David spoke up, "Maybe we should have shelled those peas before we cooked them."

"Naw. They'll be jist fine. "Sides, they'll be more fillin'," Josh said, his eyes glued to the pot.

I have eaten many fine meals, but none ever matched that one. We licked our fingers with contentment when it was over, then leaned our backs against whatever we could find. After many days of half or no rations, we felt as if we had died and gone to heaven.

Josh wiped his face with the back of his hand. "That shore 'nuff was good eatin'. Mighty nice of the folks round here to pervide us with such good vittles."

"I don't know about the rest of you, but I could use a good nap." I stood up, moved further away from the fire, and curled up in a patch of newly green grass and fell asleep.

I awoke a few hours later, feeling refreshed. Stretching and yawning, I allowed myself to think of Clara. Perhaps we would soon be back in the vicinity of Columbia, since we had successfully completed our present campaign. I had tried not to think of her during our marching and fighting because it only made me miss her all the more. I could only hope that she was thinking of me as well, and hadn't lost interest in my absence.

In the dusky light of late afternoon, I arose from my grassy bed and went to check on Goldie. He was glad to see me. I rubbed and petted his white face, then took him to the creek nearby.

As he drank, I leaned against him with my arm across his shoulders. "Well, old boy, I guess this rest is doing you as much good as me." His thirst quenched, he turned his head and nudged me. I backed him out of the shallows and led him back to the corral, where I penned him back up with the other horses.

Unfortunately, we weren't able to rest as long as we would have liked. That evening the General got word from his scouts that a heavy Yankee column was moving from Tuscumbia in the direction of Talladega. Without warning, we were told to get ready for a forced march back to Gadsden. We were on the move within an hour.

“Ain't it jist like these damn Yanks. Had my mouth all set fer some barbecue, an' then they have ta come along an' spile it,” Josh grumbled as we left the fine city of Rome behind us.

“Don't worry. There will be other barbecues,” David said cheerfully.

“Not tomorrow, there won't. An' that's when I was aimin' to have me one.”

We arrived in Gadsden on May 7, after a day and a half of hard riding. Still exhausted from our chase of Streight's raiders, we learned with disgust that we had rushed back for a false alarm. The Yankees sighted were only Dodge's troops, and they weren't advancing but were in the process of falling back to Corinth. As we went about setting up camp we steered clear of Josh, who was in a terrible humor over his missed barbecue. Muttering over the inadequacies of our scouts, he went to sleep early. We drew sighs of relief when we saw him retreat into his blanket.

The next morning the escort met the General at the home of his friend, Colonel Kyle, where he had spent the night. As we started in the direction of

Guntersville, he insisted on carrying his friend's small son with him for a few miles. He kissed the child, then gave him back to his father. "Kyle, children are one of the few things that make life worth living."

We arrived back in Spring Hill on or about May 16, and learned that the cavalry corps' dashing commander, General Van Dorn, had been killed. They said it was by a jealous husband. Grudgingly, Bragg transferred his command over to Forrest. With two brigades, he was in charge of Bragg's left wing, patrolling a square between Spring Hill and Columbia to the south, and Franklin and Triune to the north. Although we didn't participate in any major engagements, our outposts frequently clashed with Yankee pickets, and probes sent out to evaluate our position.

David, Josh and I were temporarily assigned to the quartermaster's department, to help round up supplies and forage from farmsteads in the area. We moved between Spring Hill and Columbia, which suited me just fine, as it gave me a chance to see Clara.

Josh was far from pleased with our assignment, especially since we had appointed him to drive the rickety old wagon we were using to collect supplies. The two horses pulling it were far from spirited, quite long in the tooth. Josh was forced to apply the whip liberally so that he could keep up.

"Giddap, you old nag! Can't ya see we don't got all day to wait fer ya?"

I teased him, "You should have joined the army as a teamster instead of a cavalryman. You certainly have a way with those plow horses."

"Boy, I'd keep my mouth shut if'n I was you. I could still take ya across my knee and whup ya if 'n I had a mind to."

"Settle down, you two. We're coming up to a clearing." David pointed ahead.

We saw a small, quaint farmhouse nestled against the side of a hill. As we moved closer, a barn and several outbuildings came into view. All was quiet until we got within a hundred feet of the front porch. Suddenly two hounds appeared, growling and snapping as we approached. Josh threatened them with his whip, but to little avail.

The door creaked open. The barrel of a shotgun protruded and a female voice spoke out. "What do you want?"

I cleared my throat nervously and said, "Ma'am, we're representatives of the Confederate Quartermaster's Department, and we're here to collect supplies for the army."

"I don't got no extra supplies. Jist enough fer me an' my younguns'."

"We'd be more than willing to pay you with promissory notes for anything you have to spare."

"What's a promissory note?"

"It's just a written promise to pay you in gold for whatever you can spare, after we've won the war, Ma'am."

A sudden cackle issued out of the house, followed by the woman. She was short and plump, with a toothless grin and a worn gingham dress. She sauntered out to the edge of the porch, still pointing her gun at us, and spit a stream of tobacco juice that landed neatly beside the steps.

"You young whippersnappers is all the same. Think ya kin come along and steal from us poor folks."

"Ma'am, we don't want to steal anything from you." I reached into my jacket and drew out the notes we had been given to exchange for supplies. "Here are the notes I was telling you about."

"I ain't innerested in yer paper. That stuff ain't worth nothin'. Now clear out!"

Josh spoke up. "Now hold on there, old woman. You ain't got no right ta talk to us like that. We been fightin' them Yanks off to perteck the likes a' you, an' we gotta eat, same as everbody else."

Flying into a rage, she screamed, " Don't you go talkin' ta me 'bout them damn Yankees. If'n ya'll was gonna whup 'em, ya shoulda done it afore now. I done give my husband an' two brothers to the Cause, an' I don't aim ta give no more!" She raised her gun and sighted it at us. "Now, git!"

Without further conversation, we turned and left. Halfway down the drive, I turned to look back. The old woman was still on the porch, her gun aimed at our backs.

We plodded toward Columbia. No one spoke for a while. Then Josh said, "We shouldn't a' let her run us off."

With quiet calm, David replied, "I'm glad we did. She was right, you know. She's given her share to the South, and it wouldn't seem right to take any more from her. There are plenty of others around here willing to give us supplies."

We reached a small plantation shortly thereafter. Quite willingly the owner gave us five or six sacks of grain, dried peas and a cow, which we tied to the back of the wagon.

As dark descended, we made camp for the night in a grove of oak trees a short distance from the main road. The evening air was hot and sultry, and as I tossed and turned in my blanket trying to get comfortable, I wished desperately that we had gotten a different assignment. War was hard enough without taking food out of the mouths of women and children. It was impossible to justify the resentful, pained looks on the faces of those who gave food to the scruffy, half-clad army that defended them.

With a full wagon and four cows, we reached Columbia two days later. Grateful to be finished, we turned over the supplies we had gathered to the quartermaster's station, then set out to find the General, hoping he would give us another assignment. We were told by Captain Baines, a member of his staff, that he had an appointment at the quartermaster's office that afternoon.

The office was full of people waiting to see the General by the time he arrived. We waited unobtrusively in the back of the room until he had a free moment. I happened to glance at the door as Lieutenant Gould appeared. I had heard the General had been successful in transferring him to another unit after his loss of the two artillery pieces during our pursuit of Streight. I remembered his hateful face the day Forrest had given him a verbal lashing, and he looked little better than he had then. White and drawn, his lips pursed so tightly a white line appeared around them, he asked loudly if he could see the General in private. Tersely, Forrest said they could talk in the hall.

Josh and I exchanged glances, then casually moved to the doorway. The hallway was wide and long, with no ornaments of any kind on the walls, the scuffed wooden floor barren of any rugs. General

Forrest and Gould were several feet away but we could faintly overhear their conversation and see the strained face of the lieutenant over the General's shoulder. In a high, quivering voice, he was asking the General to reconsider his transfer.

Gruffly, the General made his reply. “Lieutenant, I have no intention of changing my mind. My decision is final.”

I could see the young man's face. His eyes narrowed into slits, his lips pressed together as he reached into his coat, pulled out a pistol, and fired. Before we could move, Forrest grabbed the hand holding the pistol, snatched his penknife from his pocket with his other hand, opened it with his teeth, and with all his strength drove it into Bacon's stomach.

Shocked, Josh and I rushed to the General's side. He was leaning forward, clutching his abdomen, his face a familiar red from the rage and disbelief that must have filled him. I could hear a soft, dripping sound as his blood escaped through his fingers and plopped to the floor.

“Sir! Let us help you!” I cried, as Josh and I tried to support him by his arms. Furiously, he lashed out at us and bellowed, “The son of a bitch has shot me!” With that, he turned and walked out the front door, Josh and I at his heels. By now, the quartermaster's office had emptied, men boiling out almost one on top of another. They followed us out the front door. With a purposeful step, Forrest strode down the street to the home of a doctor nearby. David joined us as we waited, bewildered, on the steps with a crowd of others. Silently, we watched Captain Baines hurriedly enter the house and shut the door behind him.

"That lil' bastard better hope he dies, 'cause if he don't I'll kill him myself!" Josh said vehemently.

We heard a commotion inside the house. Out plunged Forrest, weakened but brandishing a pistol. At the top of his lungs, he screamed his intention to kill the lieutenant. He rushed down the steps and into the street, followed by Captain Baines. As he passed us, the Captain announced that the doctor had diagnosed the General's wound as mortal.

Word of the incident had spread rapidly. The street was filling up with curious bystanders. The General pushed his way through the crowd, obvious in his intent to carry out his threat. We stayed behind him but were afraid to stop him. We were well acquainted with his terrible temper, and knew there was little we could do to prevent further bloodshed.

We had gone two blocks when we came upon a strangely silent group of people gathered in a circle in the middle of the street. Looking closer, we could see Lieutenant Gould's body, limp and exhausted, lying on the ground. Surrounded by the crowd, he was effectively shielded from any further harm. As the General rushed toward the circle, one of the men broke away and addressed him.

"General Forrest, you needn't bother yourself with this young man any further. He is dying." He then folded his arms and placed himself between the General and the crowd of people encircling the lieutenant.

Somewhat taken aback, Forrest replied, "All right, I won't shoot him. But the damned scoundrel has mortally wounded me, and he must die too." He turned to us. "You, there. Get a stretcher for the lieutenant and take him to the hotel. I'll see that a doctor gets over there to see to him." He started to fall, weak from loss of blood. Baines and another member of his staff grabbed him under his arms and held him upright.

"Major Brown's house is nearby, sir. We'll carry you there," Captain Baines said. Forrest nodded his assent. The crowd churned around us as they carried him up the street and into the house. Mrs. Brown and her daughters, Clara and Eva, led the way upstairs to a spare bedroom.

I slipped into the parlor, where I had spent some hours courting Clara. Those in attendance watched as Clara and Eva scurried up and down the stairs, fetching and carrying articles for their mother. On occasion, Clara nodded at me as I sat there, feeling helpless. I would have liked to speak with her, but at the time it seemed inappropriate. A young slave girl named Alice was sent to bring the doctor, who briefly nodded to us waiting in the parlor as he ascended the stairs.

We waited silently, with dread in our hearts. Other members of the General's staff joined us, and before long the room was filled with silent, somber men waiting for news of the General's condition. Ready to explode from anxiety, I rose and went outside, hoping the fresh air would help my pounding head. I found Josh and David sitting on the front steps, and I sat down next to them.

"What are you two doing here? Why didn't you come inside?"

"Them nice ladies don't want no dirt farmer settin' in their parlor. I figger I'm better off out here," Josh said.

"I decided to stay out here with him," David piped up. "Any news?"

"Not yet. The doctor's with him now," I said, as I rubbed my aching temples. Night was falling.

Before long, the doctor made an announcement. He explained that the bullet had not damaged any vital organs. "But in this warm weather, the possibility of infection cannot be ignored. He has an excellent chance of recovery if the wound doesn't become infected." With that, he left the premises, hurrying off.

We sighed in relief. We sat back down on the steps and tried to decide what to do next.

"Should we head back to Spring Hill and rejoin the escort, or what?" I queried.

"I think we best stay right here. The Genrul will be needin' us fer somethin'." Looking at the sky Josh continued, "I'd say 'cordin' to the moon, it's about eight o'clock. Let's head over to our old camp and set up for the night."

David and I would have liked to stay, but we knew the sisters would be busy helping their mother. It had been a long, tiresome day. With slow steps, we went back to the quartermaster's office, where we had left our horses hours earlier, and followed Josh to our old campsite.

We went back to the Browns' house first thing the next morning. When we arrived Alice answered the door and asked us to wait in the parlor. Josh nervously stood in the middle of the room, his cap in hand and looking around in awe.

"By dingy, this shore is a nice place. I wish the missus could see it."

"I'm glad you like it, sir. Good morning, John and David."

To hide Josh's obvious embarrassment, I quickly introduced him to Mrs. Brown, then asked about the General's condition.

"Praise God, he is much improved this morning. In fact, I can't seem to induce him to get the rest he needs. Would you like to see him?"

"Yes, ma'am, if we could."

"I'm sure he'll be glad to see you. Follow me and I'll take you to him."

She led the way up the stairs and down the hall. We entered to find Forrest propped up with pillows, a Bible in his hands. He looked up and invited us to enter.

"What can I do for you boys this morning?"

"Genrul, we was jist wonderin' if there was anythin' we kin do while yer laid up. I mean, anythin' in perticular."

"Right now, I can't say there is anything of importance. But don't rush off. Were you able to get some supplies for the quartermaster?" We three nodded our assent. "Why don't you hang around for a few days and we'll see what develops."

"Shore thing, Genrul." Almost bashfully Josh asked, "Kin we bring ya anythin'?"

"No, I'm fine. Now you boys run along and stay out of trouble, you hear?"

"Yessir, we shore will!" We all gave him a smart salute, then made our way down the stairs.

"Well, what do we do now?"

"Jist exactly what the Genrul told us. Hang around an' wait till he needs us."

"Perhaps we should see if they need us over at the quartermaster's."

"Naw. The Genrul wouldn't like it if we went runnin' off, gettin' supplies. Let's just mosey on back ta camp an' take it easy. We'll check back with the Genrul later on."

It was early evening before we could see Forrest again. The Browns' house was filled to bursting with officers and citizens waiting to see him for one reason or another. When we finally made it into his room he look tired, and repeated the orders he had given us early in the day. Stay put.

As we reached the lower landing, Mrs. Brown was shooing out the last of the visitors, exclaiming that the General needed his rest and couldn't see anyone else. She hurried past us up the stairs, and said over her shoulder that Eva and Clara were waiting to see us in the parlor. With a knowing grin, Josh put on his cap and walked out the front door.

The girls welcomed us with warm smiles and tall glasses of cold water. "We're sorry we don't have any lemonade, but lemons and sugar are impossible to get these days," Clara said apologetically.

"Oh, this water is just fine. It hits the spot, doesn't it, David?" I replied quickly. Blushing, he nodded his head and said "yes" with vigor.

We took our usual places, Clara and I on the sofa, David and Eva on the chairs facing us. Enthusiastically, Clara began asking us questions about our capture of Streight's raiders. Briefly I explained what had taken place, trying to leave out the parts unfit for female ears.

"We've heard all kinds of stories about the General's persistence and bravery. But I can't believe it was as easy as everyone pretends it was. I imagine we lost a lot of men, didn't we?"

"Yes, we did."

"How about the Yankees? Did they lose many men?"

"Yes, quite a few."

She looked boldly into my eyes. "I'm sorry, John. It must have been very hard on you."

"No, not really. I came through without a scratch."

"You don't have to pretend. I'm sure the life of a soldier is much harder than you make it out to be."

"You're right. But there is no reason to alarm you. The General takes very good care of us, and I have David and Josh to look out for me."

Drawing back, she said, "Well as far as I'm concerned, the General doesn't take such good care of you. He's always putting his men in the most awkward positions, taking them into enemy territory, chasing armies twice as large, and practically running you all to death. Personally, I'd rather he fight like everyone else," she ended, almost petulantly.

"You're being too hard on him. As far as I'm concerned, the General is the smartest man in the army. He has the loyalty, or at least the respect, of every man that fights under him. That's more than I can say for all the other Generals I've ever heard of." Noticing the sharp look on her face, "Except General Lee, of course."

"Maybe so, but I've heard some strange stories about him. He hasn't enough education to speak of, much less any military training, and he doesn't follow the rules of war like the other generals. I don't care if he is my Father's friend."

"No, he doesn't. He uses common sense instead. Look here – doesn't it make more sense to sneak into an enemy camp and find out what's happening, instead of relying on what scouts might see? Or making sure your artillery pieces are in good condition yourself before you go into battle instead of waiting until it's too late to do anything about it? Isn't it better to pretend to have twice the number of men if it will save the lives of those who depend on you? People can say what they will, but I know the

General has saved a lot of lives by using common sense fighting this war, and I hope he continues to do so."

"I'm sorry. I didn't mean to get you upset, John. It's just that he is a hard man to get to know. Before the war when he visited, he was a kind, thoughtful person. And he still is at times. But whenever the conversation turns to war, he changes. He becomes hard, almost cruel. It gives me the shivers to be around him when he's like that."

"He's just a man with a purpose. He knows what he wants, and that's to whip the Yankees. Sure, he's hard at times. But he has to be. We all have to be, if we're going to win."

"You're right. But it still worries me, you being with a man who can put you into such dangerous situations." Looking down, she continued, "I have grown quite fond of you, and would hate it if anything were to happen to you."

Eagerly, I tried to peek at her face. "Really? Are you telling me the truth? I hope you are, because I care for you too."

Giggling, she tilted her eyes up to me and said, "Oh, you're such a flirt!"

"But I'm not. I mean every word. Your concern touches me, but I promise you it's unfounded. The General has a genuine feeling for all of us, and only does what's absolutely necessary. Even Josh trusts him completely, and he's as cynical about most things as a man could be."

"Are you talking about that old hillbilly that's been hanging around with you and David? I don't see that his opinion is so important."

"I wish you wouldn't talk about him that way. He's been a true friend to us. I know that before the war we most probably wouldn't have been friends. But times have changed. Even though he's a bit rough around the edges, and may only be a dirt farmer, he's honest and quite trustworthy. In fact, I would trust him with my life, which is more than I can say about most people I know. I wish you would talk to him, Clara. I think you would like him."

"Hmmm. I don't know. He has an almost sinister look about him."

Laughing, I said, "You're right. But he's not at all what he seems."

"Let's not talk about him any more right now. I just saw Mama go back upstairs. Perhaps we could go out to the garden." I nodded.

We left David and Eva. The air outside was fresh and damp, tinged with the familiar scent of blooming lilacs. We said little as we circled the garden and then rested on an old broken bench. We held hands, and a distinctly peaceful, warm feeling filled my heart. We stayed only a few minutes. As we headed to the back door, I impetuously leaned over and gave her a kiss.

"Oh, don't, John! Mama might see us!"

"She can't see us. She's upstairs, tending to the General. Besides, it's a cloudy night. Surely she knows by now how I feel about you."

She headed back to the parlor with me at her heels. David and Eva were still in their seats. Rising, David announced that we had better be getting back to camp. As we said our goodbyes, Clara kept her eyes from mine.

We arrived back at the house early the next morning. We were told by the servant girl Alice, who opened the door, to head right upstairs, as the General was waiting for us.

"Come in!" barked the General as we knocked on the door. He was lying on the bed, dressed in his plain gray uniform instead of the nightshirt he had been wearing the past few days.

"Come in, boys. I've been waiting for you. I have an errand to run this morning, and I'd like you all to take me."

"Yes, sir!" We said in unison.

Josh and I joined hands and made a carrying chair, while David helped him to his feet. He gently lowered himself down, put his arms around our shoulders, then directed us to take him to the hotel.

Awkwardly, we carried him as quickly as we could. He was a big man – well over six feet and at least 170 pounds. I felt almost sacrilegious, carrying him in such a way. When we arrived at our destination, he gave us orders.

"Lieutenant Gould has requested to see me. It seems the knife wound I inflicted on him has become infected. Josh, you will go with me to his room. I'd like you, David, to post yourself here in the street in case anyone comes looking for me. You'll need to take any messages that need my attention. John, you'll stay in the hallway and see that we are not interrupted. Let's get this over with."

The Lieutenant's room was upstairs. As we walked up the long winding flight, I began to feel the strain of the General's weight on my elbows and shoulders. Josh and I lowered him into a chair close to the lieutenant's bed when we got him into the room. As I turned to leave, I took a long, searching look at Gould's face. The change that had come over it since I had last seen him was very noticeable. No longer filled with hate and malice, but with fear and sorrow etched into his peaked features.

I stood guard calmly outside the door. Without a doubt Gould was dying. I had seen others die from the mysterious diseases that get hold of a man after he has been wounded, and the translucent look of his complexion told of the infections that were taking over his body. Curiously, I watched a large colored woman who served as the hotel maid waddle past me, shaking her head sadly as she went past the door. I wasn't the only one who had read death in Gould's face.

After several minutes Josh joined me outside the door. When I asked him for details, he grudgingly gave them.

“That there boy asted the Genrul fer his fergiveness. Said he acted out a spite, an' was glad the Genrul was spared, ta help save this here country. Said he had ta see him fore he died. Dangedest thing I ever heerd.”

“Why did you leave?”

“Well, when the Genrul started cryin' an tellin' him he was sorry fer killin' him, I kinda figgered it was time fer me to go.”

“Probably right,” I said thoughtfully. We stood there silently for a few minutes. The General's voice interrupted our silence, calling us back into the room. We went back and stood on either side of his chair.

“I must be leaving now, Lieutenant. If there is anything else I can do for you, please let me know.”

“Thank you, sir.” Weakly, he closed his eyes. His chest barely rose with each short, labored breath.

“Come on, boys.” Josh and I gripped hands as he stood and lowered himself into our makeshift chair.

I took a quick glance at his face, but only saw his usual expression of confidence. There was no sign of the tears he had shed while Josh had been present.

When we reached the street, David joined us and said the general had received no messages of any importance, just the best wishes of a few townspeople. Forrest nodded silently.

The trip back to the Brown house was silent, interrupted only by an occasional passerby wishing the General his best. He would nod his appreciation, but would utter not a word. When we entered the Browns' front door, the General told the waiting officers that he would be ready to see them in 15 minutes. We took him up the stairs to his room.

After we set him down on the bed, he drew a deep sigh and reached for the worn Bible on his nightstand. He glanced at us and said, "Thank you, boys. I hope you'll forgive my display of emotion, Josh."

Josh cleared his throat and said, "Yessir."

"I just hope the Lord can forgive my fit of rage against that young man."

"But sir, you had to protect yourself," I said.

"I know that. I don't regret that part of the situation. I do regret letting myself get so filled with rage that I would wish death on one of my own men." He opened his Bible and said, "You are free to go now. Come back this evening. I may have some work for you."

I have often heard it said that General Forrest was a cold-blooded killer. Not so. He killed the enemy because that was the only way he knew how to defend his country. He made every effort to spare the lives of his men whenever possible. Because he was not a publicity seeker and felt no need to justify himself to those who spread slanderous stories about his character, his name was often linked with the most awful stories of death and deprivation one could imagine. Those of us who fought with him knew better.

CHAPTER SIX

As we moved up the Franklin Pike through the humid heat of early June, I wiped the sweat off my forehead and glanced ahead to see how the General was holding up. Although he had been allowed out of bed only a week before, his back was as stiff and straight as ever.

The Yankees had moved their main body of troops from Franklin to Triune, a small community 15 miles southeast of their old position. The General had been ordered to investigate the enemy's forces left behind. He was given command of two brigades – Starne's, who traveled with us, and Armstrong's, up from Lewisburg.

It had been several weeks since we had seen any real action, and we moved ahead in nervous anticipation. We exchanged small talk and listened to bits of chatter that floated up from the troops behind us, but underneath it one could sense an undercurrent of anxiety and concern. The thought of facing the enemy again brought me a sense of trepidation.

We were barely three miles south of Franklin when we ran into some Yankee pickets. Yahooing in excitement we spurred our horses forward and gave them chase. When we reached the outskirts of town, where the huge Yankee tent camp had been, along with their fort, we slowed to allow the rest of our troops to catch up. The General began shouting orders to his officers – we were to spread out and move in on the encampment, keeping the houses between us and the well-fortified enemy.

Scattered, useless shots were exchanged as we moved slowly, irrevocably forward. Suddenly, a shout rang out, and a young trooper from Starnes' Brigade pointed ahead to the breastworks of the Yankee stronghold. Squinting, I could make out some sort of flag flying next to the Union colors. I turned and headed toward the General, but he had already seen the flag himself.

"I can't quite make out what sort of flag that is, but perhaps it indicates a truce. Captain Anderson,

Lieutenant Boone, let's get our truce flag out and ride ahead," the General said heartily.

As the three of them moved forward, Josh, David and I posted ourselves behind a rundown outbuilding close to the side of the road. Leaning over, Josh spat and said, "Hot day."

Exasperated, my eyes darting ahead to check the progress of the truce party, I said, "Is that all you can say at a time like this? We may have just won the easiest victory of the war!"

"Maybe, maybe not," he replied calmly.

The General and his officers had only gone a short distance before a voice shouted out from behind him. "Turn back, General! That ain't no truce flag, it's a signal flag fer help!"

Immediately, the three men wheeled their horses around and headed back, but not before Forrest raised his hat in the direction of the voice, silently thanking whoever was responsible for correcting his mistake. When they returned safely, he gathered his staff together for a brief conference.

We were barely on the outskirts of town. The fort was placed on a bluff at the other end, the northern side. Some of the civilian population had taken shelter within the walls of the fort, while others had closed up their homes and taken shelter inside them. Yankee pickets, sharpshooters and skirmishers had taken up positions within the town itself, using whatever cover they could find.

Never one to waste time, the General ordered our two artillery pieces unhitched from their horses, dismounted us and positioned us behind them, and moved forward. The gunnery crews sweated, strained and groaned as they rolled the pieces up the main road heading to the fort. They stopped often to shoot at the breastworks and houses hiding Yankee soldiers. We moved cautiously but quickly behind our spitting shields and sought shelter wherever we could find it.

Part of Starnes' Brigade managed to clear the Yankees out of the town jail, and freed several political prisoners being held there. A large quantity of commissary supplies, stored in various buildings, fell into our hands, and we were thankful for them.

We were moving in on the fort when a long column of dust was sighted to the southeast. The General determined that reinforcements were coming to relieve the weary soldiers in the fort, and that they were moving against Armstrong's Brigade, posted to guard against any such emergency. Quickly he ordered a retreat, in order to insure a way back to our headquarters at Spring Hill. He knew full well he didn't have the manpower or supplies to withstand a full-scale attack.

We moved south and joined up with Armstrong about three miles from town. Wearily, we made camp for the night. Before going to sleep, we quietly discussed the day's action, and agreed the supplies we had captured had been well worth our effort. Our army had suffered only a few minor casualties, and we had determined the majority of Yankee troops had moved to Triune. Thankful to be passed over for picket duty, the three of us got a good night's sleep.

We arrived safely back at Spring Hill the next day, but didn't remain there long. General Rosecrans, in charge of the large Yankee army in Triune, was determined to push the Confederates out of Tennessee. General Bragg was equally determined not to face him until we had the Tennessee River at our backs. Our entire army began an orderly but quick retreat southeast to Chattanooga. Forrest's command was given the responsibility of securing and holding the pass through the Cumberland Mountains at Cowan so that Bragg's forces could get through.

Although there were a few Yankees scattered about in East Tennessee, we had very little trouble securing the pass. We held it with ease while most of Bragg's army marched through. They had been pursued by a sizable cavalry force through the rolling countryside, but General Forrest ordered us to guard the rear and make sure every Confederate made it to safety. We followed the main army through the pass toward Chattanooga.

Just as we reached Cowan, a small village perched on the eastern shoulder of the Cumberland Mountains, the Yankee cavalry force that had pursued Bragg for so many miles caught up with us. Only the escort, led by the General himself, was left in the village to greet them. We fired a few rounds, but saw we were vastly outnumbered. Forrest ordered us to retreat, and we moved out in an orderly fashion. A toothless old woman scurried out of her ramshackle house and stood by the roadside, shaking her fist at us.

"Turn an' fight, you devils!" she screeched. Blind to the stars on his collar, she looked toward the General. "Turn an' fight like a man, you big coward! I shore wish Forrest was here! He'd make you fight, 'stead of running like the dogs you are!"

Laughing uproariously, Forrest spurred his horse and led us at a gallop out the road leading through the pass. "Boys!" he yelled out, "I think I'd rather face a whole battery of artillery than that old woman!" Laughing at the picture in our minds we all shouted our agreement. Halfway through the pass we turned and saw the enemy wasn't making any great effort to catch up with us. We slowed our pace, and soon caught up with the tail of the main army.

Bragg set up his main camp in Chattanooga, but we saw little of it. Forrest's command was on constant picket, scouting and forage duties while Bragg's army sweltered through the hot, stifling weeks of August, nestled in a valley flanked on three sides by the Cumberland Mountains.

Ever since we had entered east Tennessee, David and I had been overcome with homesickness. Although at times we were less than forty miles from home, we dared not ask for leave. Overworked and overtired, our small army had need of every man. Josh knew how we felt. He told us that whenever we traveled into Middle Tennessee, he had the same feeling. Since he had joined the army he had only been home once. Even then, he only stayed two days before his guilt overcame him and he headed back to the General.

"Boys, I jist felt like I was shirkin' my duty. But that don't mean ya'll can't go home. If'n ya ast the Captin, he'd prob'bly letcha go."

"David, what do you think?" I asked eagerly.

"Lord knows I'd like to go home. But maybe we should wait until this campaign is over. Maybe then we'll have some free time and could risk it," he answered quietly.

"Yeah. Maybe we'll beat them damn Yanks back to Kentucky here perty quick. Then we can all go home," Josh said contentedly.

"So you think there will be a big battle?"

"I can't help but think it. Them Yanks is brewin' fer a fight, an' the only thing I kin see is to oblige 'em. Course, that don't mean to say them bigwigs sees things the same as me."

"What do you think our chances will be?"

"There ain't no tellin'. Jist depends on the time an' place, an' who makes the most mistakes."

CHAPTER SEVEN

The Yankees dawdled along, finally crossing the Tennessee River at Caperton's Ferry on or about the 27th of August. We left our position at Chattanooga and found ourselves back in the familiar area of Rome. Forrest received a small wound in the arm during a sharp skirmish to keep the Yanks from cutting off the railroad there. He shrugged off the incident moments after it occurred, as if he couldn't be bothered with such a trivial incident.

For the next few weeks we were given a free hand, Forrest covering the army's right while Wheeler's command covered its left. We spent the nights in our saddles, striking at the enemy wherever we could find a weakness. Our army was hungry and ill-clothed, so we did what we could to alleviate their suffering. Forrest sent out one scouting party after another so that he could stay informed on the enemy's position and their plans. He was not above sending out members of the escort as deserters to give out false information. He kept in close contact with General Bragg so that he could relay any news that fell into our hands.

A group of us captured a Yankee courier sneaking out of Chattanooga, headed north. Trembling in fear, he gave us his message without a word when he noticed the ferocious look Josh directed at him. Growling, he snatched it from the young man and handed it to me.

"Open it, an' let's see what them Yanks got ta say."

"Shouldn't we take it back to the General and let him read it first?"

"Ain't you got no sense? If'n it's real important we gotta know so's we kin git back quick. If'n it ain't, we kin take our time and pervent gettin' kilt. Open it, boy."

Squinting in the pale light of the moon, I opened the letter and held it close to my face. As I read, I began to chuckle and shake my head.

Querulously, Josh said, "You gonna let us in on the joke?"

“It seems General Rosecrans is worried about us. He wants General Burnside to come down from Knoxville to protect his left flank from Forrest's raiders.” I laughed again and tucked the letter into my coat pocket.

We carried the message and the courier back to the General. Still shaking, the Yankee was taken to the prisoners’ compound while Forrest reviewed the message. After reading it, he handed it to Captain Anderson and dismissed us with a nod.

It was near dawn by then, and when we got back to our bedrolls I commented on the General's unenthusiastic response to the captured letter. “I should think he would be pleased to know the enemy finds him so dangerous.”

“Hell, that's jist what he wants 'em ta think. He don't need them ta tell him he's doin' a good job. He knows he is.”

Chattanooga fits snugly into a narrow valley, Missionary Ridge on the east, Lookout Mountain to the south and west. Both are characterized by thick woods and tall, rocky cliffs, and form a trap that could mean death to an army.

From the outset, September 18, 1863 was unlike any other day I had yet experienced. We found ourselves in a situation over which we had no control. Under normal conditions we could always look to the General to guide our every move, but not so on this early fall day. Bragg was in charge, with the General his subordinate. Dark forebodings shadowed our outlook.

How do I adequately describe the sights and sounds of an army of better than 60,000, poised, on the verge of battle? To be sure, we had been scattered loosely along the snaky curves of Chickamauga Creek, many of us held in reserve, but each segment of our force knew the existence of the others and felt somewhat comforted, even though we knew the strength of our enemy and that a herculean task lay before us. Tens of thousands of men on each side, determined to come out alive, even though they knew there would have to be a large number of casualties if either side was to claim victory.

We knew we were immersed in a set of events that could not be denied. I felt as if the devil himself was blowing his hot, fetid breath down the back of my neck, urging me to participate in something I would ever afterwards regret. From the faces of those around me, they felt the same as I. We had the General with us to provide confidence, but we knew the impending battle could never be under the control of one man. We would be pushed along with the tide of events, ever onward, without even a piece of driftwood to cling to.

Buckner's small corps had been pulled out of Knoxville to join up with us, and he was quickly replaced by the Union Army in that city. This meant that Athens was probably swarming with Yankees. The thought gave me the shivers. My father would be considered a traitor. It was not unlikely he would be mistreated or forced to leave. Surely not, I prayed. He was a skilled physician, therefore he provided a necessary skill. Perhaps they wouldn't turn out a man who could prove to be a benefit both to the army and the civilian population.

Forrest's command was placed on the right flank of the main army, or to the north, as Chickamauga Creek runs in a north-south direction. We were somewhat to the west of Reed's Bridge on the creek when we clashed with the enemy. The General's force on hand had been whittled down to about 300 men – the escort and the part of Morgan's men who had made it out of Ohio. Valiantly, dismounted, we stood our ground against a heavy onslaught of men in blue, but were slowly, inexorably, pushed back.

We hated to give up even an inch of precious ground to the blue tide that opposed us, but the force of their numbers was too great. We made a stand at Reed's Bridge, shielded by the sloping bank of the creek, as well as the bridge itself. The enemy's bullets plinked around us, shooting up little spurts of earth and grass. Several of us were hit before the General grudgingly ordered us to retreat across the bridge. We carried wounded comrades with us. Others covered our retreat from the eastern side. We watched dolefully as the Yankees crossed Chickamauga Creek.

Shortly after 4 p.m. We were relieved, and ordered out on scouting and picket duty. David, Josh and I felt lucky to be sent out as scouts. There is nothing worse than to watch, wait and listen while on picket duty, knowing full well the enemy could strike at any moment. We could relieve our tensions on horseback, one of the best remedies I know for almost any problem.

We were ordered to the right of the battlefield, between it and Chattanooga. Later that evening, the General had us set up camp behind the rest of the troops.

I slept fitfully that night, tossing and turning in my blanket. My mind's eye kept turning to the sights and sounds I had seen and heard that day. The murderous blue wave converging on us, the screams of horses and men as they fell in bloody huddles, the pitiless cries of the wounded, always calling for water, the stark terror in the eyes of those around me, even as they moved to do as commanded. Before daybreak I finally loosed myself from my tangled, sweaty blanket and sparingly splashed a few drops of water on my face from my half-empty canteen.

A harried courier came clattering up and left a message for the General. We were ordered to mount and followed Forrest in a northwest direction, back toward Chattanooga. Word was passed along that we had been ordered again to the right side of the battle line, where we were to confront the enemy as soon as we could. As I leaned sideways in my saddle to pass the word along, I glanced at Josh. His face had a sour, sober look about it. I could see he was no happier about our orders than I was.

We soon found what we were looking for. We dismounted and arranged ourselves for battle, joined by Pegram's division, fighting as infantry.

It didn't take long for us to discover we were badly outnumbered. Uneasily, we eyed the overwhelming numbers that faced us, and our worst thoughts were aptly expressed by Josh: "That damn bastard Bragg! I knew we shouldn'ta trusted him. He's done shifted the whole damn battle line in the wrong direction! Lookit here! There wasn't half that many Yanks there yestiday!"

He was right. Sometime during the night Rosecrans had been steadily shifting his forces toward Chattanooga, to insure a safe place of refuge. Our troops, however, had been doing the opposite, which meant our right side now faced a greater number of troops than it had the day before.

Minutes ticked by and our exchange of fire grew more intense. We were sure the General had sent for reinforcements, but none arrived. We held our ground through a virtual shower of bullets. Men were falling all around. I turned and saw Forrest behind us, his aides at his side, exhorting the men not to give up. I saw him abruptly turn to Captain Anderson, and with a great waving of arms, send him off to the rear.

We faced a solid line of infantry, but we couldn't be classified as much more than a skirmish line. Desperately we held on, hoping and praying we would get help. David and Josh both looked a fright as they squinted through the dense smoke, their sweat-streaked faces covered with dust and gunpowder. None of us shot at anyone in particular – we just aimed in the direction of the enemy and fired. The shifting smoke made it impossible to get a clear view of the Yankees.

A ragged cheer reached us as Captain Anderson returned with Dibrell's Brigade. Although we were in desperate need of infantry, we got another brigade of cavalry. We dug in harder.

Forrest was still imploring for more help, but received no answer from his superiors. Angrily, he gathered several of his officers together, told Pegram to hold his ground at whatever the cost, and galloped off to the rear for more troops.

As if by instinct, the enemy increased their fire. Volley after volley of artillery fire withered the air. Intense heat and smoke rose around us, burning our eyes and throats. Ammunition carriers distributed their wares, litter bearers removed the dead and wounded within their reach, but I was hardly aware of them. My only thoughts were load, aim, fire; load, aim, fire . . .

Mercifully, the General returned with two brigades of infantry, commanded by Wilson and Walthall. They were placed to the left of us, and so began to take the brunt of enemy fire. Determined to show us up, owing to the natural rivalry between infantry and cavalry, they fought like the very demons of hell, and forced the enemy by short charges to give up the ground they had so easily held but a short while ago. Their determination pushed us all along, as they captured a battery of artillery and forced the Yanks to withdraw even further west. Elated, Forrest ordered them to halt and await for further reinforcements.

We had a short breathing space until Ector's Brigade arrived, just enough to look around and gauge our surroundings. We knew the horse holders were at the rear, somewhat shorthanded in order for every available man to be in the fight. Wistfully, I thought of their relative safety, but soon shrugged off the idea that I would rather be where they were.

By this time, we were thoroughly mixed in with Pegram's and Dibrell's brigades, on the extreme right of the battlefield, with Ector's newly arrived men on our left and Wilson's men on the left of them.

Before our reinforcements could get good and settled in, a sizable group of Yankees positioned themselves to the left of Wilson's Brigade and opened fire. A killing crossfire resulted, and caused our entire line to fall back in retreat. We moved slowly, firing from every stump and hole that could afford some shelter. The General was beside us.

He fought with rage, especially when he realized that we would have to leave behind the battery of artillery we had captured. He had used the pieces to great advantage, like shotguns, rolling them forward to short range and savagely firing. But they were too heavy to roll back quickly enough, and all horses close at hand had been killed.

“Damn! I can't lose all of them! John, run get some horses and let's save at least one of 'em from those son-of-a-bitches!”

“Yes, sir!” I ducked as low as I could and ran several hundred yards to the rear. Breathlessly, without any explanation, I snatched the reins of four horses from the hands of a holder, mounted one, and rushed forward. Three other men grabbed more horses as I headed to a big gun, stranded in the field, dead and dying horses and men scattered around it. Hurriedly, we took harnesses off the dead horses and strapped them to ours. Liberally using the whip, we slowly moved the gun to the rear.

The General strode up to us, just as a sweat-drenched courier reached him. As his horse reared at us, he saluted and stuttered, “Sir, I have a message from General Ector, sir. He's worried his right flank will give way.”

“Tell the General not to worry. I'll take care of it,” Forrest snapped. The courier saluted and rode off.

“Thank you, boys. We'll need this gun before the day is over,” he said grimly as he slapped the barrel.

I returned the horses to the holders, and searched out David and Josh. As I crouched forward and flopped to the ground, Josh handed me my rifle.

“Thought I'd save this fer ya. Figgered you might have a need of it.” Josh spat and sighted down the barrel of his gun.

The grueling fire continued. Word was passed along that Wilson was being forced back. Forrest raged behind us, stopping now and then to fire at the enemy. The courier returned and addressed him. The General's answer could be heard over the cannon fire.

"By God, tell Ector I am standing firm, and will take care of his left flank also!" The courier wheeled in fright and galloped away.

"It's a damn good thing we got the Genrul here, else the rest a' these lily livered, sniveling fools woulda' given up last week!" Josh snorted in disgust. We nodded in agreement.

Suddenly, we found ourselves relieved. Forrest's cavalry was ordered back while fresh infantry took over. Like sleepwalkers, we moved to the rear and made camp. It was only 1:30 in the afternoon, but it seemed like eternity since we had broken camp that morning. Tiredly, we gnawed on cold cornpone, the only food we had. We shared what water we had with others.

I couldn't keep myself from nervously glancing back over my shoulder, toward the slaughter I knew was taking place. I looked about and noticed many missing faces. The men who were left wore empty, frightening expressions, their faces smeared with dirt and grime, their clothing in tatters, most sporting a bloody rag tied around an arm or leg or hand. I shuddered and thanked God for still being alive.

♦ ♦ ♦

Sunday morning dawned, and my head still rang with the sound of the axes that had steadily been chop, chop, chopping through the night. While we rested, the Yankees had not been idle. They had been busy fortifying their positions, and I knew they would be harder than ever to dislodge.

Again, we were positioned on the right flank of the army, with orders to join in a general attack at dawn. As the sun rose we patiently waited for the signal to start the battle again. Minutes drifted by and the General grew restless. He paced behind us, the familiar signs of anger showing on his face. His eyes grew bloodshot, his face dark red, as he sent off courier after courier to find out what the holdup was. We were quiet, contemplating the task before us. Would we ever drive the Yankees away, and if we did, at what cost?

Around 9:30 the signal was given. We inched forward against an enemy so deeply entrenched we knew we could never budge them. Helplessly we fired, reloaded, fired again, to little avail.

Before long, orders were passed along to move to the north, to try and get around their left flank. We obeyed, and there found little resistance as the enemy was forced to extend their line. Still wary, we breathed a little easier, until our scouts reported a Union column moving toward us from the direction of Rossville. Tensely, we awaited the onslaught.

Have you ever had a premonition that something terrible was going to happen moments before it does? Like a flash, an awful feeling of dread enveloped me as I saw those Yankees heading for us. Sweat trickled furiously down my face, and my hands began to tremble.

Suddenly, I was thrown backwards as a searing pain shot through my upper left arm. I landed flat on my back, and saw David turn and lean over me.

Fear swamped his face and he started to speak. His look changed to one of surprise as his body jerked horribly in a long spasm. His limp body fell over mine.

I screamed, "Josh! Josh! Help!"

He pulled his head around, crawled to us and pulled David off me. Wincing in pain, I huddled over his body and asked, "Is he dead?"

"Naw, but he's barely breathin'. Looks like he took one in the back. Better git the two of ya to the rear. Here, boy, help me lift him."

"No. You stay here. They need you. I'll manage okay."

He grunted in agreement and turned back to his position. As I started to half drag, half carry David away, he shouted over his shoulder, "I'll come check on ya when these damn Yanks have had their fill of us."

It was rough going, back through the dense brush to the hospital tent. A fellow soldier with a wound to his shoulder helped me with David for a short way.

When we reached the tent, I could tell the surgeons were shorthanded. There were rows upon rows of the wounded lying out in the weather. Those who could speak were pitifully calling for water.

I pulled David to the best spot I could find, a short distance from the others. The stench of unwashed bodies, blood and infections was unbearable. I took off my cap and used it to fan David's face.

His condition was not good. He had lost a tremendous amount of blood and his breathing was very shallow. I sent up a silent prayer, but in my heart I knew it was useless. David could not live.

By and by, a doctor made his way over to us. He took a cursory glance at David, lying with his head pillowed in my lap, then shook his head. I bowed my head and cried.

Although the fighting was not far from where we were, I had completely forgotten about it. My mind wandered back, down trails and over hills I hadn't seen since childhood, my trusty rifle in my hand and my best friend at my side. Together, we had spent many an hour exploring the hills around Athens, until I got old enough to pursue other matters. How I wish I had appreciated those times while I lived them.

I paid little attention to my arm, as it had stopped bleeding. I didn't bother to get any medical attention.

The doctors were busy attending others who were in far greater need of their skills. Besides, I knew there was nothing they could do. The bullet had passed through the fleshy part of my arm and must have missed the bone completely.

David's breathing had grown shallower. I wiped my eyes and held his hand. I thanked God he had not awakened. The pain would have been greater than he could have borne. I grew drowsy from pain and dozed off.

When I awoke, night had fallen and Josh was gently shaking me. I started, then looked down at David. I didn't have to check him. He was dead.

"He's gone, boy."

"I know. I kept hoping, though."

"Have ya had somebody take a look at yerself?"

"No. I'll be okay."

"Well, we better take care a' David."

"No! Not yet. Please, Josh."

"What do ya mean? We gotta get him buried. We can't leave him here."

"No!" I screamed hysterically. "I can't let that happen yet. I'm not ready."

"Calm down. Take it easy. Here, I'm gonna go back to camp fer awhile. I'll be back as quick as I kin."

After he left, I slumped forward and cried. I couldn't bear the thought of leaving David in this hellhole, buried ignominiously with the thousands of others who had died there. He belonged home, with his parents, buried honorably alongside his ancestors in the family plot. We had left home with the intention of taking care of each other. He had died because of his concern for me, and I couldn't leave him.

I looked up wearily when I felt a hand on my shoulder. The General looked down at me, weariness and concern on his face.

"What's this I hear, John?" I saw Josh hovering at his elbow.

"What do you mean, sir?" I asked, brokenly.

"Why won't you let this soldier be buried? He was a brave man and deserves a decent burial."

"That's just it, sir." I gently laid David aside and jumped up. "He's more than just another dead man. Why in the name of God should he be buried here, where no one will remember where he lies? I can't accept it, sir, I just can't!"

He laid his hand on my shoulder again. "I understand, I really do. But I just can't see any other way."

"He's right, boy. There ain't nothin' nobody kin do."

"Yes, there is," I answered. As the General shook his head, I said, "Please, sir, hear me out. Athens is only about fifty miles from here. I could get him home in less than two days if I had your permission."

"Now how can I do that, son? There's no telling how many Yankees there are between here and Athens. Besides, I need every able-bodied man I can find right now."

Josh cleared his throat. "Well, Genrul, sir, I wouldn't exactly call this boy able-bodied. See, he's been shot there in his left arm. He ain't very much use to us in his condition."

"Another reason I shouldn't let him go. He needs medical attention."

"General, my father is a doctor. He can take care of me fine once I get home. Please, sir. I'll never be able to face David's parents again if I were to leave him here, so close to home. You see, he's an only child."

"Josh, run get Captain Anderson. I'll get him to fill out some leave orders for him." Sternly, to me: "I don't know why I'm doing this. But remember – I expect you to report back to me personally within a month's time. If you don't, you'll be shot as a deserter. If I were you, I'd take a very wide path around these damn Yankees." Gently, he continued. "Tell David's parents he was a brave and honorable soldier and I was proud to have fought with him."

"Yes, sir," I said, as I held back tears. The Major arrived and wrote out a pass for me. I found our horses and carefully tied David to the back of his, mounted Goldie, and waved goodbye to Josh.

It was hard going that night. I was weak from loss of blood and short rations. I circled the vicinity of Chattanooga as widely as I could, but was still able to hear the sounds of an army in motion. The Yankees were moving back to their city stronghold.

I stopped in the early hours of the morning to bathe my wound at a deserted well. It hurt terribly as I wrapped it with a bit of cloth I had torn from my sleeve. I watered myself and the horses and moved off again.

As the hours of darkness moved on, my head grew clearer and my grief more intense. My palms were sweating at the thought of telling David's parents of his death. What I was bringing home to them, a dead body strapped across a scrawny horse, was not what they had sent off with me. I almost wished it was I who was strapped lifeless to the plodding creature stumbling behind me. At least then David would be alive and I wouldn't have to face the grief of his loved ones.

The night was eerily still, a slight breeze whispered through the dense brush.

I kept looking over my shoulder, half-expecting to find a Yankee patrol with rifles raised, ordering me to halt. I shivered at the thought of spending months in a Yankee prison. We had heard stories concerning the conditions in such places and I knew I could never survive such a place if I were caught. I tried to hurry Goldie along, but he was going as fast as he could, his gaunt sides heaving with the effort of picking his way among the rocks and boulders that littered our path. I finally sighed and calmed myself with the thought that, whatever happened, I could do nothing about it.

When daylight broke, I realized I had not gone as far as I had hoped. A bare twenty miles lay between me and the battlefield, where I imagined the two armies were still butting heads.

My fear of capture abated with the rising sun. Now I could see any danger that approached. I decided to keep to the small path I was following, even though it wound about the rolling hills with seeming aimlessness. My sense of direction told me it was irrevocably leading me north toward my destination.

Around noon I heard the distant clatter of moving men. I eased off the trail in a westerly direction until I felt sure I could not be seen or heard. I found a small clearing with a creek running along its edge, so I decided to take a short rest. I inspected my wound but found no sign of infection. I rinsed out my bandage and re-wrapped it tightly around my arm.

I had nothing to eat, but was too bone-weary to search for food. I allowed the horses to graze for a few minutes, then tied them to a tree in the shade. I had covered David's body with a blanket to keep the flies and bugs away, but I knew the heat of the sun would do more damage than anything else. I wanted his parents to be able to see his face before he was buried.

I pulled my tattered blanket off my saddle and lay down close to the creek. I told myself I would not go to sleep, but only rest my eyes until all danger from the moving men I had heard was past. But loss of blood and lack of rest fought with me and I was soon fast asleep.

I awoke a few hours later, berating myself for my carelessness. I scrambled up, grabbed my blanket and retied it to my saddle. I didn't see the boy until I went to untie the horse carrying my dead friend.

He couldn't have been more than ten years old, and was hunkered down behind the trunk of a tree, his eyes wide with fright. I looked at him for a moment in surprise, and then called to him.

"Hey, boy, what are you doing?" What do you want?"

He didn't answer.

"Come here."

He scuffed forward, his head bowed. He stopped a few feet away.

"What are you doing here?"

"Please, suh. I wuz jist passin' by an' seen ya' sleepin'."

I looked quickly around and asked, "Where do you live? Where is your family?"

He pointed vaguely off to the south, but gave no answer. I could tell by his manner that something was wrong.

"Okay, boy. I've got to get going, so if there's something you want from me, you better speak up."

"Please, suh. I's skeered. The Yanks done chased my fam'ly off."

"Your Ma and Pa?"

"No, suh. I don't know where my Ma and Pa is. The Peterson's done bought me away from them two years back."

So you've lost your white folks. Well, where are the rest of your people?"

"They done run off. There was only four of us."

"I don't know what to tell you," I said as I mounted my horse. "Perhaps you should go to a neighbor's house until your folks can be found."

"Please, suh," he cried as he grabbed my stirrup. "All the white folks 'round here been run off. An' I's skeered of the Yanks. They don't like black folks. I seed 'em runnin' some black folks off that was only tryin' ta git somethin' ta eat. Take me with you, suh. I won't be no trouble, an' I don't eat much."

I looked down and saw a pair of big brown eyes brimming with tears and fright. He looked as if he hadn't eaten in days, and his clothes were torn and muddy. Impulsively, I leaned over and helped him up behind me. I could hear him snuffling as I made my way back to the path leading north.

We didn't speak for quite awhile. The signs showed at least ten men had moved south along the same route, but were long gone. Still, I stayed alert to any movement along the trail.

"Scuse me, suh, but who is dat on the horse we're leadin'?"

"He was my best friend."

"What happened to him?"

"The Yankees killed him. Back there around Rossville."

He was silent for a moment, then asked, "Where we goin'?"

"Athens."

We rode without another word until dusk. I stopped again for water. The boy went into the woods while I was taking care of the horses, and came back with a handful of wizened, dried up blackberries. While we ate, I decided to ask a few questions.

"What's your name, boy?"

"Matthew, suh, like in the Bible. But most folks call me Matt."

I nodded silently. “I don't understand something, Matt. Why did you come to me for help?”

“I dunno, suh.” He stopped chewing and scratched his head. “I know the Yanks is tryin' ta free us an' all, but they ain't very nice folks. When I seed you, I know'd you was a nice man.”

“I don't know about that. I'm sure they're just like us, some of them good and some of them bad.”

“Maybe so, but I ain't willin' ta take the chance,” he replied emphatically.

We mounted back on Goldie and continued on. Matt had given me something to think about. He had acquired a knowledge of the world in which we lived, even though he was a young slave boy growing up in the woods of Tennessee. Perhaps it was his condition of life that had given him his skepticism, or perhaps it was the war. Either way, it was a shame to hear such a young boy speak so knowingly of the ways of the world.

I sighed and slumped a little lower in the saddle. Clara entered my mind, and I wondered what she would think if she could see me. I stank with dirt and grime, wounded, my clothes in rags, and my face hadn't felt a razor in many a day. My best friend was dead, and now followed behind me, tied to a horse that was more dead than alive. I had left my responsibilities with the army, aided by an emotional fit that seemed more childish the more I looked back on it. I began to feel remorse at leaving during a time the General needed every available pair of hands.

Another Yankee patrol forced us off the path about 10 p.m. I figured we were only about five miles from Athens when we returned to the trail. I goaded Goldie to his fastest trot. He picked up his head and seemed eager, as if he recognized familiar surroundings.

The town was dark when we arrived. Since I didn't yet know whether there were any Yankees about, I skirted around to the west side of town and made my way up a back street to the Knox's home. I left Matt with David's body and the horses in the stable, then went through the garden and up to the back door. I held my breath as I knocked. The house was dark. After a short time, the door opened.

"Mastah John!" the startled voice of Beaulah, the housemaid who belonged to the Knox family, exclaimed. "Come in, suh! Where's Mastah David?"

"Are Mr. and Mrs. Knox home? I must see them immediately. It's urgent." A look of fear entered Beaulah's eyes as she nodded and left me in the kitchen.

The Knox's appeared. As they entered the kitchen, I could see they already knew why I was there. I cleared my throat and spoke before they could ask any questions.

"I'm sorry. David died yesterday. We were fighting outside Rossville, near Chattanooga. I've brought him home to you."

"Where is he?" Mrs. Knox asked, brokenly.

"Out in the barn, ma'am. Shall I bring him in?"

"No," Mr. Knox said quietly. "Beaulah!" he called.

"Yes suh?" she answered from the hall.

"Get Adam." To me, he continued, "We'll have to bury him tonight. This town is crawling with Yankees, and they might ask questions if we were to wait until tomorrow."

I could hear the sound of wailing as Adam entered the kitchen. He bowed his head as he was given his instructions. Mrs. Knox had seated herself in a chair by the fire, a dazed and glassy expression on her face.

Mr. Knox turned to me. "Forgive me, John. Can I get you something to eat?"

I looked into his tormented eyes and shook my head. "No thank you, sir. I've got a young boy waiting for me out in the stable, so I had best be getting on home."

"Thank you, John. We can never repay you for what you've done."

As I shut the door behind me, I heard David's mother begin to sob. I stumbled to the stable and got my horse. As Matt silently climbed up behind me, I took a last look at David.

"Goodbye, old friend. I'll never forget you."

I backed Goldie out of the stable and headed home.

My father looked at my arm first thing. Since the war put such a strain on the supply of medications, he had nothing but whiskey to put on it. It stung like the devil, but I knew it would help. I put myself to bed afterwards. Matt slept on the floor next to me.

I awoke late the next morning, still feeling groggy. It had been a long time since I had slept in a real bed, and I was no longer used to it. The bed groaned as I swung my legs over to get up.

My father had heard me stirring, and he entered the room. "Did you sleep well?"

"Not very. I'm used to a blanket and the stars."

"You look thin and worn, son."

"I laughed off the worried tone in his voice. "Don't worry about me. I'm managing."

"How long can you stay?"

"The General wants me back in a month."

"There's something we need to discuss. We've been having a lot of problems with Yankee patrols. Did anyone see you in town last night?"

"No, sir. Only the Knox's."

"Good. You'll have to stay indoors during daylight hours. If you were seen by the Yankees or one of their informers, you would be taken."

I nodded. "I was afraid the situation here would be like that."

"The war has reached even to Athens," he replied grimly.

"Where's the boy I brought?"

"He's in the kitchen."

"Sorry I had to bring him. I didn't seem to have much choice at the time."

"Let's go try and find something for you to eat."

We went down to the kitchen. Matt was there, gnawing on some old corn bread and some cold peas. I joined him. Not much, but after going so long with nothing to fill my stomach, I considered it a fine meal.

Matt offered to go to the barn and tend to Goldie. "Make sure he doesn't get any oats or corn, you hear? After what we've been through, it's liable to kill him. Just give him lots of hay for now."

My father piped up. "No worry for that. We haven't had grain around here for quite some time."

"Yes, I guess not."

We entered the office space in the front of the house, and my father got busy tending to his patient records. He looked older and more stooped than I remembered him, but seemed to be in relatively good health. When he looked up, I asked him for some paper and a pen.

"David had a girl in Columbia. I need to write to her."

"Of course. Let me see now . . . I put a few sheets of paper away to save for an emergency, which I guess this is."

He left me alone in his office. As gently as I could, I explained to Eva the sequence of events that had led to David's death and how I brought his body home. I tried to express my sorrow at his loss as simply as I could. After finishing I wrote a short note to Clara. I closed both letters and left them on the desk. No telling how long it would take before I could send them.

There were plenty of vegetables from the late summer garden, so Father and I managed to throw a supper together for the three of us. He explained that he didn't have Miss Mattie's services any more. She had run away about six months ago. "But Old Ned still comes around, although I haven't been able to pay Mrs. Willis for his services lately. No one has cash money any more. She says I can pay her back when the war is over."

"Any news of the war, Father? When I passed by Chattanooga the other day I heard the Yankees falling back into the city. If they gave up the fight, we won a major victory."

"I haven't heard anything. But I do have war news," he replied soberly.

"Paul Scott died two months ago in Virginia. So did Russell Fargate."

I lowered my head. Both had been close friends, almost as close as David.

"I didn't want to write you about it, since we knew it would be such a shock. But Charles Cooke is still in Virginia, and his parents report he is doing fine."

Silence. Then he continued. "Some of the boys fighting for the Yankees are dead, too. Clarence Morgan, for one."

I nodded briefly, but said not a word.

"You still look tired, son. Why don't you go back upstairs and get some rest?" my father asked.

"I think I will."

I dozed fitfully through the afternoon. The sun was following its fiery red path to its resting place behind the western hills when I climbed from bed. I watched for a moment out my window, then clumped downstairs.

Father was out, probably tending to a patient. I paced nervously around the house, re-examining objects I had been familiar with since childhood. I was by then too used to being outside in the open air, and felt caged in, like an animal in a traveling caravan. Matt sensed my frustration and steered clear, heading out to the barn to seek his own solace.

When father came in, we went to the kitchen, the only room in the house where he allowed himself to smoke. He lit up while I clenched and unclenched my hands in front of me.

"What's wrong, son?"

"Just restless."

"Have you checked your arm today?"

"Yes, sir. It's coming along fine. No sign of infection."

"Good. You were lucky."

"I guess. Listen, do you mind if I go out tonight for a ride? I'll wait until it's good and dark."

He pondered a moment, then nodded his head.

"Did you hear any news while you were out? About the battle, I mean."

"I suppose you could call it news. Rosecrans pulled back into Chattanooga, while Bragg has fortified the mountains surrounding the city. Neither side gained much ground."

"I don't believe it. All those thousands killed for nothing," I said, incredulously.

We both were silent for a moment. A waste, a waste. Over and over my mind repeated those words. I finally shook my head and looked up. Father spoke.

"War is the most useless invention man ever created. It solves nothing, only prolongs hate and misunderstanding among us. I wish to God we could solve our problems in a more humane manner."

"So do I."

We both sighed heavily.

"I've been approached by a member of one of those peace societies that have begun to plague us, especially since Gettysburg. Being a member of the medical profession, I suppose they thought I was an ideal candidate. I considered joining it, but I'm afraid the only way to end this bloody mess is to have total defeat, by one side or the other."

"I still have my beliefs, but I would gladly give them up if it would save your life." His eyes looked at me, filled with pain and a love I would not understand until I had children of my own.

"I'm going back, father. I have obligations."

"I know. I would never ask you to stay. You must do what you have to."

I waited until close to midnight before I left. As quietly as I could I made my way out of town, then spent an hour riding some old, familiar paths. When I got back to town, I went to the cemetery and searched for the Knox plot. I eventually found it, and

David's grave, despite Adam's excellent attempt to conceal it. I only spent a moment there. It too vividly reminded me of my loss.

The house was quiet when I slipped back home. I stumbled over Matt's sleeping body as I climbed into bed.

The days dragged slowly. Father's patients kept him busy. I spent many hours reading in the parlor, and several more with Matt in the kitchen before the fire. We hardly let him out of the house for fear someone would notice him, but tried to keep him busy with chores about the premises.

One Sunday, while my father was at church, I joined Matt by the kitchen fire. I sighed at the prospect of another long day.

"Mastah John, you sho' must be tired a' settin' 'round here wif nothin' ta do."

"I am, believe me."

"Must be awful excitin', fightin' in a war."

"Sometimes. But, come to think of it, soldiers have to sit around quite a bit, too."

"You shuckin' me, ain't ya?"

"No."

"Did you all just sit?"

"Oh, we'd find something to do, I guess. Mend saddles or sew on our clothes, sing songs, or listen to someone who could play the fiddle. I've always kept my Bible with me, so I've had that to read."

"Listen to music, huh?"

"Yes. The General has a real fine bugler. Sometimes at night he'd give concerts."

"That musta been mighty fine," he sighed. "Maybe I'll jine up when I git big enough."

I laughed out loud. "But the question is, which side would you join?"

"Don't rightly know, suh." He grinned. Maybe the Yanks."

"Well, I hope to God this war will be over long before you have to make up your mind."

The nights were easier. Father would be home, worn from the demands placed upon him, but always willing to talk. We would go to his office after supper and while away the hours discussing the war or local news.

Father was quite interested in the General. He had become a folk hero to the people of Tennessee. They enjoyed telling stories of the many ways he managed to sting the Yankees, and I took the opportunity to clear up a few misconceptions, at least in my Father's mind.

"I hear the General has no education. Amazing."

"Well, no formal education. He has a horrible time spelling. That's why Captain Anderson takes care of most of his correspondence. But he was a very successful businessman before the war and can express himself very well. Of course, he still has a backwoods accent."

"What kind of business was he in?"

"He was a slave trader for years, or so I've heard. Most recently, he owns and runs a couple of large plantations. In northern Mississippi, somewhere."

"Hmmm. For a man who comes from the backwoods, he has managed to work his way into the planter class."

"Yes. And very much pro-slavery. Even Josh, who could never afford to own a slave, is as pro-slavery as a person can get. The only way I can figure it is that the free black man is more of a threat to the poor than to anyone else."

"True. I hadn't thought of it that way. If the slaves were freed the poor man would have to compete with him for jobs and land."

"Which means, Father, if we lose we could find ourselves in the middle of a different kind of war."

We sat in silence for a moment, contemplating.

"What does the General have to say about the war?"

"The only thing he can say – that we will win. Forrest isn't a philosopher or a politician. He was born to lead men into war. If you could only see him on the battlefield you would understand. He has no fear, and cannot tolerate anyone around him who is unable to control theirs. He fights by instinct, as if there is another person inside him that always knows what needs to be done."

I stopped and shook my head. "It's impossible to explain. You'd have to see it."

"He doesn't sound like a very tolerant man."

"He can't afford to be. His brand of war demands total obedience. If the men thought they could do as they pleased, they would. We don't have any deserters or troublemakers in our outfit."

"I can imagine."

"But he doesn't demand anything he would not be willing to give. And he doesn't always follow the rules just because they're there. He uses his head more than any other general I ever heard of."

"So we've been told. Some of the rumors we've heard have led us to believe he can be vicious. I've been worried about you, son." He leaned over and put his hand on my shoulder.

"Don't be. The General is a determined opponent, but he is fair. He takes prisoners whenever possible and treats them as well as anyone else. And he doesn't allow his men to take advantage of civilians. He only takes what he needs. Really. We aren't allowed to drink or carouse, and woe to the man who mistreats a woman."

"Good."

"I've been meaning to talk to you about something."

"I know you're restless. I've seen it. But don't be in too big of a hurry to get back to the war, son."

"I've been home almost a week, and my arm is healing fine."

He sighed heavily and rubbed his puffy eyes. "Please, John. Stay awhile longer."

"But they need me. And what would happen to you if I were turned in?"

"At least stay until you're all healed."

I slept restlessly that night, the image of our ragged, dirty army burned into my mind. We had heard little about the war since I returned home. All we knew was that the two armies were stalemated at Chattanooga, both of them battered and worn. I had no idea where Forrest was, or even whether he and his little corps had survived. I felt stifled, shut up in the house. I prayed my arm would heal quickly so that I could return to the fight.

CHAPTER EIGHT

Saturday, September 26 seemed to arrive too early, after the almost sleepless night I had spent. Matt and I arose before the sun and went out to the barn to check on Goldie. At the kitchen table for breakfast we were joined by my father, dressed and ready for the day.

"Good morning!" he exclaimed cheerfully. I grunted at him. He consumed his meal and then scraped back his chair.

"I guess I'll be going. I'm off to the Jackson's. They're expecting a new addition to the family and are probably waiting for me."

The morning proceeded normally until shortly before noon, when I heard Matt's small black feet slapping down the hall toward me. He rushed into the kitchen, his face alight with excitement.

"Hurry, suh! Your Pa is headin' this way, an' he's got his ole mare at a trot!"

"Go help him unsaddle her," I told him as I jumped up and headed for the back door. He entered, his worn cravat askew and his hat gone.

"What's going on? What's happened?"

He spoke quickly, despite his hard breathing. "General Forrest is coming! He met the enemy on the banks of the Hiwassee and outflanked them. They'll be here before long."

"Matt, go upstairs and get my pistols." He scampered off.

"What are you going to do, son?"

"Why, I'm going out to see if I can help."

"But . . ."

"Don't worry, I'll be fine."

Matt returned with my guns and the two of us went to the barn and saddled Goldie. We could hear the sound of gunfire in the distance, as well as trotting horses and shouts from the street. Father joined us before I could mount.

"John, be careful."

"I will. And don't worry – with all the commotion about, I don't believe anyone will notice me."

He nodded his approval, a gleam of excitement in his eye. I got on Goldie and steered her out the gate.

The streets of Athens were bedlam. People rushed to and fro, the sound of panic in their voices. The clogged avenues echoed the clamor of horses' hooves as people fled the approaching storm. As I had assumed, no one paid the least attention to me.

I arrived at Main Street in time to see the Yankees pass through, heading north. They moved in an orderly fashion, although it was easy to see they were worn out. Their horses had the unsteady gait of animals that had been ridden hard. The men had the stony glare of tiredness, their faces covered with dust and the traces of gun smoke.

I did little to conceal myself, since the Yankees had other things on their minds. There were a few onlookers, people familiar to me, but they looked past me without recognition. Their eyes were glued to the procession before them, some with sadness, and others with looks of grim satisfaction.

I turned Goldie and made a swinging curve about the town, then headed south on the main road. Before long a warning shot was fired, and I halted. As soon as the scouts recognized me, they waved me on.

I spurred Goldie to a gallop until I sighted the General at the head of his escort. I pulled off the road into the thick pine woods and waited for him to approach.

He wasn't surprised to see me. He waved me next to him and we rode together at a trot.

“Did you see them?” he asked sharply.

“Yes, sir. Heading north. They're worn out but not in a panic.”

“Damn! I almost had 'em back there at the river!” he said vehemently.

He called over his shoulder to his staff and ordered them to a gallop. As they pushed their horses to greater speed, I slowed Goldie down and fell in with Josh.

We were silent until we reached the outskirts of Athens, when the General slowed us to a trot.

“How's the arm?” Josh asked.

“Fine. It's healing well.”

He cleared his throat and glanced away. “Did ya git David taken care of?”

“Yes.” Embarrassment colored my face. “I want to apologize to you for my behavior. I don't know what came over me.”

“It's okay, boy. Grief kin do funny things to a fella.”

I blinked, then changed the subject. “What's been going on?”

“Not much. That fool Bragg done messed everythin' up, jist like I knew he would. We coulda let them Yanks have it whilst they was filterin' back to Chattanooga, but Bragg was too busy presidin' over his little sewin' circle – I believe he's president. Anyways, the Yanks is safe 'n sound in the city an' we're camped around the town. I don't figger we'll never root them out," he replied bitterly.

We continued on through the town at a trot, a town that looked decidedly different now. I felt more comfortable and at home in the saddle with my comrades in arms and the General. I could see Athens and its people more objectively, and saw plainly that my allegiance to my former life had shrunk considerably. The well-kept square with its imposing courthouse, the familiar stores grown dingy and worn since I had last seen them, and the neat houses that had sheltered me in the past had changed. These things and what they represented were still dear to me, but for different reasons. My place was with the General, to do what I could to protect it. I no longer thought of Athens as a shelter, a place of refuge, but as a place I was duty bound to protect.

As soon as we reached the north side of town we returned to a gallop. We could hear gunfire ahead as our skirmishers harassed the fleeing enemy.

We were about five miles out when the General sent word back that he wanted to see me. I rode forward.

He glanced at me as I came alongside him. “You'll have to wait until dark before you can get back into town. I'm sure you know there are plenty of spies and informers around these parts.”

“Yes, sir. But I was hoping I could just stay with you.”

“No,” he replied sternly. “That would never do. I promised you a furlough and a furlough you shall have. Your family deserves some of your time. Stay with them awhile longer. Then head south. I'm not sure where we'll be, but inquire around Chattanooga, and I'm sure someone will know.”

“I will. And thank you, sir.”

He waved me aside, and I dropped back next to Josh. I rode with him until dusk began to fall, and then headed south. It was good and dark by the time I reached town. I slipped through side streets, now quiet after the day’s excitement, until I reached home.

The next morning from my window, I saw a Yankee patrol move down our street. It passed slowly, the men lazily looking at each house as they passed. They were unwashed and unshaven, and their horses were ill-treated.

I left three days later, after dark. My last day at home was pensive and sad. Matt didn't want me to leave, at least not without him. Since I had only found him I couldn't claim him as mine, but he didn't see it that way. The only life he had ever known or comprehended was that of a slave. He declared he was mine and that he belonged with me.

"I can't take you, Matt. A war in no place for a young boy."

"Please, suh. I don't eat much an' I won't make no trouble."

"I'm sorry. You'll have to stay here until the end of the war. No telling where your masters are, so we'll have to wait and see what to do with you."

"Yessuh," he said sadly and drooped his head.

"Now don't carry on. My father will take care of you until I get back. Try and make yourself useful, do you hear?" I said cheerfully.

Supper was quiet, as most farewell meals are. We waited in the kitchen until it was time for me to leave. Finally I stood up and said, "Well." Matt grabbed my pack and took it out to the stable.

Father walked me out to where Matt was saddling Goldie. He cleared his throat several times before he spoke.

"Be careful, son. My prayers are with you."

"I will."

"Write if you ever get the chance."

"Yes." I turned and shook his hand, then hugged him about the neck. I led Goldie out of the stable and mounted him. Despite the darkness, I could see the two of them, a tall, stooped gray man and a small black boy, waving at me as I rode off.

CHAPTER NINE

I headed south, along the same path I had come. The night air had a deep touch of autumn coolness to it. Goldie, feeling it, held his head up and pranced smartly. I patted his neck and thought, you might not be moving so fast, old boy, if you knew where we were heading.

The night air kept me awake and gave me a chance to clear my head. I would miss home, no doubt, but I was glad to be heading back where I belonged. My stay had made me realize my place was no longer in Athens. I was now a man in my own right. Sometimes I wonder why we expect life to teach us our lessons the way we want them to be taught, and find out too late our expectations are unreasonable. I certainly never expected my manhood would be achieved through heartbreak, trials and tribulations. I immaturely thought war would be fun, and that growing up would come along because it had to, not because I earned it.

The only good thing I had received from the war was the people I had met. People I could respect. I hadn't been able to tell my father much about Clara. Perhaps it was superstition. Perhaps I had been afraid that if I told him, something would happen to me. I didn't want to share her with him. At least not yet.

The letters I had written explaining David's death were still on my father's desk. He had promised to send them along at the first opportunity. I hoped they would reach them before I did.

As I expected, it wasn't an easy task finding the General. After several inquiries from different groups of soldiers still holding the mountains around Chattanooga, I continued on to Rome, Georgia. I had been told by a scruffy, odorous young sergeant that he could possibly be found there.

From what I could see, our troops didn't look very well. Most were haphazardly clad, and morale seemed low. Their situation was far from promising.

Bragg had thoroughly bungled the Battle of Chickamauga, and they knew it.

The weather turned cooler and the trees were busy turning colors. I set out from the Chattanooga area with the intention of enjoying my ride to Rome. I knew once I reached my destination it would be many months before I could enjoy true peace or calm.

I found my comrades camped close to the same place we had occupied before, after our pursuit of Streight. I was directed to the spot where the escort had settled, and was happy to hear Josh's loud, complaining voice before I reached it. At least, I thought to myself, he hasn't changed.

He greeted me with a wave and asked what had taken me so long. I shrugged and laughed.

"You best git over to the Genrul's tent. I expect he'll be glad to know ya didn't fergit us."

The General shook my hand and asked after David's family, then told me to get settled back in. I told him I was proud to be back, then returned to Josh.

Things had changed somewhat since I had been gone. For one, we had a whole new set of messmates. They seemed different, somehow – quieter and more taciturn. Life had become harder than they had been led to believe.

Everything in camp looked tattered and shabby, from the men's garments to the dilapidated tents and horse's gear. Josh commented that the food was even worse than when I left, a fact I found hard to believe until I had been back a few days.

I asked him about our situation. He looked at me piercingly for a moment, then asked, “You heerd anythin'?”

“Not much since I saw you in Athens. Only that Bragg's been busy babysitting the Yankees holed up in Chattanooga.”

“You mean you ain't heerd about the Genrul?”

“No, What about him?”

Josh heaved a sigh. “That dang fool Bragg jist about ruint this here war fer all of us. Not long ago he took away all the Genrul's men and put 'em under Wheeler agin.”

“Surely you're joking,” I said, aghast. “Doesn't he know how the General feels about Wheeler?”

“He shore does now. The Genrul let him know right quick he didn't like it none. He resigned.”

“Whew!” I whistled. “That must have shook everyone up. But I guess it got straightened out, or we wouldn't be here now.”

“Jist by the skin or our teeth.”

“What happened?”

“Fer some reason, President Davis jist happened to see the Genrul's letter sayin' he was getting out.”

He chuckled. "Davis told him he would make things right. The Genrul jist got back from meetin' with him a few days ago."

"So, how did he make things right?" I asked impatiently. I had forgotten how much Josh liked to draw his news out.

"Seems we'll be headin' out any day now, fer northern Mississippi. President done gave us an independent command."

"Great! We won't have to worry about these dunces anymore."

"Huh! Shows how much you know, which means not much, boy. First off, this ain't our own private fight, an' we'll always have ta tell our goin's on ta somebody. An' then there's the fact they 'bout cut our men down ta nothin'." He looked at me soberly, then vigorously spat into the fire. "We ain't got but three hundred men with us now."

"I noticed the camp seemed smaller than before. Must have been quite a blow to the General."

"Yup. They even took away the old Forrest Brigade. Them fellas shore was mad, an' so was the General. But since, he's been jist as chipper as ever. Seems ta be almos' glad we been cut back. I guess he feels like we'll be startin' over fresh agin, an' maybe things'll go right this time."

"He could be right, you know. Is that the General's wife I saw over at his tent?"

"Yup. She come as soon as we got moved here. She's a real lady, too. Religious. We been havin' preachin' two, three times a week."

"The General's lucky to have her along."

"Yup," he sighed wistfully.

We were busy over the next few days getting ready for our transfer. I had almost forgotten how efficient and demanding the General could be when there was a task at hand, but was soon reminded. Our force was much reduced, and he still took upon himself most of the details of our move.

By the time we left, I had fallen back into the old routine, and except for the fact that David was no longer with us I found it hard to believe I had ever left.

Our new messmates – Bradley Stephens was from northern Alabama, around Decatur. He was young, only 17, but seemed capable. He hated the Yankees with a passion. His family were sharecroppers and had recently acquired their own piece of land, but the war had interfered with their plans. He had been conscripted, and vowed to kill as many Yankees as he could so he could get back home. Ironic that, instead of placing the blame on those who had dragged him into the war, he consumed himself with loathing for the only ones he could fight against. At first, his intensity made me wary, but I soon learned to cope with it. He was a fine soldier, and followed orders promptly.

Thomas Burns was another matter. He had been conscripted too, but under different circumstances. He was the son of a wealthy planter and had been busy dodging the war since its start. He was 25 years old and as lazy and shiftless as the day is long. Perhaps that's why his father was no longer willing to pay to keep him out of the army. Lord knows how he wound up in the escort. Josh kept a sharp eye on him, and only by threats and intimidation was he able to keep Thomas in line.

Fred Moreland, on the surface, reminded me of Bradley. He shared the same background, but was older. He had a wife and family in Tennessee, and had been in Starnes' regiment almost from the beginning. He, too, was an excellent soldier, and had been transferred to the escort as a reward. He was remarkably amiable and easy to get along with. He could give and take a joke as well as any other man of my acquaintance.

Although Forrest's command had been greatly reduced, the escort had been replenished again to 65 men. Our little band was indispensable to the General. We were his eyes and ears, his good right arm, so to speak. I heard Captain Anderson once call us the "companion cavalry," like Alexander the Great once had.

We traveled west along the same path we had followed last year in pursuit of Streight. Josh and I relived the memories of that grueling chase, and we both agreed it had been one of our finest hours. We didn't know what lay ahead of us, but we were sure nothing in our future could compare to what we had already been through. If we had only known . . .

I realized the further west we moved the longer it would be before I could see Clara again. It pained me to think it might be months before we would be in Tennessee again. I resolved to write her again once we settled into some sort of permanent camp.

We arrived in Okolona, Mississippi around November 18, and spent several days setting up camp. We were welcomed with open arms by our neighbors, proud to claim the General as one of their own. He had two plantations in Cohoma County, as well as his hometown close to Memphis, in northern Mississippi.

The Confederate force there, however, didn't welcome us with much enthusiasm. The General looked grim when he entered Colonel Holston's tent, the man in command. Josh and I noticed the men seemed undisciplined. They were grubby, their equipment was falling to pieces because of lack of attention, and there was an overall atmosphere of despair. We exchanged knowing glances when the

General left Holston's tent, his taut body and bulging eyes telling us all we needed to know.

The General had sent for another regiment, under Colonel Richardson, but when it arrived it only contained about 200 men. Instead of complaining, he got to work. He planned on conducting a major campaign into western Tennessee, where he knew he could find plenty of young men willing to fill his ranks. He sent ahead a small force under Colonel Tyree Bell to spread the word of his coming.

West Tennessee was as good a place as any to gather supplies and men. The Yankees were supposed to be in control, and had thousands of men stationed around its perimeter. But the interior was free of Yankee soldiers, and once there we could move with little interference.

We had only a week to get things in order before we left. All of us who had been with Forrest did what we could to get the others ready for the coming ordeal. We had never followed any sort of routine discipline, but we were rough and tough when it came to keeping things repaired and in good working order. Our newer members were used to a slacker routine, but they soon found out this attitude wouldn't do if they were to remain with the General. By the time we were ready to leave, our equipment was reasonably in order.

We left Okolona on December 1. The General took his usual place, astride his horse on the side of the road so he could watch his men pass. He checked everything carefully before galloping to the head of the column.

Despite the cold, we were in good spirits. After all that had happened to us in recent months, it was invigorating to be on the road again, against enemies we could fight.

We had only enough horses to drag two big guns with us, with a scant five wagons of ammunition, but we knew what the General was capable of. Our lack of manpower and artillery bothered us none at all.

As we neared Memphis, Forrest shrewdly sent some men in that direction, a feigned attack we hoped would fool the Yankees enough for us to get past their troops stationed along the Memphis and Charleston Railroad. Just as he knew they would, all the troops were pulled into the city to defend against what they thought was a major attack. We crossed into Tennessee on December 4th.

It had been raining for days and days on end, making the roads nearly impassable. Even the smallest creek was swollen and filled with debris. We slogged onward and tried our best to ignore the weather.

We escaped a confrontation with the enemy until we reached Bolivar. There we had a short, stiff skirmish, and the Yankees gave way. Before we moved on, the General sent scouts off toward Memphis and Corinth to keep us advised of enemy movements.

We had forage and food waiting for us in Jackson, and we set up camp while the General began recruiting. He intended to return to Mississippi with enough fighting men to become a viable force in the war.

General Bell had done a fine job. Not only were we well supplied, but we had several hundred men waiting for us so they could join up.

Captain Anderson cheerfully volunteered Josh and I to help persuade men in the area to join us. Some of them had previously served or had recuperated from wounds, so were happy to join us rather than go back to their previous commands. Others had just come of age, or had been skipped by the conscription. We spent the next several days talking and cajoling, explaining the kind of adventures we had been through and what it was like to fight under Forrest. We glossed over the hardships as best we could.

I felt a little guilty about that at first. But Josh pointed out we couldn't afford to be completely honest. We needed men. Before long, I got into the swing of things and could spin a yarn almost as good as Josh.

The men would slouch up to our station point. "How's the food in the army?"

"Ain't too bad," Josh would answer. "The Genrul sees we git the best he kin find. Course," he would say nonchalantly, "not all them Genruls and such-like got much int'rest in what us soldiers eat."

"Is that a fact," they would say.

"Yup. The Genrul sees we are took good care of. Ain't that right, John?"

"Yes," I would stammer out. "Remember when we got those fine new rifles after we beat the Yanks up around Nashville? I still carry mine with me." I would then show off my rifle, which I always kept well oiled and gleaming.

"This here army life is bettern' workin', boys. I wouldn't lie to ya. Now, sometimes we git a mite tired and worn out, chasin' these damn Yanks round the countryside, but somebody's gotta do it. This here's our country, ain't it? They ain't got no right runnin' round, scarin' our womenfolk, stealin' our food an' horses, an' worse."

"That's right," someone would growl. "They been a burnin' and stealin' hereabouts fer long enough. Ain't you been hearin' bout all the murderin' and outrages they bin doin'? Where do I sign up?"

We would point the way to the recruiting tent, and then settle back and wait for the next group of curious, would-be soldiers to come along.

The General set up recruiting stations in every county in West Tennessee. Because most of the major towns were held by the Yankees, we were forced to proceed in secret. Not above taking firm measures, Forrest issued orders to conscript any young man who was diffident about signing up. Once we got those draftees south to Mississippi, they would make fairly good soldiers. Until then, we took turns guarding them, so they wouldn't run off on any unnecessary errands.

After a while a ring of Yankees began to close around us, moving south from Kentucky, from Fort Pillow on the Mississippi River, and north from Memphis and Corinth. We hadn't tried to conceal our presence. The Yankees knew Forrest was a very dangerous man. By the middle of the month we began preparing to pull out.

We were pitifully short of arms, so the General sent Colonel Russell ahead with a small, armed force to protect the new men who had no guns. He also sent a message to General Joe Johnston, the top commander in the West, asking for any spare troops he could muster to meet him just this side of the Memphis and Charleston, to help him remove the extra supplies he was bringing. General Chalmers was sent toward Memphis from the south as a diversionary tactic.

He divided us into three columns. Most of the raw recruits, led by Bell and accompanied by the General and the escort, formed the largest one. We were encumbered by the two cannon, several hundred head of cattle, and forty or fifty wagons of supplies. Josh and I were grateful for our status as veterans – the new recruits had to herd the cattle and wagons along.

The second column was headed by Colonel Wisdom, and was sent in a southeasterly direction to dispute any enemy headed toward us from Corinth. The last column, led by Richardson, was sent ahead to secure a landing for us across the Hatchie River.

We were the last to leave. The citizenry of Jackson so hated to see us go they threw a big party for us. The night before we left at dawn, we were warmed with eggnog and danced to the tune of several fiddlers. We had a mighty fine time with the pretty ladies, who vied for a chance to dance with a member of Forrest's cavalry. Even Josh got into the spirit of things and tromped on the toes of several young ladies, with as wide a grin on his face as I ever saw.

As we moved out, Forrest kept us far to the rear of Bell's column, hoping the supplies and men the army so desperately needed could reach safety. We remained calm, despite the reports brought in by scouts. The ring the Yankees had formed was slowly growing tighter.

The nights turned bitter cold. Miserably, we huddled against each other for warmth. The General would permit no fires. When we woke in the mornings, our clothing was crusted with frost.

We had been gone from Jackson three days when we were first set upon. We fought doggedly, and though we were outnumbered we managed to repel the attack. Without hesitation, we continued southwest.

When we reached the Hatchie, we found Bell and the supplies had made it to the river. Richardson's column had run into a large enemy force and was waiting for us on the opposite bank. Tiredly we crossed on an old dilapidated ferry, hoping we would be allowed to warm ourselves with fires when we reached the other side.

Just as we landed, a courier dashed up. Richardson's pickets had again run into trouble, five miles further down the road toward Bolivar.

Forrest picked ten men out of the escort and sent them east toward Memphis to scout out the possibility of enemy reinforcements. He led the rest of us south along the road to Bolivar.

We joined up with Richardson's men and took the lead. Before long, we ran smack into a Yankee picket. We gave chase and soon burst through a grove of cedars and into the midst of about 40 Yankees. Alarmed, they hastily mounted their horses and fled.

The General stopped. Up ahead he could see the scattered campfires of the enemy's main camp. He called for Captain Nathan Boone.

"Captain, scout out the camp ahead. I'm going back to see if I can hurry up the rest of the men." He turned his horse neatly around and galloped off.

"Okay, boys, you heard the General. Let's spread out here, give each other lots of room," Boone said authoritatively. "Let's make this a good one. Let's ready the charge! And speak up, will you? It would be a shame if these Yanks thought they were being run off by only fifty men!"

We moved forward, slowly at first, formed into a semi-circle with ten paces or so between each man. The officers began calling orders. "Forward, men! Company advance!"

The frost was thick on the ground. We could hear the enemy scuttling about, trying to get mounted and formed into some sort of a battle line. We came to a dry cornfield, all that stood between us and them. Boone stopped, raised his saber and yelled, "Forward, Brigade. Charge!"

We galloped through the cornfield, whooping and yelling. The stalks crackled loudly with the frost, bending and breaking under our horse's hooves. The excitement of the moment warmed my insides and made me impervious to the cold air.

We neared the edge of the field in time to see the Yankees break and retreat in disorder. As we swept through their camp we looked hungrily at the food cooking over their fires, but Boone refused our entreaties to stay and eat. We kept after the enemy and did not return until we had chased them a good two miles down the Somerville road. By the time we got back, Richardson's men had taken care of the victuals.

"Wouldn't ya know it," Josh whined. "We done all the work, but them's the ones that gits the reward!" All I could do was laugh and shrug my shoulders. Josh liked to complain, but he was usually right.

We returned to the river, where Bell was desperately trying to get the supplies ferried across. Since we had only one ferry with which to work, it was a long, slow process. We slept in shifts throughout the bitter night, and were rewarded soon after daybreak. We had gotten everything safely across and had lost only two horses and one man. Wearily, we again took up the march.

We moved south through the wan winter sunshine. Tensions increased, along with our exhaustion and hunger. I imagined the new recruits were now realizing army life was not what they had pictured it to be.

Scouts arrived sporadically and conferred briefly with the General, before heading back to their stations. The Yankees had us trapped neatly between the Hatchie and Wolfe Rivers. There were strong detachments from Bolivar south to Grand Junction. Yankee infantry swarmed along the railroad from Collierville to Corinth. To make matters worse, they had burned all the bridges across the Wolfe. There was no doubt they were trying to put an end to us.

Just as we were beginning to believe they had us cornered, a mud-spattered scout rode up with a message for the General from an old acquaintance. There was a bridge near Lafayette Station that the Yankees had only partially burned. The General smiled grimly. He ordered Bell to pick 300 men and march ahead to begin repairs on the bridge. He ordered the rest of us to follow the path taken by the enemy we had ambushed the night before.

Richardson's men took another route. They had gotten within a few miles of Somerville when they were attacked. A youngster who couldn't have been more than 15 rode to tell us the news. Wasting no time, Forrest gathered the escort and a detachment from McDonald's Battalion and we rushed to their aid.

When we arrived, it was soon obvious that we were vastly outnumbered. Forrest took command. He threw every available man into battle formation, even those who were unarmed. As we came face to face with the enemy, the cold seeped into our brains and we began to shiver.

We lost quite a few men in that fight. Our losses were greater than the enemy's, due to our lack of weapons. Despite that, we managed to gain their rear and they retreated in disorder.

Among the injured was Lieutenant Boone, the big gruff man who had led us so courageously on many occasions. We also lost his younger brother in this skirmish, a sergeant in the escort. Although I did not know his brother well, his loss was a great one.

Grim and determined, we moved forward. It was slow going, what with the weather and the huge amount of supplies we were transporting. There was a deep impenetrable silence among us as we realized how deeply in trouble we were. We could not hope for assistance, since we were deep into enemy territory. The noose around our necks felt tighter and tighter, as our scouts dashed in and out, always reporting the Yankees moving closer.

The night of the 26th – Christmas Day had come and gone without our realizing it – the General began preparations for our crossing of the Wolfe River. He sent an advance guard ahead to the railroad, where they felled trees and placed other obstructions across the train tracks, two miles on the other side of our planned crossing point. He sent a detachment off toward Memphis again to create a diversion, hoping the Yanks would be tricked into believing we were headed that way.

We reached the remains of the bridge at daybreak of the 27th. There was a small group of Yankees nonchalantly camped on the south side, but a surprise attack soon got rid of them. We got to work hurriedly, chopped down trees with whatever our imagination provided us, and within a few hours had repaired the floor of the bridge. We sighed with relief when our main column came into view, and without further delay we hustled it across.

Josh and I were sent out as scouts. Mud-spattered, cold and weary, we were nevertheless thankful to be away from the tensely unhappy column of men. We had been with the General long enough to know he would get us out of the fix we were in one way or another, but most of the men were not as optimistic as we were.

South we headed, into a peculiarly silent, brooding landscape. It was an overcast, wet day, the wind hardly moving the bare branches and dead winter grasses along the roadside. We passed a few weather-beaten cabins, the doors and windows shut tight. The people had either fled or were inside, huddled around cold fireplaces. I couldn't blame them. The Yankees had been rushing about for several days, and the people knew from experience the best course of action was to stay out of their way.

Josh sighed wearily and swore under his breath. I kept my mouth shut and breathed in the eeriness around me. It seemed to fit my mood. I was tired and hungry, bitterly tired of being chased about the country. I wondered if we would find safety even if we made it to our destination.

"There's a crick up ahead. I need ta fill my canteen."

We stopped briefly, watered our horses, filled our canteens and moved on. The country was empty of any living thing. We jumped nervously when a mongrel barked at us, protecting an empty cabin. Josh growled angrily back at him, but the dog didn't seem to notice.

We plodded on for several hours, seeing and hearing nothing. Josh finally swore vigorously. "Let's git back. There ain't no Yanks within 20 miles of us."

"If you say so. I guess the column is well past the bridge by now."

We returned the way we had come. Within a surprisingly short time we came upon the column. We rode directly to the General's side and made our report.

“Good, good!” he exclaimed jovially. “I didn't figure there would be any Yanks south of us, but you never can tell. Fall back in line, boys. We'll be camping soon.”

“Wouldn't ya know it,” Josh grumbled. “We been out lookin' fer nothin’.”

Everyone else had upon occasion lost confidence in Forrest, but never Josh. I had no idea what had gotten into him. But that evening Fred Moreland got him spinning yarns about our earlier expeditions with the General, and before I knew it Josh was laughing right along with the rest of us as he recounted the many times we had managed to elude the Yankees in the past.

“Dumbest bunch a' soldiers since the British,” he shouted jovially, after he repeated a much-embellished account of our last journey into West Tennessee.

Happily, we moved on to Holly Springs, Mississippi soon thereafter. We were cheered on by another happy populace as we set up camp. But the small cloud that had appeared on our horizon at Chickamauga was slowly growing larger.

CHAPTER TEN

Good news reached us after our return to Okolona. Forrest had received a promotion for our gallant excursion north to Jackson, and was now a Major General. He was now in charge of all Confederate troops in northern Mississippi and western Tennessee. Josh had gotten his hands on some local moonshine we jokingly called whiskey, and we had our own private celebration. I woke up the next day with a terrible headache.

We set to work training the new recruits, which on the whole were a sorry lot. They were either very young and inexperienced, or shifty eyed, worthless souls who had been dodging their obligations since the beginning of the war. To whip them into a cohesive fighting force was no easy job.

Most of them had joined in small groups that had to be consolidated. Typically they were resentful of the General's attempts to appoint officers over them. They wanted to elect their own, irrespective of their ability or experience. There was so much dissension the General was forced to form four brigades, composed of the bare minimum of men. Richardson had command of 1,500, McCulloch had 1,200, Bell 2,000, and his own brother Jeffrey had 1,000.

Since they were country folks, the men could all ride and shoot, but they knew nothing about marching, tactics or following orders. Those of us who had experience in such matters were used as examples and demonstrated the maneuvers necessary to our survival. It was slow, tedious work.

Before we had been at it very long, the General called the escort to a meeting. We gathered before a brightly burning campfire one damp evening, restless but attentive to the message Forrest had to give us. He stood tall and straight, his arms crossed in front of him. We grew silent as he cleared his throat.

"Boys, I've decided to rescue you from your training duties."

As we began to cheer and clap, he grinned and motioned for quiet. "Before you get all worked up,

I'd better tell you that I have a much harder job for you." He let us murmur and shuffle about for a moment before he continued.

"As you know, we've been having a lot of trouble with these new recruits. For some reason they don't feel obliged to fight with us. They want to go home, they say, to take care of their farms and families. They say we've lied to them, and those we've conscripted say we forced them into the army against their will." A few chuckles and guffaws erupted here and there.

"Now, I just can't afford the loss of these men. There is trouble brewing – big trouble. I've had reliable reports that the Yankees are planning to march through this great state and ruin its use for the Confederacy." His voice grew brittle and hard, his hands tightened into fists. "If we lose these recruits, we will be hard pressed to defend this area."

"I'm going to send you out to all the roads hereabouts leading north. You are to stop all persons you suspect to be a deserter and bring them back at once. We will have to deal harshly with these men if we expect to maintain our discipline."

Josh and I looked warily at each other. From the sound of his voice, it was clear the General meant business. We left quietly and returned to our messes. The next morning we were assigned to groups, each given a specific road to watch.

Fred, Thomas, Bradley, Josh and I were in charge of a small road, not much more than a path, that ran haphazardly north between two larger thoroughfares. We set out shortly after receiving orders, leaving our tents and most of our gear behind.

We situated ourselves on the west side of the road and settled in for a long wait. Fred had a worn pack of cards and we idled the time away by playing games. Anyone would be foolish to attempt to leave during daylight hours.

As darkness descended, we put out our fire and posted ourselves at intervals on both sides of the road. I was thankful to have never given in to the habit of smoking. Thomas always grew fidgety when he couldn't smoke.

The first night was long and fruitless. We slept late into the next day, then played cards until the sun went down. Again, we guarded the road, this time with more success. About midnight, two scraggly young men, little more than boys really, wandered up the road. Bradley, posted furthest to the south, ordered them to halt.

We quickly converged on them and took away their rifles. They were on foot, with no extra rations. They looked frightened when we told them they would have to return to camp.

“But the General!” one stuttered fearfully.

“Yeah, boy, he ain't gonna be too pleased with ya'll. An' I haven't figgered out jist where you two was headin' with no food or horses.”

“We was goin' back home,” the other said, belligerently. “We didn't ask ta be brung down here, an' we ain't aimin' to stay.”

“That's what you think,” Josh snapped back. He spat and wiped his mouth with the back of his hand. “We's getting' awful tired a' fightin' yer fights. It's time ya'll did a little a the work, 'stead a hidin' behind mama's skirts.”

The boy grew livid and had to be restrained by Bradley and Thomas. “I tell ya, I ain't gonna fight fer someone else's slaves! I'd a soon be dead!”

“That's jist fine,” Josh replied, his voice silky smooth. “But if yer gonna die, ya might as well do it defendin' yer country 'stead a' bein' shot tryin' ta run away. Bradley, tie these two younguns up, an' we'll take 'em back in the mornin'.”

We spent one more night on the lookout for deserters, and caught one more for our effort. We returned the next day, and were told to stay put.

Altogether, the escort captured twenty recruits heading north. Most of them were young men who had not volunteered, but there were a few who had changed their minds about army life. When they realized it involved more work than play they tried to slip away, hoping to get past the Yankee outposts along the Tennessee border any way they could.

That afternoon, the General gathered all his men on the parade ground. We were ordered to stand at attention while the deserters shuffled past, hands tied behind their backs. There was no defiance in their faces now as they realized the gravity of their situation.

We waited at attention while they were tried. The other new recruits watched restlessly. They were much impressed by the proceedings. I doubted many more would be heading north any time soon.

An announcement was read. All the men who had deserted would be shot, as ordered by the court martial board. An audible gasp rumbled through the ranks, and even Josh was shocked. Death by firing squad was a standard consequence of desertion, but we weren't a standard outfit. It seemed a foolish practice since we needed every man who could carry a rifle.

The camp was unusually quiet that evening. There was no singing or boisterous laughter. After supper rations, most of the men went to sleep, but I'm sure those new recruits who had contemplated leaving had a restless night.

Shortly after dawn a somber train of rickety wagons filed through the center of camp. The deserters were in them, each sitting on his own coffin. They were a sad lot. Some were crying pitifully, others had their heads in their hands. A few looked about, and their eyes registered the fear and desperation that had engulfed them.

We were drawn after them. Silently, the whole camp emptied and tramped slowly after the last wagon. The train stopped several hundred yards away from the horse corral.

There was a straight line of open graves waiting. Each man was placed before his own. As their sentence was read, several of them fell to their knees and shed tears of anguish. Except for their lamenting, silence enveloped us as we waited for their sentences to be carried out.

The group of soldiers that had guarded the wagons shuffled into line and marched the required number of paces in front of the prisoners. Before they could raise their rifles, a lone horseman galloped toward us.

I sighed with relief when I recognized the General. He reined in his horse when he reached the firing squad, and looked sternly at the sentenced men.

"I hope you realize the seriousness of your situation. Since you have refused to serve your country, we have been forced to take these grave measures. However, if you promise to serve faithfully from this day forward, I will pardon you."

Broken sobs of relief erupted from the convicted men. The General continued in a louder voice, so that all could hear. "I am only doing this as an example to the rest of you. I will not be so lenient next time." He wheeled his horse and galloped back the way he had come.

The prisoners were set free. There was great shouting and clapping of hands as we all returned to camp. The General's leniency had won him new respect, but now his men knew he was capable of doing whatever was necessary to maintain discipline.

By 1864 the Yankees had split the Confederacy along the Mississippi River and were desirous of splitting it again. If they could capture Selma and Mobile, to the south, they could control some of the richest farmlands of the Confederacy.

General Sherman had a plan. If he could send out two large forces, one from Vicksburg and one from Memphis and have them join together at Meridian, Mississippi, they could capture Selma and Mobile with relatively little trouble.

We were alerted that Sherman had left Vicksburg on the 3rd of February, and he moved swiftly after dividing his 20,000 infantry into two columns.

General Polk commanded our infantry in that area, but could only call for reinforcements as he fell back to the Alabama border. Our own force was too small, and it would have been suicide to get in their way. We could deal, however, with whatever kind of enemy cavalry force emerged out of Memphis.

General Sooy Smith's cavalry left the vicinity of Memphis around February 11, heading south to join up with Sherman. He had about 7,000 fighting men and 20 pieces of artillery. Forrest shrewdly kept a closer eye on this newer threat, instinctively knowing they presented a more reasonable target. General Polk or forces out of Mobile would have to take care of Sherman, while we could take care of Smith.

The scouts and escort were kept busy day and night, sent off in groups both to the north and to the south to keep an eye on the enemy.

As Smith advanced, Forrest moved us south of the Tallahatchie River. He divided his force this way: Richardson's, McCulloch's and Jeff Forrest's men were sent east and stationed close to West Point and Columbus. He took Bell's brigade and the escort to the vicinity of Grenada. Restlessly, he moved us again, and we arrived in Starkville around February 18. In case of emergency, he posted Bell's brigade along the Tombigbee River, which the Yankees would most likely have to cross before they could reach Meridian.

We were in a tight spot. Sherman had gotten safely to Meridian and Smith was heading in that direction, burning and killing as he went. We were tremendously outnumbered and badly equipped. Our scouts reported Yankee detachments being sent out from the main column with orders to destroy anything useful they came upon. Pillars of smoke could be seen in every direction, and large crowds of slaves had abandoned their plantations. We waited, frustrated and tense, for the General to give us an opportunity to end the destruction.

Forrest seemed calm and cool. He had been instructed to draw the Yankees as far south as far as possible and then destroy them. In order to accomplish this, he had to bide his time and wait for the right moment. He waited.

The Yankees were in prairie country by this time, a flat, lush area in Mississippi that some called the Land of Egypt. Their scavenging intensified. The local populace fled in all directions, desperately attempting to save what valuables they could carry, while their homesteads were plundered in their absence.

When the Yanks reached Prairie Station, the General decided to show himself. He placed his brother's troops several miles outside West Point, with instructions to resist the southward march of the enemy. Vastly outnumbered, they did as they were told, but were slowly forced south of the town. By nightfall they reached Sakatonchee Creek where they camped that night on its northern shore, determined to keep Ellis's Bridge open.

Most of Forrest's men were camped within ten miles of each other that night. The next day would be a decisive one, we knew. The veterans among us could almost smell the impending conflict, as if there was something in the air that foretold a major confrontation. And we were always more comfortable when we were taking the initiative. There is never a more desperate feeling of dread than when someone is chasing you. To be able to decide when and where you will meet the enemy – that is the desire of every fighting man.

Early the next morning, the Yankees attacked at Ellis's Bridge.

Word was brought that about thirty Yankees had crossed farther downstream and were raising havoc. General Forrest gathered the escort together and we took out after them. Their capture was a simple matter since we placed ourselves between them and their return to the bridge. When they rode back to rejoin their comrades, laughing and crowing at their sport, we captured them with relative ease.

We returned to the creek to find both sides hard at it. We found our positions along the battle line while Forrest went forward to see how things were progressing.

We had been there about an hour when the enemy literally vanished. Josh looked at me in amazement and scratched his head in confusion. Suddenly, a light flickered in his eyes and he grinned in glee. “Well, what do ya know! I think them damn Yanks is wantin' us to chase 'em! Yessir, I guess we was more than they could handle. If'n I had a nickel, I'd betcha they done skedaddled outta here!”

I squinted, searching the place where the Yankees had been but a few moments before. “You know, I think you're right. Now, I wonder why they would do such a thing?”

“Ain't no telling. When you fight such peabrains fer a livin', you kin never tell what they're liable ta do.”

Forrest moved quickly. He sent two companies of Faulkner's Twelfth Kentucky, under Captain Tyler, after the Yankees, and sent for all his scattered troops. Colonels Jeffrey Forrest and McCulloch, along with the General and the escort proceeded at once on the heels of the enemy. His orders were for everyone to meet at Okolona.

We moved north, most of us in good spirits. Despite our fast pace, we chattered and laughed among ourselves, and shared jokes that had become old months before.

Bradley related a fresh piece of gossip to me while we were riding along. As he told his story, he wore a look of intense satisfaction that gave me the jitters.

"While we was skirmishin' back there, Forrest found one a' his men tryin' to run away. He'd lost his horse an' most a' his gear an' was headin' to the rear when the Genrul seen him. He got right off his horse and threw the coward to the ground, got him a switch off'n a bush an' beat the tar outta the youngun. Then he turned him loose and told him to skedaddle back to the fight 'fore he really lost his temper." Bradley chortled with glee.

"I really don't see the humor in that," I said slowly.

"Ya don't?" he asked innocently. "I think it's kinda funny. I've about had it with these greenhorns. I was forced into this here war same as they was, but ya don't see me tryin' ta get outta my duty."

I looked at him coldly, and realized how fruitless any reply would be, but answered him anyway. "If I were you, I wouldn't talk about being conscripted. If you were truly interested in your duty, you would have enlisted." I looked at him fiercely before riding ahead and joining Josh.

“Don't be so touchy,” Josh told me. “Bradley's here, ain't he? An' turnin' out ta be a good soldier, besides.”

“True. But he shouldn't be laughing at someone else's misfortune. I can't help it. He has a cruel streak in him I don't like.”

“Ya don't have to like him. Jist fight the Yanks with him.”

Forrest received a report from Captain Tyler that the enemy had passed through West Point and were headed north to Okolona. He pushed us harder, hoping to catch up with Tyler before he had to face the enemy alone with his small command.

We came upon their battle lines six miles north of West Point. The Yankees had a thick stand of trees to their backs, several pieces of artillery and at least 1,500 men. Tyler was out of artillery range awaiting our arrival. Since we had come at a gallop we had left the majority of our men behind us. As we waited for them to catch up, the General decided to test the waters. We advanced a short way, but were forced to retreat by blasts of artillery fire.

By now, Forrest had grown impatient, ready for the action to begin. He left Tyler where he was and led the escort in a flank movement. As the Yankees saw us moving around them, they gave way. Tyler immediately moved ahead and captured most of their rear guard.

"Damn!" the General shouted disgustedly. "Where is McCulloch? We could have captured the lot of them if we'd had more men." He raised his saber and ordered us to the chase.

We followed behind Tyler and his men. We met the Yankees again a few miles up the road, where they had placed themselves among the outbuildings of a large plantation. Tyler impetuously threw his men at them with a charge, but was forced back.

McCulloch's brigade finally arrived. Forrest sent them, dismounted, to the front while he, the escort, and Tyler's men rushed them at their rear. The Yankees broke and ran, but not before a blue-bellied cavalryman turned and fired at the General. He missed. The General calmly raised his navy six and killed him before he could fire another shot.

We doggedly followed the enemy until nightfall. At last we rested while the remaining part of our small army caught up with us. Our scouts reported the Yankees had continued to retreat, but had finally made camp around midnight about two miles south of Okolona.

Forrest had us up long before dawn. With the escort and McCulloch's men, we charged through Okolona at daybreak, the enemy's rear guard running before us. When we reached open prairie country outside town, we spotted the enemy battle line, poised and ready. We rode a bit further and soon spotted men of our own – Bell's brigade had boldly declared itself ready for battle. We hastily joined them, knowing they didn't have enough men to defend themselves. But their maneuver had saved us. If the Yankees had attacked us as they intended, we would have been easily overwhelmed.

McCulloch's and Jeff Forrest's brigades were still coming up, but the General would not wait. His experienced eye spotted a weak point in the enemy line. He stood in his stirrups, bellowed "Charge!" at the top of his voice, and galloped forward. Caught up in the excitement of the moment, we followed.

The Yankees were not expecting us. They gave us one good volley, then retreated behind their second battle line. The General called a halt and dismounted us behind a fence. Our skirmishers stayed ahead of us. The enemy attempted to rush them but were soon encouraged into retreating.

Our reinforcements caught up with us about this time. Under orders, we quickly remounted and surged forward. We got amongst the Yankees, every man surrounded by them, but half the enemy weren't fighting, just raising their hands or holding their rifles in the air, stock up. Utter confusion reigned for several minutes. When the dust settled, we found ourselves in possession of ten Yankee cannon, and prisoners too numerous to count. But the General refused to be satisfied and we were off again.

Five hard miles followed. The road was deeply rutted, and the trees let down their limbs to slap us across our faces. Forrest was like a wild man, urging us along, determined to catch every last Yankee in the state.

The enemy had built another battle line across the road. The Yankee dismounts had been ordered to let their cavalry through and hold us off for as long as they could. They accomplished their objective for several minutes, then fell back about a mile to a stronger position.

By this time Bell's brigade had fallen behind, exhausted from the seemingly endless riding and fighting. The General ordered McCulloch's and Jeffrey's brigades to form into columns of four along the road to help protect themselves from the artillery fire. They advanced on horseback, and when the bugle sounded, the columns eased into a battle line, as smooth a maneuver as I've ever seen. The artillery and the men fired at the same time, an ear-splitting sound that rent the heavy, windless air about us.

Our line wavered, then halted. Josh and I looked about in confusion, and a question rushed to my lips. Why were we stopping? The enemy hadn't moved. Why didn't we forge ahead?

There was a confusion of movement at the head of Colonel Forrest's brigade. I saw the General gallop over and throw himself off his horse. He was cradling someone in his arms. Jeffrey's been hurt, I thought.

While I watched the General, the men along the line dismounted and moved ahead, shooting from behind whatever cover they could find. They slowly passed the General where he knelt beside his youngest brother, whom he had practically raised like a son, but Forrest didn't see them. Josh, Fred and I gave up our places on the line and went to him.

Jeffrey had been shot through the neck and must have died instantly. The General was still kneeling beside his lifeless body, sobbing, when we reached him. Other members of the escort were there, as well as several officers. They whispered above his head, wondering if he would be able to resume command. As they wondered, the General called for his adjutant, Major Strange.

"Major, I leave you in charge of my brother's body. See that it is taken care of." He mounted his horse as a part of Bell's brigade came in sight. He eyed them, then turned to observe the enemy. He briskly ordered part of Jeffrey's brigade to mount and flank the enemy to the left. He bellowed orders to his aides to have the rest of the men mount and prepare to advance.

As he waved his saber over his head and ordered the bugler to sound the charge, I remembered my own reaction to the death of someone close to me.

He must have been just as grief-stricken, but couldn't ignore his duty.

How strong he was! But how pitiful he could not take the time to mourn the passing of his favorite brother.

He led us in the charge, careening ahead of the escort as if he intended on being killed. Hitting their line, he hacked away at every bluecoat within reach, careless of the attempts made to unseat him. Josh stayed at his side, with a look on his face that gave mute testimony to the terror that filled his soul. If anything happened to the General . . .

The Yankees broke to the rear under our uncompromising onslaught. Forrest followed them as if he would bring about their end by himself. The escort kept up with him, but the rest of our little army soon fell behind.

The General turned a corner in the road, and involuntarily slowed his horse. Ahead of him was a cordon of enemy soldiers, protecting an artillery piece and several wagons and caissons that hadn't been able to keep up with their retreating comrades. There were several hundred of them, ready and waiting for us. Aghast, we watched as the General charged them.

We had no choice but to follow. We went at it, harder than we thought possible. We did our best to protect Forrest, but he really didn't need our help. He slashed and hacked at the Yankees while the rest of us did our best to protect ourselves. Several of our members were seriously injured, but we didn't have time to tend to them.

I thought we were just about to be swallowed up when part of McCulloch's brigade arrived to help us. They all pitched right in, even McCulloch himself, who had received a serious wound in his hand earlier in the day but had refused to leave the field. The enemy were not prepared for our ferocious attack and soon turned and ran.

Without a word to anyone, Forrest resumed the chase. We obediently followed, knowing it was our duty, but also frightened by the idea that something terrible would happen to him if we didn't.

After another mile, we came upon them again. While we charged them, they opened up on us. They had been able to set up an artillery piece while they waited for us, and they used it. A piece of hot iron killed the General's horse. Seemingly unperturbed, he ordered a member of the escort to dismount so he could take his horse. The Yankees ran again, but put up another fight just down the road.

The General lost another horse, but it was soon replaced by one of his favorites, King Phillip by name.

That was an unusual animal. He was a gray gelding, much bigger than the average horse. He had acquired a mysterious talent during his lifetime. When in battle, he became extremely fierce and excited, and whenever he came close to a blue coat he would rush at the wearer with teeth bared. On this occasion, he didn't have much of a chance to show his dislike for the enemy. Almost as soon as he was brought forward, the enemy dispersed.

The Yankees refused to offer us any further chance to capture them. They never again turned to face us, but ran straight for the Tennessee border.

We rested that night while the state home guards chased them as far north as Tallahatchie, scooping up stragglers along the way. We were bitterly disappointed we had not captured the lot of them, but were eternally grateful that the General had been spared. He could have been killed dozens of times that day, but hadn't.

Forrest was never quite the same after his brother Jeffrey's death. The change was not evident to those who didn't know him, but the sparkle in his eye had dimmed. He was still confident, brave and foolhardy, but there were times he seemed more thoughtful and silent than he had been in the past. The war was coming home to us all.

CHAPTER ELEVEN

We returned to Starkville, and then on to Columbus, near the Alabama border. Our horses had become worn and thin from our excursions. They had been on short rations, and we had lost more of them than we could afford. Riding stock was hard to come by, since the Yankees controlled most of the area where we depended on getting them. The government scraped together what they could, but they were usually the sorriest animals one could imagine.

Goldie was still with me, but he no longer had the bouncing gait of a young animal. I tended him as best I could, but there was no getting around it – he was worn out. Josh had lost two horses since the war began, so I felt lucky I still had Goldie with me.

Camp was set up in the usual manner, with the General's tent surrounded by those of the escort. The recruits we had picked up in Tennessee were loosening up after their first encounter with the enemy, and were learning to adapt to whatever they were thrown into. They began to resemble real soldiers, with steady looks and swaggering strides. We had lost a good many chasing Smith, but the ones we had left were now veterans.

Somehow, a letter from home arrived while we were in Columbus. I was much easier in my mind about my father since my journey home. I had seen he could manage without me. He had nothing of any importance to write, except Matt was growing like a sprout and was quite handy with his horse. I returned a letter home at the first opportunity, with a few details of our latest campaign.

We hadn't been in camp long before Josh learned we were being sent more men. One thing I always admired about him, and still do, is that he could sniff out news like a bloodhound. I always suspected he came by his information dishonestly, by listening at tent flaps or sneaking around campfires. But I finally had to admit he had ways of gleaning news that were honest and straightforward. He would innocently start conversations with the right people, and before you knew it he had the information he was after. And it was not unusual for officers to freely confide in him.

Because our recent campaign had been recognized as a success in Richmond, we were sent three skeleton regiments from Kentucky led by Brigadier General Buford. They came on foot, but hoped we could supply them with horses. With them also came the hope the General would be able to recruit back to full strength. Forrest welcomed them with open arms, but the rest of us viewed them with some trepidation. Their arrival meant we would have to make another foray into enemy territory.

Josh grouched and grumbled while we prepared to move out, and none of us could blame him. We figured that sooner or later the odds would catch up with us and we would be captured in enemy territory. A worse fate could hardly be imagined. I took vicarious pleasure in hearing Josh complain; it seemed to come more naturally to him than to me. His gruff voice had a calming effect on me and helped to relieve my own fears.

About the middle of March we quickly moved north. Surprise was the only advantage we had, since we were so drastically outnumbered.

The General paused us briefly in Jackson and left some of our men there to wait for Buford and his men to catch up. He then took the escort, the Seventh

Tennessee and the Twelfth Kentucky regiments with him to Trenton to begin recruiting. While we worked feverishly, using coercion and any other method we could think of, Forrest sent the rest of his force, consisting of McDonald's battalion and Faulkner's and Duckworth's regiments, north to capture Union City. This they did with little difficulty, and soon rejoined us with extra supplies.

Josh was still grumbling about moving so quickly back to Tennessee. His negative attitude pervaded him so completely that the General was forced to have a stern talk with him. He assigned him to scouting duty to keep him away from the recruiting. I must say I missed his easy banter. He could so easily persuade these simple folks to join our ranks. Without him it became an odious task, and required me to try and fill his place.

We had hoped the General would return south with the recruits we had gathered before he attempted to invade Kentucky, but he would not wait. He was determined to get what he came after, no matter how many Yankees he had to go through to get it.

We had been in Trenton four or five days when the General directed us to head north. He sent three detachments ahead to Paducah with orders to drive the enemy troops there into the town’s fort and wait for the rest of us to catch up.

The cold spring sunshine did little to cheer us as we moved ahead. The beauty of the Tennessee spring could have saved itself for another time. We moved silently through its stillness, oblivious to the power of nature all around us. Our recruits moved sluggishly, finally becoming aware of what we were leading them into. We had to prod and push them into keeping up with us.

We straggled into Paducah and proceeded to the western side of town, where the enemy's breastworks nestled against the Ohio River. Their fort was surrounded on its other three sides by a deep ditch, which was fronted by several yards of jumbled, dead timber.

While the rest of our troops caught up with us, we began to fire vigorously at the fort. We had been at it but short time when the General sent the enemy a flag of truce with a demand for immediate surrender. His request was refused.

Forrest contemplated their reply for a moment, then turned to his aides. "That's fine, boys. I'm not really looking for a fight today anyway. We have a lot of green recruits with us, and I hate to sacrifice any of them until they are trained. Here's what we'll do – post half our men here to keep the Yankees in their hole, while the rest gather up all the supplies and horses in town."

This was done. We were directed to leave our places at the fort and get busy gathering supplies. We worked hurriedly, hoping we wouldn't be trapped in town. Meanwhile, an unauthorized attempt to seize the fort was made by one of our brigade officers. It was a failure, and caused us not only the loss of the officer in question, but several other men as well. The report of the attempt threw the General into a rage. It was a sorry waste of his preciously few men.

We were in Paducah most of the day. After we got through burning what we couldn't use, which included a steamboat and almost a hundred bales of cotton, we headed south in good order.

Before we crossed the Kentucky border, the General gave us an unusual order. All the men from West Tennessee were directed home on furlough, to report back to Trenton and the General on April 3rd. We were drastically short on supplies and horses, and I suppose Forrest hoped the men could get more rations at home than he could supply them with.

The rest of us muttered about having to remain, but we knew it would be impossible for any of us to go home and return safely. We figured Forrest must be planning something important, or we would have all returned to Mississippi.

Our food situation was deplorable. Most of the country we passed through had been picked clean, and the new crops were just going in. There was no fresh meat to be found. We could sometimes find some flour or dried peas, cornmeal or dried beef, but not always. Josh was beginning to look like a scarecrow, his normally lean body and face turned scrawny, and his clothes barely hung on him, threadbare and worn as they were. I don't imagine I looked much better, but then it's easier to see someone else withering away.

When our troops returned from furlough, we had something else to think about besides our own hunger.

They came back beaten, bitter and as hungry as when they left. They returned from families as hungry as they were. Quietly, they wandered back into camp, but it wasn't long before stories of what they had left behind filtered through camp.

It would be hard to equal the stories of outrage, murder and assault we heard. Hundreds of lonely women and children had seen the very food on their tables snatched away, as well as every animal they owned. Homeless families wandered about in the woods, thankful for any kind of roof over their heads, after being burned out by the Yankees.

The men returned determined to wreak revenge. Many of them had been unable to locate their families while others found them in destitution. Their attitude infected the rest of the troops, and brooding discontent soon hovered over our camp.

Perhaps the hardest thing for the men to accept was that Fort Pillow, where most of the ravaging Yankees were stationed, was the home of colored troops who had participated in the scavenging antics of their army. These colored troops were, on the whole, ex-slaves, and our men couldn't believe they had been turned loose on a helpless populace. Maybe worse was that the other soldiers at the fort were Tennesseans who had refused to join the Confederacy, and held personal grudges against those who did.

Trouble was brewing. A few of us tried to calm down some of the men by telling them most of the stories they had heard were blown out of proportion. After the men had been back a few days, they seemed to calm down, but nerves were still taut.

Josh and I eyed each other with some dismay when we found out our next campaign would be against Fort Pillow.

Fort Pillow is directly west of Jackson, Tennessee, on a bluff above the Mississippi. As we marched to our destination, the General ordered Buford back to Kentucky to create a diversion. It was also hoped he could collect more supplies, which we desperately needed.

Conversations were short and brief as we headed westward.

"Doggone it, I wish't the Genrul would take us back ta Mississippi. We need ta be gitten back fore we get caught in sompthin' we can't git out of," Josh whined as we rode side by side.

"I agree." Silence for awhile.

"I think I'm gittin' too old fer this. It jist ain't as fun as it used to be." He sighed and spat loudly.

"Oh, I don't think you're too old. Things have changed somehow. It's not as easy as it used to be."

"You kin say that agin. We used ta git almost enough ta eat, and so did the horses. Men were better, too. Not so young an' lazy."

"True. Seems like we've been scraping the bottom of the barrel all the way around." With a sharp pang, I remembered David, young and healthy, now filling a spot in his family's plot.

"You need a rest, Josh. Maybe when we get back you can slip home for awhile."

He snorted. "Tain't likely. Besides, I don't even know if I got a home no more."

"Haven't you heard from your wife?"

He looked at me with exasperation. "Now how kin I hear from her if she don't even know how to write?"

"Oh. Well, maybe they're okay. You can always hope, you know."

"Yeah," he said with disgust.

Fort Pillow lies on a triangle of land formed by the Mississippi and a small stream called Cold Creek. It had been built shortly after the war broke out, to protect the river from Yankee traffic, but had been abandoned when we were forced out of Memphis in 1862. Since then it had been occupied by the Yankees.

It was protected by two lines of outer earthworks and a deep ditch in front of the main fort. The terrain was rough with knolls and depressions, and the heavy brush had been cleared away for about 400 yards in every direction. In the fort's walls there were six protected openings for cannon, and rifle pits on either side. On the south side there was a ravine which sheltered two rows of cabins, used to store supplies and to house the white soldiers. The Negroes were billeted in tents within the fort and near the riverbank. There was a collection of shabby tents and cabins round about where the enemy's collection of women and children stayed.

While we approached the fort, a detachment was sent south to Memphis. Some of the troops still in Mississippi moved in that direction also, and a rumor was spread about that General Stephen Lee was planning an attack against the Yankee stronghold. Large pontoon bridges were built across the Wolf River, as if a sizable force was readying to move against the city. In this way, the General could be sure no reinforcements would be sent from Memphis to rescue Fort Pillow.

General Chalmers had been sent ahead to force the Yankees to keep within the confines of the fort until the rest of us could catch up. We arrived with Forrest about 11 o'clock in the morning to find the enemy pinned within the fort by Chalmers' men. The women and children had also taken refuge behind its dirt walls.

The General spent several moments mulling over our position before he gave us orders. Abruptly, he directed McCulloch to take the cabins close to the fort. If they could be captured, the enemy's artillery would be unable to bring themselves to bear, and our sharpshooters could pick off the cannoneers. This was promptly done.

The rest of us were scattered along the front of the fort on foot, with orders to get as close to the enemy as we could. Fortunately the hillocks, holes and dead timber afforded good protection. Several of the knolls were high enough to be even with the fort, and our best sharpshooters were directed to these. Our casualties would be fewer because of these tactics.

Despite their lack of artillery, enemy fire remained heavy. They had been joined by a Union gunboat, the *New Era*, which fired at us from the river.

The General lost a horse shortly after the fracas started. It reared and fell on him when it was shot, but only bruised him. Captain Anderson begged him to stay on foot, but he only replied that he was just as likely to be hit one way or the other. He continued on horseback.

He ordered Colonel Barteau with the Second Tennessee into the ravine running off Cold Creek, which was protected from the gunboat shelling. We all advanced our positions slowly until about three o'clock, when a flag of truce was carried in by three officers.

Forrest demanded unconditional surrender, with a promise that all those captured would be treated as prisoners of war. He claimed to have received a fresh supply of ammunition, and could not be responsible for the fate of those inside if his demands were refused.

As the officers neared the fort, one was sent back at a gallop to warn the General that a steamboat full of troops was approaching. Cursing, the General spurred his horse and hurried to a rise from where he could see the expanse of the river.

The report had been correct. Soldiers were sighted on the vessel, which headed directly for the landing by the fort.

Forrest raged as he ordered Anderson and 200 of McCulloch's men to the bluff below the fort, where they were ordered to fire if there was any attempt to reinforce the enemy. The same order was sent to Barteau, then at the mouth of the ravine near Cold Creek. As these orders were given, the smoke of two more steamboats was spotted, approaching from the south.

Three warning shots were fired at the closest steamboat. It turned and continued past the landing.

We waited nervously in the spring heat for the enemy's reply to the request for a surrender. The Yankees finally answered with a demand for an hour's consultation between the fort's officers and the gunboat. The General snorted contemptuously when their reply was brought to him.

"Tell them I don't expect the gunboat to surrender. They have 20 minutes before we storm their works."

The flag of truce was planted in plain view outside the fort, easily seen by our men. Shortly after the General's second demand was carried in, he was brought forward to the flag by one of our officers. We learned later that the Yankees did not believe they were being attacked by Forrest in person.

As we bantered and jeered with the Yankee soldiers hanging over the fort's walls, the enemy's reply was brought forward. Written on a dirty, torn piece of paper were the words, “Your demand does not produce the desired effect.”

Forrest straightened furiously in his saddle while this communication was read to him. “Send it back. I want a straight answer – either yes or no!” He returned to his position in the ravine with Colonel Barteau, in part to get away from the jibes and obscene gestures thrown at him by the Yankee soldiers hanging over the walls.

I do believe the General was sure the Yankees would surrender. We had them outnumbered and surrounded, with little hope of receiving aid from any direction. It was always his policy to gain victory with as little bloodshed as possible. He could not have known what was about to happen.

Captain Goodman brought the enemy's one word reply – “no.” The General ordered an immediate assault.

It wasn't much of a battle. It took us less than fifteen minutes to gain the walls of the fort. The fighting was bitter and bloody, reduced to man against man. Those of us who had sabers used them, and those who didn't used their rifle barrels and butts. It has been said we fought cold-bloodedly and inhumanely against the defenders of Fort Pillow. As far as I can recall, we fought no differently than we had anywhere else, and certainly no differently than the fort’s defenders.

Suddenly, a Yankee bugle blast was sounded, and the enemy began moving down the rear bluff toward the bank of the river. We later learned that Major Bradford, in charge of the fort since Major Booth had been killed earlier in the day, had arranged for the gunboat to protect the men under the bluff if they were forced to give up their position within the fort. The Yankees turned and fired at us as they made their way to the river. They left their flag flying.

The protection they planned on receiving at the riverbank was never given. Afraid of his own capture, the captain of the gunboat never fired a shot to protect his comrades huddled along the river.

As soon as the General arrived inside the fort, he and Captain Overton lowered the Yankee flag and ordered a ceasefire. This order was carried out within minutes inside the fort, but down below the bluff the men didn't hear it right away, and the melee continued.

A lot of the Yankees drowned trying to swim out in the river, or were picked off by our men. Others attempted to escape south but were shot or driven back. With McCulloch's men on one side and Badeau's on the other, the enemy was hemmed in. Altogether, seven officers and 219 men were captured, out of the original 557 defenders. When we arrived, we had a total compliment of 1,200 men.

The officers in command of the fort, because of their arrogance and stupidity in defending such a position against a force that possessed twice their numbers, caused the death of over half their men.

The commander, Major Bradford, asked permission to bury his dead, which we granted. Captain Anderson attempted to communicate with the Yankee gunboat, so that the wounded could be taken away, but to no avail. It left in a hurry as Anderson neared it in a rowboat.

We found half-full barrels of ale scattered around the walls of the fort, and canteens filled with whiskey on the bodies of the Yankee dead. It was only with a great amount of discipline that our officers were able to keep our own men from using the liquor we found.

A Congressional Committee was later appointed to investigate the "slaughter" at Fort Pillow. As could be expected from a Union Congress judging a Confederate general, they decided our actions against the fort were inhumane. They decided we had violated the truce and had mercilessly killed the defenders after they had surrendered. If I may be so bold, I would like to say their findings were nothing but hogwash.

It is true that the General ordered three warning shots fired at the steamboat loaded with Yankee soldiers that had approached the fort's landing, and that he also ordered men to move their positions into the ravine after the truce was called. His reason for these actions was to prevent the reinforcement of the fort. It is also a violation of civilized warfare to attempt to aid a beleaguered position during a truce. The shots fired and the soldiers moved had little effect on the outcome of the battle, whereas if the fort had been reinforced, our efforts to capture it would have been for naught. Forrest's actions at the time were justified. It seems to me the fault here lies with Major Bradford, then in command, who hadn't signaled the approaching steamboat the news of the truce.

Let me also point out that we would not have killed the defenders after the surrender, as there wasn't one. The General himself helped lower the Yankee flag, and immediately ordered a ceasefire. Since our forces were scattered all the way from the fort's outer walls to the riverbank, it took a while for the news of this order to reach everyone. Some soldiers were no doubt killed after the flag was lowered, but only because our men under the bluff had not yet heard the order to cease fire.

A number of our men, including Bradley Stevens, fought like avenging demons during the battle and were a bit overzealous. I didn't approve of the way Bradley dealt with one surrendering man in particular. But one must remember their heads had been filled with stories of what these Yankees had done to the women and children of Tennessee. Many of our soldiers had relatives who had been burned out, raped and stolen blind. Personally, I was surprised they showed the restraint they did, considering the circumstances. The defenders of Fort Pillow had been waging warfare on women and children, intolerable in our minds.

The Congressional Committee also raised a fuss over the high percentage of Yankee casualties. The rate was higher than during other battles – Shiloh, Sharpsburg, Gettysburg, Chickamauga. Again, it wasn't the General's fault so many Yankees were killed, but Major Bradford's. It was his decision not to surrender, and so he should be held accountable for his folly.

At the time, the General did not believe the black man was equal to the white. He had been a slave trader before the war and owned many slaves himself. But to say he was willing to see the black soldiers slaughtered, as if they had no redeeming value, would be a falsehood. He had offered to treat all the soldiers at Fort Pillow as prisoners of war if they would surrender. Many of the enemy soldiers who survived our assault were black.

There were women and children killed at Fort Pillow, members of the contingent that had lived in rude quarters around the fort. In the heat of battle they had been shot, and no one was proud of that fact. But they had been at the scene of battle, a fort under attack. A risk is taken whenever civilians live near such a place.

The General had been a thorn in the side of the Yankees ever since the war started. He had proved to be impossible to catch and capable of destroying more than the Yankees were willing to give up. He was considered a major threat, one the enemy would go to any means to destroy. If his professional conduct was besmirched, so much the better. Perhaps that would induce Yankee soldiers to try even harder to eliminate him if they believed he was the devil incarnate.

News of Fort Pillow spread like wildfire. Even to this day I have found some of our own people believing the slanders spread by Yankee newspapers at the time. Forrest would forever be dubbed as a killer.

As a witness to the incident, I can say without trepidation that the General was unfairly condemned. He was by no means perfect, but he was a true, professional soldier, the likes of which we will probably never see again.

Until the end of the war, we would be haunted with the shadow of Fort Pillow. It was brought up to us time and time again by Yankee prisoners as well as our own countrymen.

CHAPTER TWELVE

"That's jist what he gits fer bein' too nice to the bastard," Josh told me vehemently, as we discussed the escape of Major Bradford the night after capturing Fort Pillow. "He shoulda' know'd ya can't take the word a' these lyin', thievin' Yanks."

"But the General believed him when he promised not to try to escape. What else could he do? The Major was an officer," I said in defense.

"So? The bastard let his men burn an' steal everythin' round here that warn't tied down. Seems the Genrul shoulda know'd he couldn't be trusted."

"Well, it's done and over. Nothing to be done about it now."

"Yup." Josh rose from the side of the fire, rolled himself up in his tattered blanket, and was soon snoring peacefully.

We returned to Jackson and prepared to leave the state. We were exhausted and needed rest, and our new recruits needed proper training before they could be reliable, although they had held their own against the fort.

Before we left, we learned the unfortunate end of Major Bradford. He had been captured by scouts and sent along to the General, but before he could reach us, his guards took him into the woods and shot him. A sad but fitting end for a man who had helped instill such terror and fear in the hearts of the civilian populace.

It was toward the end of April before we made it safely back to Mississippi. Surprisingly, we had little opposition on our way south. It almost seemed as if the Yankees hated to see us go, which wasn't far from the truth.

At that time, Sherman was gathering his armies south of Chattanooga, readying to spring against Johnston at Dalton and march onward to Atlanta. The presence of Forrest anywhere near him caused General Sherman great anxiety. If we would stay in West Tennessee, he could be assured we would be unable to hinder his campaign.

Forrest had ideas of his own. He proposed plans to attack and destroy Memphis, but his superior, S. D. Lee, did not approve them. He then immediately asked permission to move against Sherman's supply lines in middle Tennessee. General Lee consented to his plan.

We rested and trained our recruits for a solid month. Since our recent foray into West Tennessee, we were fairly well equipped and supplied. At least we now had enough horses for all the men, and clothing to go around. We moved out of camp on the morning of June 1, 1864.

The thought of returning to middle Tennessee brought me much joy. I had tried to keep Clara out of my mind, because thoughts of her filled me with the most bitter sadness, but the thought of seeing her again changed all that. I began to picture her again in my mind's eye – her sparkling brown hair and eyes, her slim waist, the tilt of her head and the way she fluttered her hands as she talked. I determined to tell her my feelings when I next saw her, and if I made it safely through the war I would marry her.

Josh's spirits also perked up considerably as we moved east. The General had promised him a short furlough so he could check on his family. He became his old self again, full of half-hearted criticism and sarcasm, over-simplified philosophies and keen observations on the foolishness of man.

"Here, boy, go git us some firewood, and be quick about it!" Josh snapped gruffly at Thomas, who was dawdling aimlessly about the camp as we tried to set up for the night.

"By dingy, ya'd think we wus the greenhorns and him the old timer 'round this place."

"He isn't exactly a greenhorn any longer. He's been in two campaigns."

"Well now, is that so? I'd never woulda' guessed it, seein' as how he can't seem ta remember from one day ta the next how we all have to work aroun' here. Or, maybe, jist don't wanna remember."

"That's probably closer to the truth. He's just lazy."

"Yup. I tell ya, 'tween his laziness and Bradley's cussedness, I'm purty near findin' me another mess ta stay with. If'n it warn't for you an' Fred, I'd a cleared out a long time ago."

Josh stroked his beard, as he did when he was thinking. "They ain't too respectable, neither. I never thought ta say this about any man in this here outfit, but that Bradley is jist plain mean an' cruel. You see'd how he was at the fort. Gives me shivers jist thinkin' about it."

"I know. But he's one of us, and we have to learn to accept him as he is. That's not to say we won't have to keep an eye on him, though, just so he doesn't get out of hand. At least he follows orders well."

"Yeah. Almost too good."

"Let's talk about something else. What do you figure on having your wife cook for you when you get home?"

We wandered off into a discussion of the various ways chicken and homegrown vegetables should be cooked, Josh preferring them to be all thrown together with a little bacon grease, while I liked mine cooked separately, with lots of butter on the vegetables and the chicken cooked until crisp.

Our hopes of seeing our loved ones soon were short-lived. We had reached the outskirts of Russellville, Alabama, when we were overtaken by a courier sent by General Lee. The Yankees had sent a large expedition south from Memphis with the intention of ransacking and pillaging Mississippi, and we were immediately recalled.

General Samuel Sturgis was sent into the prairie country with approximately 8,500 men – infantry, cavalry and artillery – with express orders. He was to dismantle the railroad as far south as Okolona, and work on the one headed east to Macon. Upon completion of these orders, he was to return by way of Grenada to Memphis.

We were in trouble again, all right. Counting all our scattered reserves, we had maybe 5,000 men. We were in our own territory, which was to our advantage, but were outnumbered and under-equipped compared to the enemy.

Forrest hustled us back to Mississippi with the confidence and bravado of a man who faced the best possible odds. We swallowed our fears and tried to assume the same air of assurance, a task not easily accomplished.

Our disappointment in not getting back to middle Tennessee soon vanished under the strain of returning to the battlefield. We knew we would have enough on our minds in the next few weeks without cursing our luck at having to return.

We converged on Booneville, a small hamlet that eyed us with suspicion as we swarmed through it. General S.D. Lee was there to confer with Forrest. They set right to work making plans for the upcoming operation.

We received orders to cook three days' rations and load all unnecessary supplies onto a waiting train, to be sent south with General Lee. With much regret we also sent two batteries of artillery because they would only hamper our speed.

Lee decided it would be wise to draw the Yankees as far south as possible, away from their source of supplies in Memphis. After he left that evening, the General held a conference with his top officers – General Buford, Colonel Rucker and Captain Morton of the artillery. Although Generals

Lee and Chalmers had planned on concentrating their forces around Okolona, where we could fight in the open prairie country, the General planned for emergencies. General Lee had given him orders to lead the enemy as far south as possible, but if need be he should face them in battle if it became necessary.

We moved out at daybreak, June 10, the sun at our backs. It had rained heavily the day before, and we could tell even at that early hour the day would be hot and muggy. The enemy had camped at Stubbs Farm, five miles from Brice's Crossroads, where the highway from Ripley to Guntown crossed Tishomingo Creek and met with the road from Baldwyn to Pontotoc. Here is where Forrest decided to meet the enemy.

We knew we were outnumbered, but the dense woods and undergrowth around the crossroads would be to our advantage. The enemy would be unable to judge our numbers, which meant they might be fooled into believing we had greater strength. The road the enemy was taking was narrow and thick with mud, a fact that surely would slow them down. They would lead with their cavalry, leaving their infantry to catch up just when the sun was hottest. We would have some advantages if we could meet their advance at the crossroads.

We came upon the enemy's cavalry suddenly, and moved to the edge of the dense woods. There was a lone dwelling, Brice's place, with a few cleared acres across from it. Captain Tyler was already there with a couple companies of Kentuckians from Lyon's Brigade. They had just retreated across the open field, driven back by Yankee cannons placed within the dense foliage across the way. The General took charge.

The Yankees dispersed their troops on either side of the road to Pontotoc, directly in our path. They had placed their artillery on two rises behind their position, and occupied the edge of the clearing. Their dismounted cavalry deployed among the brush, while it looked like more men were joining them all the time.

At this time, we had less than 1,000 men with us – Lyon's brigade, the Escort and Gartrell's company. The artillery was still some distance away and could be of no help to us. We faced an enemy of thousands of men accompanied by three or four batteries of cannon.

"Damn!" the General raged. "They're as strong as I feared." He moved his horse restlessly back and forth in front of us. "We'll have to do something before they charge and overrun us." He turned to Captain Anderson. "Take a small detachment and head back to Booneville. When you find Bell, order him to move up fast and fetch us all he's got."

He stretched us out in a semi-circle around the clearing. Hurriedly, we began to fortify the fence we found there with logs and brush, anything we could get our hands on.

Lyon was ordered to advance. He threw out two skirmish lines, their horses prancing and pawing in excitement. They were welcomed with artillery and scattered small arms fire, but to little effect. They feigned a charge and moved about the field as if they had good sense for about an hour. The Yankees, as if put in a trance by their antics, remained where they were. They must have been waiting for their infantry to catch up, but during that wait the rest of our men were coming on the field.

Colonel Rucker and his brigade joined us. The General immediately dismounted two battalions of our reinforcements to the left of Lyon, and kept one battalion in their saddles to help protect our left flank. The odds were beginning to even up.

Another diversion was ordered as we waited for the balance of our men and artillery to arrive. We rode forward, careful to keep out of rifle range, and fired our weapons at the blue swarm in front of us. Part of our line had advanced too far and were forced to fall back, several men carrying wounded comrades with them. More reinforcements, about 500 strong, rode up.

Again, we entertained the Yankees, this time to the right. The answering fire was slow and irregular, and we withdrew.

It was now almost noon, the heat and humidity oppressive. The sun glared down, and its rays bounced off the rifle barrels of the enemy. The trees around us filtered out any breeze that might have given us some relief.

There was no water to be had, and we were broiling from the lack of it.

The General could not wait. Although more than half his troops and all his artillery were still trying to reach us, he rode along the entire length of his line, calling out encouragement. All of us would be thrown forward in a desperate attempt to dislodge the Yankees.

"Have to go forward, men, before those rascals realize how short-handed we are! If we can overwhelm the cavalry we can make short work of the infantry! Let's all pitch in, boys! We need every last man of you. Don't worry! We've faced mightier tasks than this. We can do it!"

He was greeted by whoops and cheers, with a few groans mixed in. We waited nervously for the general charge.

When the bugle sounded, we sprang over the fence on foot, wild, ragged yells hurtling from our throats. I don't believe we had any illusions about what lay ahead of us.

The Yankee line wavered as we fired and ran forward. They fired back desperately, but couldn't deny us our goal. We quickly gained their position.

There is nothing quite as dreadful as hand-to-hand combat. It has been glorified by poets and authors for centuries, but I can't for the life of me see why. It's bloody, ruthless and terrifying. The smells are enough to turn a decent man's stomach, the sounds can ruin a man's dreams for a lifetime. As for the sights – dead and wounded falling grotesquely about, blood spurting, men running in fear, vicious looks of loathing on the faces of friends and foe alike.

We had the Yankee cavalry on the run. They didn't seem to care for our kind of fighting. As they fell back we could see a brigade of infantry move up and mix with the cavalry units we had just defeated. These were Illinois troops under Colonel Hoge, as we later learned from prisoners. They swarmed toward us.

At this fortuitous moment, more of our army came up. The enemy halted their movement as they saw our reinforcements arrive. At this point we had nearly 3,000 men on the field, while the Yankee cavalry was calling it quits and they still had half their infantry on the other side of the creek, many of them straggling on the road.

The General quickly placed Bell's troops, with himself in charge, to the left of the field. In a moment, they had filled the holes and gaps of our position. The right wing was put under the command of General Buford.

The heat was stifling. Bell's troops had marched hard all day, and a few dropped in their tracks from sunstroke. Our animals were suffering just as much, and most of them turned sluggish and uncooperative. We were ready to join in battle again, anything to help the hot afternoon to pass.

Forrest sent me to Buford with a message. He was to push hard to the right, as we could see the Yankees massing for an attack on our front. As I returned, the battle rejoined. I hurriedly gave Goldie's reins to a horse holder and joined the melee.

The escort fought with the General, on the left with Bell's men. We crept forward on our hands and knees through the dense brush and pecked away at them. Part of Bell's troops gave way, and the Yankees took this as a signal that they could force a general retreat if enough pressure was brought about by a general assault.

Fortunately, Forrest was one step ahead of them. He called most of the escort to him, and we found our mounts and rushed to the aid of Bell's troops that had been driven back.

Once there we dismounted and tied our horses to whatever we could find and joined in. The General himself was there, brandishing and firing his pistols in the front ranks of his men. We cursed and screamed as we fought; we never were able to give up a fight if there was the slightest chance of victory.

Soon enough more of our men arrived on the field, catching up with their commands, and Bell's troops rallied enough to stop the gap. We began to advance. Slowly our entire line began to surge forward and the bluecoats gave way.

The General received a message from Buford. Colonel Barteau, with the Second Tennessee, had gone off to the right and was harassing the enemy's reserve infantry. They had been thrown into confusion. The Yankee cavalry had moved to the rear to see what could be done.

"Come on, men!" Forrest shouted as he rode along the lines. "We've got them on the run! They're being attacked to the rear by Barteau. One more good push and we've got them!" His excitement seemed to rub off on us. We drew on our last reserves of strength and fought on.

Shortly, the escort was remounted and ordered to the right. We were told to wait there until we heard the sounds of a general engagement, then rush at the enemy's back and prevent them from reaching the Tishomingo Creek bridge.

We heard our comrades converge on the Yankees. We heard Morton's battery booming at them, loaded with canister and rolled within shotgun range, as the General had ordered. As the shots sprayed into them, the enemy began to turn and run in our direction.

There were so many of them, they overwhelmed us. A wagon had overturned on the bridge, but this didn't do much to impede them. They crawled over it, pushing and shoving at each other until it was reduced to kindling wood. Others tried to swim across the creek. The ones that made it left screaming comrades to die a watery death.

Lieutenant George Cowan ordered part of us to follow him. Despite our thirst, we didn't even stop for water as he led us across the creek, a short way from where the Yankees were crossing, and into the flank of the enemy.

We fired indiscriminately at the fleeing, wild-eyed mob. We managed to cut quite a few of them off and captured them along with a cluster of wagons. Before we could resume the chase, we felt the searing fire of our own artillery, still popping away from the high ground of the crossroads at the Yankees around us.

“Stupid, no-count gunners. Can't they see us, or have they turned into Yankee lovers?” Josh screamed ferociously. He snatched our flag out of the hands of a wide-eyed young color-bearer and rode into a little clearing in plain view of our advancing troops. He began to furiously wave it back and forth.

“There, ya blame fools! It's us! Can't ya see? I'd come over there myself an' knock the stuffin' outta ya, if'n I warn't busy on this side!” The gunners saw the flag and began to shift their fire away from us. Josh returned the flag to the holder.

“I swear. If'n ya cain't trust yer own people not ta shoot ya in the back, who can ya trust?” he stormed at no one in particular.

“Enough,” Cowan told him. “We have work to do.”

“That's the thanks I git fer savin' our skins,” he muttered darkly at me. He spurred his horse and obediently followed the Lieutenant.

The rest of our troops caught up with us. The General had taken command of the men assigned to hold the horses during the battle, as they were relatively fresh. He took them to the lead. We clattered down the road, and came upon the enemy's last feeble attempt to make a stand. As soon as the guns came up and fired a couple of rounds at them, they retreated again.

Forrest sent the freshest of his men after them while those of us who had fought the most rested until the wee hours of the morning. We slept like drunken men, although it had been many a day since any of us had tasted liquor. We gnawed at the cold rations we had left before we resumed the chase.

We didn't let up the next day, although we had killed or captured at least half of the enemy and all of their supplies and big guns. The weather was still fiendishly hot and caused us many casualties that day, due to heat prostration and sunstroke. Our horses barely wobbled along, some perishing from the heat as well as exhaustion.

The sun was beginning to settle into the western horizon when a sudden commotion at the head of our column caused us to pause. The news was passed along that the General had given in to the heat.

Josh scrambled ahead with me at his heels. We found the General under a tree in a dead faint with his aides huddled about him. Dr. J.B. Cowan was busy trying to revive him. He had been overcome quite suddenly and had fallen from his horse.

The doctor had been warning the General to slow down and take some rest, but he had refused. Not even his closest aides could get him to heed the doctor's advice.

"I don't like seein' him down like this. If anythin' were to happen to him, I dunno what we'll do. Prob'ly die, cause a' some ignorant Genrul who don't know what he's doin'," Josh declared.

The pursuit was brought to a halt immediately, although I don't imagine the General was ever satisfied with it. The rest of us were, though. We hadn't destroyed the enemy completely, but had managed to come as close as possible. We had stopped cold a major threat to the safety of the state and felt satisfied with our accomplishment.

CHAPTER THIRTEEN

We had hoped the enemy would leave us alone after their resounding defeat at Brice's Crossroads, but we were mistaken. We had been back in camp only two weeks when the Yankees again attempted to ransack our territory.

General S.D. Lee took charge of the defense this time, and it didn't go as well as before, when Forrest was in command. We met the Yankees at Harrisburg, a rather unsatisfactory battle since the Yankees refused to stay and fight. They dug in along a ridge and just let us attack them, to no avail. Then they hightailed it back to Memphis and were only half-heartedly pursued.

We lost many men at Harrisburg, men that couldn't be spared. Too many of that number had been officers or veterans who could never be replaced. Although I'm sure General Lee was a good man and a good soldier, he could not take the place of our General. He couldn't control the troops who had grown to be Forrest's men. And because he couldn't, we lost far more that day than we should have.

It would have gone better for us if Forrest hadn't been wounded. It was only a foot wound, but a very painful one through his toes. We were afraid he had been killed when he was carried off the field, white and still. But he soon returned and spurred us on to even greater feats. The enemy left the field, and because of Forrest's condition, were not vigorously pursued as they otherwise would have been.

The war was beginning to show on the General. He was too pale and too thin, but was unwilling to take his doctor's orders for a prolonged rest. He had asked to be relieved of duty the day we met the enemy at Harrisburg because of poor health, but General Lee would not consider it.

After he received his wound, he ordered up a buggy with a frame contraption built on the front to elevate his leg, and made his rounds among his troops. He looked quite out of place, as he tried to whip up some spirit out of the old nag that pulled the dilapidated, worn-out buggy.

I received a letter from Clara.

June 25, 1864

> Dear John,
>
> I have smuggled this letter out of town and hope it will find you. We have heard you are fighting somewhere in Mississippi, so I am sending it south.
>
> Eva and I received your notes. Eva is heartbroken over the loss of David. We cannot seem to get her interested in anything. We had hoped the warmer weather would help her, but it hasn't so far.
>
> The Yankees have taken over this part of the country. We see their patrols daily. They haven't caused much trouble, except food is nearly impossible to find. The necessities of life have all but disappeared from the stores, and we do without simple things we never lacked before. So many of our friends and neighbors have left to go south, where they

> think it is safer, but Mother refuses to leave. This is her home, and she cannot bear the thought of leaving it.
>
> We have heard from Father. He is alive and well, but seems to be losing heart. General Lee is fighting a desperate war at Petersburg in the east, one Father says we can never win.
>
> Mother and Eva both send their regards. We all hope you are in good health and that you've not been hurt. We have heard stories of your attack on Fort Pillow. Surely it was not as vicious as the papers have made out. Mother says General Forrest is an honorable man and that the Yankees are slandering him because he has been so successful against them. I surely hope so.
>
> Hoping to see you again soon,
> Clara Brown

I tucked this letter in among the others I had been saving in my saddlebag, but not before I had read it a dozen times. It warmed me to know she was thinking of me. Her Mother's approval meant the world to me. She would not have sent her regards otherwise. I knew there was hope for me if I ever made it through this blasted war.

It was also good to hear that people were defending our actions at Fort Pillow. We had become painfully aware of the nefarious stories about our ruthlessness. Many of the Yankee soldiers we had captured at Brice's Crossroads and Harrisburg were terrified of us. They believed we would gather them up and slaughter them unmercifully under direct orders of the General. When we turned them over to be transferred to prisoner of war camps, many of them shed tears of joy.

Josh also received some news. His oldest son had sent a note on the merest scrap of paper saying they were all alive and well. Josh figured the preacher's wife had taken it into her head to teach the boy to write, since he had never attended school.

“Didn't figger he'd never need ta know 'bout readin' an' writin'. I never did. But it shore is nice ta hear they're makin' it.”

Our foraging parties were forced to travel further and further away. Food was scarce. The local farmers were growing less because seed was hard to come by. Besides, it seemed that whatever they grew it was snatched up by either us or the Yankees. Since it was summer, we could depend on being supplied with a few fresh vegetables, but meat had become a luxury. After a raid, we usually acquired a few barrels of beef, but it wasn't nearly as good as fresh meat. Yet we couldn't really complain. We knew that, on the whole, we ate better than any other army in the Confederacy.

While out foraging for the quartermaster's department, Josh and I stopped in Tupelo to visit Bradley Stevens, who had received a leg wound at Harrisburg. Our downed comrades had been placed in the houses of the citizens of the town because there were no hospital facilities. Bradley had been lucky. He stayed in one of the nicer homes and received better than usual care.

Josh hadn't wanted to stop. His dislike of Bradley was growing daily. I insisted, however, that he go for courtesy's sake. Once there, he was barely civil to the poor man, and I was inclined to agree with his attitude.

Bradley had turned from a brash, vengeful young man into a hardened, hateful adult. He had nothing good to say about anything or anyone. We stood at his bedside with our hats in our hands while he vented his feelings to us.

"If it wasn't fer the damn Genrul, I wouldn't be in this here mess."

"He's just doing his duty. You can't blame him if you got wounded."

"The hell I can't! I don't see why we always gotta be right in the middle a' things. I'm surprised any of us is still alive."

"Boy, if'n you want sumpthin' ta blame, ya oughtta look ta the Yanks. They're the ones started this, not the Genrul."

"I hate the Yanks, too. They shoulda jist stayed where they belonged, 'stead a getting' the Genrul all riled up."

"Can we get you anything?"

"Yeah." he answered fiercely. "You kin git the hell outta here. I never asked you to come. And you kin tell the Captin I'm aimin' ta transfer outta the escort, if'n I kin ever git outta this damn bed. I ain't wastin' any more time ridin' around gittin' shot at. I aim to go to the infantry, where a fella don't git shot at so much. Leastways there's a chance I kin slip away and git back home where I belong."

We left him there, huddled in his bed. We didn't say a word to each other the rest of the day, until after we reported Bradley's sentiments to Nathan Boone that evening. The Lieutenant looked at us warily from under his bushy eyebrows, but made no comment.

"I told ya. That Bradley's nothin' but trouble," Josh said with some satisfaction as we ate our meager supper. "He might as well jist go home fore he winds up makin' a mess a' trouble fer the rest of us."

"Maybe so," I said tiredly. "I feel sorry for him. He doesn't have much to look forward to, does he? I mean, he'll wind up hating everyone he comes in contact with. He's so full of bitterness he could bust."

"Yup. He's turnin' into a bad apple fast." Josh yawned. "We best git some rest now. We're back on foragin' duty agin tomorrow."

I took my blanket some distance from the fire and rolled up in it under the protection of a large oak tree. But I slept restlessly that night, a picture of Bradley's bloody behavior at Fort Pillow on my mind.

It was early August, humid and sticky in Mississippi. The Yankees again invaded us from the north, but we had so few men and supplies it was hard to imagine how we could stop them. The scouts reported they had well over 20,000 men, and we had been whittled down to less than 5,000. It didn't matter. We were off.

It had begun to rain. The Tallahachie River was on the rise and the enemy made slow progress. General Chalmers was sent ahead and did an admirable job of impeding their progress by destroying bridges across the numerous creeks that crisscrossed the state. He picked and prodded at the enemy and contested every foot of ground they gained.

Bradley had rejoined us, though only God knows why the Captain had not transferred him to a different unit. We were told to keep an eye on him and report any attempt he made to desert. Josh watched him like a hawk, unrelenting in his belief that Bradley would only cause us trouble.

Although the General's foot had not completely healed, he could not sit while the enemy was about. When Chalmers was forced to retreat at Oxford, we were there to meet him.

Outnumbered, we faced the enemy there. Despite all our efforts and three days' hard fighting, we found ourselves outflanked by the superior numbers of the enemy. The General had no choice but to withdraw.

We were tense and quiet about our campfires during those days. We had fought often long and hard for the General and against great obstacles, but it seemed we were facing a situation that even he could not get us out of. The energy and enthusiasm we usually felt when fighting were lost, gone with the assurance we normally had – that we could whip a numerically superior force if need be. The odds this time seemed far too great.

A cloud of gloom descended on us, but it was short-lived. An order went out for us to cook rations and prepare for a hard-riding mission. An inspection was held, with the horses and men in the best condition ordered to get ready immediately.

The level of noise in camp rose as we prepared to ride out. Even those who had not been picked to go out first got into the spirit of the occasion and helped us get our rations and horses in order. There was laughter and excitement in the air again, and it reminded me of the old days.

Josh and I had been chosen to ride ahead. Because Bradley's loyalty was in question he was brought along, even though he did not hesitate to tell us he had no desire to come. Fred would have liked to join the expedition, but was suffering through an attack of dysentery and had to be left behind. Lazy Thomas had allowed his horse's back to become infected with saddle sores, and so remained behind.

We rode out in good humor, despite the heavy darkness and the drenching rain. Taking the initiative was always fine with us. Today I wonder at my sanity. I suppose one of the advantages of being young is that one is less likely to be afraid of the unknown.

It was rumored we were heading to Memphis, where the General planned to attack the base of the enemy's expedition. It seemed perfectly logical to me. If you can't oppose the enemy from the front, you must try to get at them from the back. We laughed at the audacious plan, one truly inspired by a most desperate situation. And one we were sure could not fail.

The rain poured down on us, but it didn't dampen our spirits. We slogged away despite the weather, and reached Panola in the early dawn. We rested there while our stragglers caught up.

We were inspected again. A hundred of us with weak horses were sent back to wait with the others, leaving less than 2,000 in the expedition. Those of us who remained drew sighs of relief when we learned we could go ahead.

The sun, weak but shining, came out as we pressed ahead. Despite the muddy conditions of the road, we reached Senatobia by nightfall. Since all of us were quite worn, we camped there for the night. We had to cross two streams the next day and would need to be rested before we attempted them.

Hickahala Creek was a force to be reckoned with. It had a deep, wide channel, swollen from the rains. We fell to discussing different ways to cross without using a ferry, since using one would give our expedition away. Josh and Bradley grew heated as they talked it over, but their quarrel ended quickly at the appearance of the General.

He raised his voice so that the whole column could hear him. “I need ten volunteers from each regiment.”

Almost immediately the required number of men rode to the front, including Josh and I. We all knew that whatever task the General had in mind, it would not be easy, since he only called for volunteers when he knew what he had in mind would be difficult. He grinned at us as we gathered around him.

"Now boys," he pointed to about half of us, gathered on his right side. "I want you all to go to the houses and cabins round about and tear up their floors. Get the planks down to the ferry crossing. The rest of you – I need you to cut down those telegraph poles and drag them to the crossing."

"But Genrul," Josh whined. "We can't do that. We ain't got nothin' to drag 'em with."

"Sure you do!" he replied, cheerfully. "Use your horse's tails. Braid 'em around those poles and get them to the creek!"

We did as we were told, though Josh cursed as he tried to braid the skimpy hairs left in his horse's tail around a pole. "That's it, damn it! I ain't volunteerin' fer nothin', not ever agin. Of all the stupid . . ."

"Cut it out, Josh, and let's get going!" I said impatiently.

"Keep yer pants on, sonny, I'm a comin."

By the time we arrived at the creek, preparations to cross were well under way. A ferry had been anchored about in the middle of the stream.

Grapevines had been cut and strung across the creek, while two huge trees on each side had been felled across it. Our poles were tied together with vines and made into rafts, none too sturdy but good enough to suit our purposes. These were put into the creek on either side of the ferry, and tied to the cable that had been made out of vines. Other poles were laid, then topped with pieces of flooring we had requisitioned from nearby dwellings.

Before we began to cross over, the General dumped a wagonload of corn we had gotten in Senatobia and ordered each of us to carry an armload across. He scooped up a huge amount in his own arms and led his horse across our makeshift bridge.

We followed him in twos, leading our horses. It wasn't much of a bridge, but we all made it across. We looked back at it once we were all across, but couldn't see it any more. It had completely submerged into the depths.

We rode hard for seven miles, until we reached the bank of the Cold Water. We repeated the same procedure we had used to cross the Hickahola, and crossed it before sundown. We traveled about ten more miles until we reached Hernando, the General's hometown, before we were allowed to rest for a short while. Josh had just begun to snore when we were called to mount again.

We moved ahead through the darkness, and didn't slow up until we were about four miles outside of Memphis. By this time, many of the scouts and spies the General had sent ahead reached us with accurate information on the whereabouts of the enemy within the city. Not only did they report where the troops were stationed, but they also knew in detail where their horses and mules were kept.

The General called a conference and gave his officers their assignments. One detachment, under Captain Bill Forrest, was to get past the pickets and capture General Hurlbut. Josh and I were placed in his command. Another detachment was sent to guard the main junctions of the railroad and steamboat landing in town. Another was ordered to capture General Washburn – this one led by Jesse Forrest. Yet another was sent to the main camp of troops. The General kept a sizable number of men in reserve. We were all told to keep quiet, and anyone caught plundering would be shot.

As we began to move out, a thick, wet fog settled around us. We were thankful for it, since it would help us to stay concealed.

We all moved ahead. Not long after we got started, we were challenged.

"Who goes there?"

As instructed, I answered, "A detachment of the Fourteenth Missouri Cavalry, with prisoners."

Silence. Then, “Advance.”

The captain, wearing a captured Yankee greatcoat, moved ahead of us. When he reached the picket, he hit him over the head with his rifle. The man fell to the ground. The rest of us rushed forward and overpowered the other pickets. But one of them managed to fire off his gun.

“Damn!” Josh whispered. “The Genrul ain't gonna like that one bit!”

We moved stealthily ahead through the deserted streets. The fog hid us from anyone who might have been about. The weak, early morning sunshine did little to disperse it.

The charge was sounded. All took off at a gallop, each detachment to its own assignment.

The Captain led us at a full gallop down the street until we reached the Gayoso Hotel, where General Hurlbut was billeted. Bill Forrest didn't wait for us to dismount, but rode his horse right into the lobby, an act that would not be forgotten for many a day.

The rest of us burst in behind him and began to round up enemy officers. Ladies were screaming, not all in a bad way, and men were shouting. We searched the hotel thoroughly and managed to capture a few members of Hurlbut's staff, but the Yankee general himself was nowhere to be found. The hotel staff was frightened out of their wits by our appearance, but couldn't tell us his whereabouts. Disappointed, we left the hotel, prisoners in tow.

A resistance had been organized, and by the time we found Forrest things were getting hot for us. The Yankees began an earnest attack, but not before we helped ourselves to horses and gear from a couple of livery stables. Forrest gathered us all together as a hen gathers her chicks, and then we began to withdraw.

At first I thought that our secret raid had not been much of a success. Neither general we targeted had been captured, though we had several other officers in tow, along with a couple hundred others, some still in nightclothes. They were better than nothing.

Our rear guard was attacked as we galloped out of town. The General called together his escort, and we countered the attack. Our intensity was too much for them and they were forced to withdraw.

We rested a bit at Cane Creek Bridge. The General sent Captain Anderson back under a flag of truce, with a note asking for an exchange of prisoners. He also asked for clothing for the Yanks who had been captured before they could get dressed properly.

"Better send these back, too, General," spoke up his brother Jesse, sheepishly waving the suit of clothes he had stolen from General Washburn's room.

"Yes, we had better. We wouldn't want the General to catch cold," Forrest said, a wide grin on his face.

When Anderson returned, he brought a message from Washburn that stated he had no authority to exchange prisoners, but he sent clothing and two wagonloads of food, enough to get the prisoners back to our main camp. Later, he would send our General a suit of Confederate gray made by his tailor in Memphis, in gratitude for the return of his dress uniform.

It turned out that our raid had served its purpose. The Yankee invasion of Mississippi was called off, and after those troops were recalled to Memphis, most of them were transferred to Missouri. They never suspected the daring raid by our General, which was in turn thanks to the diversion created by General Chalmers and his hard-fighting men.

No one in Memphis appreciated the General's humor in raiding his own town. They thought it was scandalous that he would do so – even his fellow Confederate friends there. He had interrupted the security of their world and they didn't like it one bit. Their attitude didn't bother the General. He had accomplished what he had set out to do.

CHAPTER FOURTEEN

We learned of the fall of Atlanta from a courier on his way south with a message for Forrest's new commander, General Taylor. The news left us stunned. We knew it had been a desperate fight, one that had taken the best the Confederacy had to offer in the western theater of the war. That, on top of our losses in Virginia, was enough to make us certain we were fighting for a lost cause.

Looking back, it is easy to see the mistakes made by the military and political leaders of our struggling republic. For one, they were blind to the potential of many of their leaders on the battlefield, the General included. They centered their attentions on the east, giving up the potential for victories in the west.

Our superiors were too busy with their political wranglings to pay attention to the most important matter at hand – winning independence. Our capital was rife with jealousy, back-biting, gossip and greed. There was no cohesiveness between the states and their leaders. Each one was eager to feather their own nest and could see no further than the end of their nose.

But then, I am not qualified to analyze the faults and shortcomings of the Confederacy. All I know is that those of us who fought so long and so hard became increasingly bitter as we played out the final chapters of the war. So many had given their lives and fortunes for a cause that could only end in defeat.

And then, one must look at the enterprise as a whole. Was the principle worth the sacrifice? Speaking only for myself, I was beginning to doubt it.

At the news of the fall of Atlanta, the General was called south to Meridian to confer with his superior, General Richard Taylor, the son of President Zachary Taylor. We waited restlessly for his return, sure that a major campaign was in the making.

Since our return from Memphis, the General had reorganized the troops. Because he understood the loyalties of his men, he had placed all the

Tennesseans in his command in one brigade, with Colonel Rucker at its head.

Southern men are hardheaded, stubborn and independent. We prefer to be asked and not told, and even though we had been fighting for a long time, these qualities had not been erased. While the General was gone, our camp exploded.

Colonel Rucker was considered a junior officer by many of the other colonels placed under his command, and they refused to take his orders. Fine men, one and all, but they still had not learned to swallow their pride when necessary. They tried to embroil the rest of us in their petty, political arguments. Before the General returned, the men were taking sides, either for or against the General's decision to appoint Rucker. Fistfights broke out among us. General Chalmers called us together and spoke, but it was clear the disagreement could only be settled by the General himself.

Josh and I let it be known we had no choice but to stand behind the General in this matter. He had brought us too far to have his authority questioned. Bradley, of course, took the opposite view, and he and Josh came close to blows over it. I drew a sigh of relief when the General returned, knowing he would clear the matter up.

He did it quickly and with little fuss. He immediately arrested Major Allen and Colonels

Green, Neely and Duckworth, and sent them south to his commander in Mobile. With the instigators gone, our camp quickly settled back down. Except for a few mutterings here and there, the incident was quickly put behind us.

We hustled about and prepared to move out. Josh told me we would be moving back into middle Tennessee. My heart skipped a beat and my mind whispered, "Clara." Before long I would see her again, no matter the cost.

It was early September, but the heat of the summer was still with us. We sweated and cursed under the hot, humid sun as we readied our gear and horses. Some of the men without mounts were busily building a platform and Josh and I took a brief respite to watch them.

"I wonder what that's for," I asked quizzically.

Josh cackled behind his hand, "You'll see."

The day before we left, we were all called to the platform. As we gathered together, the General mounted the steps and watched us with a calm eye.

We soon quieted to hear what he had to say.

"Men, I have some good news for you. We have been ordered home to middle Tennessee, to see what damage we can do to General Sherman's communications. As you all know, he is deep into Georgia, stealing as he goes." He grinned sarcastically. "Let's try and make his journey a little more difficult, shall we?" A few of the braver men answered his statement with whoops and yells.

"Now, I'm expecting you to conduct yourselves as you have in the past. There will be no looting on this expedition." His voice deepened to a sterner tone. "You will obey all orders or face the consequences." His voice rang louder and even harsher. "I will not tolerate any more disobedience to the officers I have appointed to command. This army has always relied on my best judgment and will continue to do so. Those who could not understand or accept my authority have been punished. The same, or worse, will be in store for any man of this command who questions my orders." He stared at us through burning eyes that seemed to pick us out individually. He relaxed slightly and continued on in a milder tone. "We move out in the morning. May God bless us on the campaign we are about to begin."

We moved out in two columns. The first went on horseback to Cherokee, Alabama, under General Buford. There were 3,000 of us, strong and ready to march back into the state we loved. The second column was with the General who went ahead of us by rail, with a little more than 400 men who had no mounts.

As the General was preparing to board the train at Tupelo for the journey to Alabama, he was accosted by an irate Colonel who claimed to have been insulted by something Forrest had said. As the General paced the train depot, deep in thought, the young man stumped up to him and said, "General, I wish to speak to you. You have offended me and I demand an apology."

The General looked at him abstractedly, as if he weren't there, then moved off to another area of the depot and continued his pacing. The Colonel refused to be ignored and followed him. "You can't get rid of me that easily, sir."

Forrest snapped. He reached out, grabbed the Colonel by the scruff of his neck and threw him down. He stepped over him and continued walking back and forth. The colonel presently stood up, brushed himself off, and wandered away with a dazed look in his eye. He discovered what the rest of us already knew – don't interrupt the General when he has important matters on his mind.

Our two columns merged in northern Alabama on September 18. Chalmers stayed in Mississippi with a brigade of men to take care of things while we were gone. We were instead to have General Roddey in Alabama to help us. It was also rumored that General Wheeler would be there, too.

We were down to the bare essentials, insofar as supplies were concerned. We were allowed one change of clothing and one blanket apiece, four days' cooked rations and 100 rounds of ammunition per man. Our raid would have to be lightning quick if we were to make it back alive. We were warned not to straggle because the column couldn't wait for anyone to keep up.

General Roddey was in ill health and would not be able to accompany us, but sent about 900 men. Wheeler had just returned from a raid up around Murfreesboro, which had been an utter disaster. His cavalry corps was completely demoralized. He had lost an entire brigade somewhere in Tennessee – either they had all deserted or been left behind and captured. He could no longer command any respect from his men and had asked to be relieved of duty. He handed over to the General about 500 men, including the old Forrest Brigade, reduced to 60 men.

This last caused the General great pain. He had turned over the brigade to Wheeler after Chickamauga. He had hated to lose the men who started the war with him, but was forced to by order of General Bragg. When we moved our base of operations to Mississippi, they had numbered almost 500.

"Sixty!" Josh muttered when he heard the news. "Damn! I started this here war with those fellas." He shook his head in despair.

Still, we started the expedition in good spirits. Most of the command were from middle Tennessee and were anxious to see how their homes had fared. We were warned, though, that only necessary furloughs would be granted. Just to smell the air and feel the sunshine of home seemed to satisfy them, however. There was very little grumbling.

We moved directly to the Tennessee River, which we had crossed many times before. The wagons, artillery and foot soldiers crossed at Colbert's Ferry under the command of Captain Anderson, while the rest of us crossed with the help of a guide near Ross's Ford. The river is a mile wide at this point, but we made if over without a mishap.

We rode hard the rest of the day and camped that night on the outskirts of Florence. We paraded through the town the next day, and were cheered on by crowds of onlookers who lined the streets to see us ride through. I thought of the cheering crowds and giggling, pretty girls I had dreamed about when I first entered the war. I had to smile at myself. Who would have guessed the kind of sacrifices I would have to make to earn the praise of my countrymen? The foolish dreams of youth. As I rode Goldie through the crowded streets, my only determination was to get home in one piece. Someone else could have the cheering crowds because they were no longer important to me.

Yet if felt good to see how the people flocked around the General as he rode King Phillip down the avenue. Ordinary people appreciated his genius and loved him despite his humble beginnings. Even though the Confederacy was fading, they still screamed and cheered for him as if the war had only started.

We moved forward with a vengeance the next day. To the surprise of the garrison at Athens, Alabama, we attacked and forced them to retire to the fort close to town. Before we could relax and enjoy the siege, the General sent the escort and the Second Tennessee under Colonel Barteau and Captain Anderson to capture a train just pulling into the station, which we did. We cut the telegraph wires, then were deployed by the Colonel along the track. We were about two men to a cross tie, and when the order was given we ripped the iron railing up from the ground. We sweated and cursed at the work, but kept it up for several hours. On our return to our comrades before the fort, we captured about 100 horses corralled outside of town. They would be of use to the dismounted troopers we had brought with us.

Early the next morning, the General began to ready us for an assault on the fort. Some of our men, under Colonel Jesse Forrest and Colonel White, were sent toward Decatur to delay the arrival of reinforcements. We then sent in a demand for surrender under a flag of truce. The Yankee commander refused.

The General was not satisfied. He didn't want to sacrifice any of his men by ordering a direct assault. He agonized for a short time, pacing up and down with his hands clasped behind his back, and then sent another message to the Union commander. He asked to meet him outside the fort to discuss the matter.

This particular fort was the strongest one between Nashville and Decatur. It was enclosed by a 15-foot ditch a quarter of a mile around. The men inside were amply supplied with fresh water and rations. Josh and I, with the escort and the Second Tennessee to the north of the fort, watched the General as he waited for Colonel Campbell to come out.

We knew of an enemy column on its way from Decatur to relieve the fort, and knew Forrest would have to have a good bluff under his hat. With a bland, confident look on his face, Forrest explained to the Yankee colonel that he commanded at least 8,000 men before the fort, with enough artillery to lay it flat. While he was so describing his small force, we were busy putting on the show we had been accustomed to giving. We mounted and dismounted, marched and moved before the fort, as if we were following specific strategic plans. Before long, the colonel had fallen for the same trick as many of his predecessors before him. He surrendered the fort, lock, stock and barrel.

Just as the 1,400 defenders marched out of the fort and laid down their arms, their reinforcements came into view. They had waged a desperate fight to get there, and were overcome by the sight of their comrades giving up the position they had come to relieve. They surrendered also. We were now in charge of 1,800 prisoners. Both sides had sustained numerous casualties along the road from Decatur. Colonel Jesse Forrest, the General's brother, suffered a painful wound through the thigh in that frantic fight.

We took no time to gloat, but immediately proceeded to the two small blockhouses near Athens. The first surrendered immediately, but the second required a little persuasion from our artillery.

Before we left Athens, the fort and blockhouses were destroyed. Prisoners and extra supplies were sent back to Cherokee Station so that we could proceed unencumbered. North we went, toward Pulaski, Tennessee. We carried along a Yankee officer who had been in command of one of the blockhouses we had just destroyed. He proved to be useful in persuading other commanders down the line to surrender, and saved us the trouble of besieging them.

We headed toward the railroad trestle at Sulphur Branch, a vital link between Nashville and northern Alabama. It spanned a deep ravine that cut into the flat plains that make up this part of the country.

It was an awe-inspiring structure. It was 400 feet wide, supported on either side by sturdy blockhouses and protected by at least 1,000 Yankees. Once our guns were placed about, a demand for surrender was sent in. When it was refused, our artillery began to work. After two hours of steady firing, they surrendered.

Captain Morton's gunners had done their job well. There were over 200 Yankee dead, scattered horribly around the inside of the fort. I averted my eyes as we ransacked the place and took out anything that could be of value to us.

Over 800 prisoners were sent south under guard. The dead were buried and the wounded cared for before we fired the place. All of us were now well mounted and equipped as we moved north again.

We continued on, destroying railroad equipment and blockhouses along the way. Curious civilians gathered outside their homes as we passed. Some of them waved and cheered us on, others just stared stonily as we passed. Most were ill-clothed and looked as if they could use a good meal. Their scruffy pastures and fields needed work, and most of their homes and barns had fallen into disrepair.

There was hardly a man left along the whole stretch of road. Women, children, and the aged made up the bulk of them.

The blockhouses and bridges across the Elk River had been abandoned. Apparently news of our coming had reached the defenders, and they left without so much as firing a shot. We gleefully destroyed the works, glad to be spared an encounter with the enemy.

We happened upon a large government corral at Brown's Plantation. As we hove into sight of the place, a shocking scene lay before us. There were Negroes, thousands of them, who had left their masters and followed the Yankee army. They lay, dirty and stinking in the sun, before a collection of the filthiest hovels I had ever seen. They were covered in vermin, and many had open, running sores all over their bodies. Our sudden appearance seemed not to disturb them at all. Their eyes stared without recognition, and few of them even stirred to see what was going on.

The General cursed when he saw them. He ordered us to round them up and see that they got their belongings out of the miserable dwellings they were living in. These were burned and the Negroes sent south under armed guard. None seemed shocked at the orders.

We met resistance at Richland Creek, but not enough to stop our destruction of the blockhouses found there. The defenders ran off and joined the garrison at Pulaski, now secure behind their substantial fortifications around the town. The General made a few feints in their direction, but did not seriously consider attacking them that evening. They were much stronger than we, and it would take some planning to attain their defeat.

That night, Forrest handed out extra supplies to all of us. There was coffee and sugar, new boots and clothes for those who needed them, and extra rations. Josh and I put our coffee together, and drank enough that night to make the average man sick to his stomach. We preened and paraded about in our new blue coats and trousers. It felt good to be almost home, with new clothing and plenty of rations.

We moved against Pulaski early the next morning. There were plenty of Yankees outside the fort, and they peppered away at us without any indication of giving up. Still, we managed to push and prod them into the fort by early afternoon. The General did not seem overly concerned at their strength, even though it was easy enough to see they outnumbered us. He gathered the escort up and reconnoitered the enemy's position, both front and rear. We got as close as we could without being shot at, but could find no weakness. We glanced worriedly at the General as we reached our own conclusions of the enemy's impregnability, but his facial expression never changed. He studied the fort carefully and quickly, then led us back to the rest of the men.

Josh was depressed at the thought of us attacking the fort. “It'd jist be my luck ta git myself kilt jist 30 miles from home. I shore wisht the Genrul had picked a better place to meet them Yanks.”

I was exasperated. “He can't always do the picking. Sometimes he has to follow the dictates of others.”

“Humpf. Not the Genrul. Didn't Genrul Taylor give him permission ta go and do what he wants here?” He paused, glaring at me. I stubbornly refused to reply. “Well, didn't he? So the Genrul didn't have ta bring us up here. He coulda gone a diff'rent way.”

“All right.” I said crossly. “He could have. But he didn't. We're here and we'll just have to make the best of it. I just wish you wouldn't get so worked up. I'm tired of hearing it.”

He swelled visibly, and his eyes protruded. “Easy for you to say, boy. You ain't a stone's throw away from yer fam'ly, who you ain't seen in years. Seems ta me I remember you gettin' ta go home not so long ago.”

"So? I have interests in this part of the country, too, but you don't see me getting all worked up, do you?"

By this time we were glaring belligerently at each other across the mess fire. Fred had watched the whole scene silently, but spoke up.

"Cool off," he said calmly. "Relax. The Genrul ain't fool enough to try to do somethin' we can't handle. Josh, go check your horse. She seemed to be limping some while we was out scoutin'."

Josh, grumbling, went off. I looked at Fred quizzically for a few moments, then got up and found my rifle. I took my frustration out on it, and cleaned it until it sparkled. By the time I had finished, my anger was gone.

The rest of the troops were busy making noisy feints at the enemy fort, but neither gave nor received any serious damage. We continued popping at them as darkness descended and ceased fire at about eight o'clock.

A tang of autumn coolness was in the air as we gathered around our campfires. Snatches of song floated on the breeze, and the smell of tobacco smoke was in the air. Men debated the pros and cons of our situation, but none could predict what the General had on his mind. There were few greenhorns among us then. We had fought with him long enough to be prepared for the unexpected.

We were ordered to build up our campfires and get ready to march. We piled them high with extra wood and built several new ones. We rode off for Fayetteville about ten o'clock, and left behind an enemy who believed we were safe and snug, wrapped in warm blankets before our roaring fires.

Josh seemed uncommonly tense and quiet as we headed east. I decided it would be best to leave him alone with his thoughts. Discussion would probably have made matters worse.

Since it was late and some of the troops had seen some hard action that day, the General camped us eight miles from Pulaski. We hurriedly made camp without the benefit of fires.

Before I could get good and comfortable, the General approached our mess. “Josh?” he called sternly.

“Yessir?” he answered as he scrambled out of his blanket.

“Saddle your horse. You've got some visiting to do.”

“Yessir!” Josh replied as he began to roll up his blanket.

“I can't spare you for long. We'll be camped north of Fayetteville tomorrow night, somewhere along the road to Tullahoma. See that you join us there.”

“I will, sir, an' thank ya kindly.”

The General waved in reply and moved off. I breathed a sigh of relief. "Josh, before you go, I have something for you." I reached around in my saddlebags and took out our supply of coffee and sugar. I stood and handed it to him. "Emma could probably use this."

"Shore she could. She prob'bly ain't seen such fer months. Thank ya kindly, John."

"Watch out for Yankees. They're swarming around these parts." He left quickly, a smile of joy on his face.

When the sun rose, we were already on the road. It was rough going. The terrain was hilly and treacherous, and the roads wound mischievously through dense woods. The byways were thick with mud from recent rains. They were so narrow we had trouble pulling our artillery through.

As we neared Fayetteville the countryside became more populated. The children turned out to greet us and waved at us from behind the fences of their homes.

The General waved and smiled at them in return.

We passed easily through the town, a small, neat hamlet alongside the Elk River. We didn't stop, but moved north along the road to Tullahoma. We camped that night about five miles outside of town.

I waited nervously for Josh's return. I had no doubt of his loyalty, and it was apparent the General didn't either. But I had a nagging fear the Yankees had somehow captured him. Normally he was very cautious and I prayed that the excitement of seeing home again hadn't clouded his judgment.

Bradley had been irritable and belligerent all day. Fred and I had watched him carefully, afraid he would take the chance to escape. I knew he was angry because the General had let Josh go, even though he had stated that no furloughs would be granted, but I didn't feel the need to explain the General's actions to him, at least not then. As far as I was concerned, Bradley didn't deserve a furlough. He would only desert if he had been given a chance to go home.

Josh rode in close to midnight. I had lain down long before, but was too worried about him to sleep. As quietly as he could, he made his way to our mess and laid down.

"How was everything?" I asked quietly.

He jumped visibly. "Boy, don't scare me like that. I thought you wuz asleep."

"Well I'm not. I've been waiting for you to get back. How was Emma?"

"Fine. Leastways, as good as I kin expect. The youngun's is growin' like weeds."

"Have they had a rough time of it?"

"Yup. Food's been purty hard ta find. Seems the Yankee patrols are keepin' things picked clean. But

Emma's purty smart. Her and my boy Frank dug 'em a special place away from the house and been hidin' some a' their supplies. Course, she hadn't been able to keep much meat. A few chickens, an' that's about it. They could be doin' worse."

"I guess she's ready for you to come home."

"Naw. She hates them Yanks like poison. Her and the kids is proud a' me, I guess, cause I'm with the Genrul. Didn't have the heart to tell her things can't go on much longer."

"Surely she knows that. News travels fast."

"She jist don't wanta be'lieve we ain't gonna win. Thinks Genrul Lee in Virginia is gonna do a miracle or sumpthin'. He sighed heavily. "Kinda pains me ta see her so damn loyal. Don't know what she'll do when everythin's over."

"She'll survive. Besides, she may be right. We may win this thing yet."

"Yup," he said blankly, with no conviction in his voice. We were quiet then, and soon both of us were asleep.

I was awakened abruptly a short time later and brought to the General. Nathan Boone was already there with 20 or so other members of the escort. We were joined by Captain Kelleher of the Twelfth Kentucky and about 30 of his men.

The General explained that he needed us to head northeast to Tullahoma and cut the telegraph there that led south to Sherman in Georgia. "I realize, boys, there's only a handful of you, but you'll have to do the best you can. I've got Yankees heading for us from every direction and I can't take the risk of putting all my eggs in one basket." He looked cheerful and self-confident. "We'll be heading your way first thing in the morning, but I doubt we'll make it that far. Join us as soon as you've completed your task."

We sleepily saluted and headed off to get our horses. The night was dark and damp, but we had a couple of good scouts with us who knew the way. Despite the muddy condition of the road, we made good time. Lieutenant Boone kept us to the south of Tullahoma, near Deckerd, and Captain Kelleher took his men north. Both parties worked furiously until dawn and did as much damage as could be expected from such a small force. We headed back quickly toward Mulberry as soon as Captain Kelleher rejoined us. He and his men told us there were thousands of Yankees in Tullahoma. They had seen their camp. We whipped up our horses at the news and were glad when we saw our scraggly army ahead of us.

Shortly after we returned the General divided his army. He sent Buford south with the artillery to capture Huntsville, Alabama. He was instructed to destroy the railroad from there to Decatur before he crossed the Tennessee River to safety. The rest of us headed west to draw the Yankees in that direction, in the hopes they would follow us instead of Buford. The General was also hopeful we could do some damage to the railroad that ran from Nashville to Decatur.

We were in a tight spot. We had gained several new recruits since returning to Tennessee, but our force had been sadly depleted by a large number of guard details sent south with prisoners. Our ammunition was woefully short, thanks to the stubborn resistance of the enemy fortifications we had encountered. It was rumored there were at least 15,000 Yankees headed for us, determined to end our raiding days forever. I would guess we had less than 3,400 men by this time, a pitifully small number to face so many well-armed troops. As usual, the General had made the right decision when he decided the situation in which we found ourselves was too hot for us to handle.

We marched all day and camped that night at Petersburg. The next day we passed through Lewisburg and my spirits began to soar. It looked as if we might make it to Columbia, where I was sure I could manage to snatch a few minutes to see Clara, but it was not to be. The General changed direction, and we headed north toward Spring Hill.

We worked all day on October 1, 1864. We destroyed as much of the railroad at Spring Hill as we could before heading back south. We overran several blockhouses and burned them to the ground. We burned bridges and mutilated railroad tracks with the help of firewood that had been piled along the tracks, intended for the use of the engines.

Just before nightfall, we came upon a blockhouse that had a large sign posted at its' gate – "No surrender." We laughed and joked at those who had posted such a sign, but realized we could do little about it. We had no artillery with us, having sent it all south with Buford.

As darkness settled about us, the General circulated about the camp and asked for ten volunteers. He soon got them. They were ordered to sneak in and burn the bridge guarded by the blockhouse. This was accomplished promptly, and we marched south by the light of the fire. We laughed aloud at the thought of the commander of the blockhouse, who refused to surrender but lost the object of his defense. We camped on the outskirts of Columbia.

"Don't be gittin' any ideas about goin' in there an' seein' that gal. There's more Yanks in that town than you kin shake a stick at," Josh said matter-of-factly the next morning as we gobbled our cold breakfast of cornpone.

I nodded slowly in agreement, then brightened. “But I could probably get a note in!”

“Shore!” Josh said enthusiastically. “That's the spirit! Got any paper?”

“No.” My spirits drooped again.

“You wait right here.” He rose and limped off, but was back shortly with a piece of paper, pen and ink. “Shore comes in handy ta be good friends with the Genrul. He kin getcha anythin', if ya need it bad enough. Better git ta writin', boy. We're fixin' ta get real busy.”

I wrote furiously as the rest of the men got ready to move out. As I was addressing the note, Josh brought Goldie to me, saddled and ready to go.

We couldn't attack Columbia itself, so we did what we could to let the Yankees, secure within the city's defenses, know of our presence. While most of our men popped away at them on the north and west sides of town, other detachments were sent south to burn bridges and trestles. The rest of us were used to gather supplies from the countryside. There was plenty of livestock about, and we took what we needed.

The country folk were glad to see us back, and readily shared what they had. I found a youngster who was willing to slip into town and deliver the note I had written, and I gave him some hard money for his trouble. His wide, freckled face lit up when he saw it. I imagine it had been a long time since he or his family had seen real money.

We left before nightfall, headed south. I looked over my shoulder at the once peaceful town as we departed, saddened by the look of war that had slipped over it. The leaves of autumn were falling, and it only enhanced the gloom of the place. I knew Clara was probably safe, but I hated leaving her there. How nice it would have been if I could have ridden in and snatched her away, away from the dirt and violence of war?

We moved quickly. As reported by our scouts, we had cavalry breathing down our necks from the north, out of Nashville, with more headed our way from Athens, and still more directly west out of Wartrace. The Yankees didn't like us marauding about. We were considered a real threat to Sherman's plans, because they realized the damage the General could do if he had a mind to. We passed through Mount Pleasant and Lawrenceburg and finally reached the Tennessee River above Florence, weary but determined to make it to safety.

We had learned never to expect the river to give us a fair chance. It has always been unpredictable and untrustworthy. I have cursed at its vagaries more times than I care to remember. It seemed whenever we needed its cooperation the most was when it was overflowing its banks, filled with either autumn or spring rains, its muddy waters filled with debris. This time was no exception. When we reached its banks, the wind had whipped its high water into large, perilous waves.

We were met by General Buford. After threatening Huntsville, where he convinced the commander that his small army was led by Forrest himself, and Athens, then reinforced with a new garrison, he had marched west to Florence and the river. He had already sent the artillery and supplies across.

For transportation, we had only three boats and ten skiffs to get us all across. The damp wind continued to whip the river into waves as we worked all day, October 5.

The General sent a detachment to slow the approach of the enemy from Athens, while Colonel Windes of the Fourth Alabama did the same to the east of us, where the Yankees were pressing forward from Huntsville.

We didn't stop, even though we were forced to drop downstream to continue our ferrying of men and horses across. Some of us were allowed to sleep in snatches while others took our places. But by the afternoon of the 6th, the enemy was almost upon us. Since there were still at least 1,000 men on the wrong bank of the river, they were ordered to mount their horses and swim to a large island, not far from the north shore, where our efforts to cross would continue. One regiment was left behind to skirmish with the Yankees and give the rest of the men a chance to get across.

We stayed on the south side of the island where we were well hidden by the thick growth of cane and trees and the high banks of the northern side. It didn't take long for the Yankees to disperse the regiment we had left behind. They scattered to the hills and continued to pester the flanks of the enemy.

After a short time, the Yankees gave up in disgust, thinking we had made it safely across the river. They fell back the way they had come. The night was cold, but we worked steadily on without the benefit of fires.

Josh and I stayed with the General on the island, and waited for the last boat to leave. Before we could go, Forrest made a last inspection of the island to make sure no stragglers were left behind. We waited by the boat impatiently, hungry for the fire, food and rest that awaited us on the opposite shore.

The General came back with four pickets. They must have been asleep on duty or they would have realized we were pulling out. The General gruffly ordered them to board the boat. Sheepishly, they each grabbed an oar and helped row us across.

Our leader was in a foul mood. I'm sure he was as cold, hungry and tired as the rest of us, since he always insisted on doing his fair share of the work. He also had the added strain of knowing we had escaped by only a hair's breadth, and couldn't even be sure of our safety once across the river. As we started across, he began to vilify anything and everything that came to his mind – the persistent Yankees who hounded us, the river, the weather, the laziness of certain members of his staff, and so on.

He was busy applying a pole to the bottom of the river, sweating with the rest of us, and had barely gotten warmed up from his efforts when he noticed a lieutenant in the boat with us, standing in the front, gazing arrogantly down at us while we worked to get us securely across.

"Why don't you take a spell on an oar and help get us across?" the General snapped angrily at him.

"Sir, I'm an officer. I'm not required to do that kind of work as long as we have privates along to do the job for us," the lieutenant replied haughtily, his arms crossed over his chest.

The General roared out, and before anyone could stop him, had swung his pole at the lieutenant. He clipped him on the side of the head and sent him sprawling into the river.

Josh chuckled aloud, and finally held his pole over the boat toward the poor man, who grabbed hold of it and was pulled aboard. As he lay in the floor of the boat, soaking wet and gasping for air, the General raged at him.

"Now damn it, grab some oars and get to work! The next time I'll let you drown!" The lieutenant did as he was told, and began to row so fast it was hard for the rest of us to keep up with him.

After we disembarked, we were allowed a short time to rest, eat and get warm before the fires. Blissfully, we took advantage of the opportunity and felt much better as we began the march to Corinth.

Since we were well away from the Yankees, the march wasn't as hard as most of them had been. We were allowed to rest periodically, and had captured enough food to keep us satisfied.

Josh and I were getting used to staying close to Bradley. He had little to say during those days, and when he bothered to speak at all, it was usually unpleasant. But, we didn't seem to mind him as much anymore. We had grown deaf to his complaining and his threats. We knew once we returned to Mississippi, we could relax our vigil.

The General was in better spirits as we moved westward. We had gathered a large number of recruits while in Tennessee. Despite the gloomy outlook of the war in general, we had not done badly.

Yet we weren't to realize until later that it was too little too late. Perhaps the General knew, but he would never speak of it. He always tried to maintain an air of optimism while he was with his men.

But Sherman was firmly entrenched in Georgia, and the Confederacy simply didn't have enough men in the west to oppose him. Even though we had caused some damage, it wasn't nearly enough to cut the tentacles with which the Yankees were gradually strangling the South.

CHAPTER FIFTEEN

We made it safely back to Corinth, where we recuperated for a short time. Thomas Burns had been hit at Columbia, but it was not a serious wound. Except for Bradley, we could relax around the fire.

I had not heard from my Father in some time, so I wrote him as soon as we got settled back in. Clara was next on my list. The anguish of being so close to her but being denied an opportunity to see her was still upon me, and the letter I sent (still in her trunk in the attic) was the closest thing to a love letter she had ever received from me.

Mrs. Forrest had joined the General at our camp, and she took some time to greet as many of us as she could. She was a fine woman, easy to look at and converse with. She always seemed cheerful, despite the fact both her husband and only son lived so dangerously. She had become a familiar sight among us, ever since I had returned from my furlough after Chickamauga. The General's moods were much improved whenever she was around. It was obvious they were still very much in love, and treated each other with the greatest respect.

Soon the General sent out a call for General Chalmers to meet him near the Tennessee border with whatever men, wagons and artillery he could muster. We were off again, with the General hoping to throw another crippling blow at Sherman's line of supply.

Since late 1863, the Yankees had been busy building the Nashville and Northwestern Railroad to tie Nashville straight to a supply landing on the Tennessee River, and it was being used to give Sherman's expedition into Georgia an alternate route of supply. The railroad ended at Johnsonville, named after the Yankee military governor, which was not so much a town as a vast supply depot on the eastern bank of the Tennessee. If it could be seriously damaged, our efforts to handicap Sherman would be advanced.

Although we were far from rested, we set out from Corinth on October 16. We joined up with Chalmers and set out for Jackson together.

If the General had hoped to forage for supplies, he was much disappointed. The ravages of war were taking effect on western Tennessee, and the people were unwilling to trade what little they had for Confederate currency. Our horses were in sad shape after our previous foray behind enemy lines, and we were forced to leave many worn-out or dead ones along the way. The rest were in dire need of shoes, and limped pitifully.

Word was passed out for ten volunteers from each regiment. Once gathered, the General ordered them out in search of iron. They were told to take what was needed from blacksmith shops nearby, and to strip the metal off any wagons they happened upon. The men galloped off in a hurry and were back by sundown. The smiths that always accompanied us were put to work. By morning, all of our horses had been shod, and we pushed off again.

We arrived safely in Jackson, and the General immediately set up his headquarters. One of the first things he did was send home all the men of the area, in the hopes they could find better mounts and some warm clothing for the approaching winter. The rest of us helped recruit and bring in supplies. We also grabbed some extra rest, since most of us had not fully recuperated from our last raid.

The General waited several days before we advanced against the river transports that moved up the Tennessee to Johnsonville. He wanted to be sure there was no major force moving in his direction before he struck out and stranded himself with little hope of rescue. When all seemed safe, we headed out for the river at the Kentucky line.

Buford went first, carrying his field artillery with him. He was in place along the river, his men and guns firmly entrenched, by about October 28th. Part of his command held the works at old Fort Heiman, with more artillery placed a few hundred yards downstream. More men and guns were placed at Paris Landing, about five miles upstream.

The plan was to capture the rich river transports headed to Johnsonville, where they would be unloaded and their cargo sent by rail to Sherman. Buford's men were ordered not to fire until the transports were safely in our trap.

The men waited patiently until the next day when the *Mazeppa*, a new steamer out of Cincinnati, obligingly came into view, and when it had steamed into position, the lower battery fired three well-placed rounds. Her crew abandoned her in a hurry when she drifted to the opposite shore.

Her capture became a dilemma. How to get her across the river and into the willing hands of Buford's men? A young private solved the problem. He tied his pistol around his neck, and using a plank for a boat, paddled across. Soon enough, the *Mazeppa* was tied up on our side of the river.

She was truly a prize. After all her supplies were unloaded – meat, flour, shoes, blankets and warm clothing – she was fired. Three Yankee gunboats had come sniffing after her, but were chased away by our artillery.

The men celebrated that night. There was plenty to eat and enough clothing and shoes to go around. Most of us slept with new blankets, warm and cozy. The coming winter didn't seem to be nearly so bleak.

Another steamer, the *Anna*, hove onto the scene early the next morning, but managed to escape our trap. Meanwhile, the gunboat *Undine* heard the shots fired at the *Anna* and came up to investigate. She rounded the corner at Paris Landing, and after about an hour's fight, limped on to a point between the guns of Paris Landing and Fort Heiman, where none of our artillery shells could reach her. Here she rested and began to repair the damage she had sustained. Her guns were loaded with shrapnel and used against the men popping away at her with their rifles.

A transport, the *Venus*, followed. The *Undine* signaled her of the danger, but she paid no attention.

On she came. She was fired upon, but the damage was slight. She wound up next to the *Undine*, protected by her guns.

Still another ship, the *Cheeseman*, with a barge in tow, approached our guns. Not as brave as the others, she quickly surrendered after several rounds were shot her way.

Chalmers arrived with several more pieces of artillery, which were placed at Paris Landing. Colonel Rucker discovered a way to maneuver some of his artillery so they had a line of sight against the *Undine* and *Venus*. This was done immediately, and the *Undine* was the first to be abandoned, followed shortly thereafter by the *Venus*.

The *Tawah*, another gunboat, had been attracted by the sound of guns. She moved down and began firing at our upper battery. Chalmers ordered several of our guns to be moved closer to her, along with two companies of sharpshooters. They proved too much for the *Tawah*, and she moved off out of range.

We didn't arrive with the General until the 31st, and he was well pleased at what Chalmers and Buford had accomplished. He said their gumption had given him inspiration, and he declared he would make their efforts worthwhile. He began to organize, and soon came up with the idea of using the abandoned Yankee boats along the river against the enemy stronghold in Johnsonville.

The *Cheeseman* was too damaged to be of any further use, so she was quickly unloaded and burned. Two 20-pound Parrot guns that had been brought by Buford were mounted on the *Venus*. The *Undine* was already well equipped with eight 24-pound howitzers. Repairs were made quickly and the General called for volunteers to man the two vessels.

Despite having no experienced men to command the boat, the General was undaunted. Lieutenant Colonel Dawson was persuaded to captain the *Venus*, and Captain Gracey of the Third Kentucky, who had some knowledge of steamboats, was given command of the *Undine*. They weren't expected to perform any miracles, and were ordered to burn the boats if they were forced to ground them. They were allowed a few hours to train their crews before we moved on.

A steady rain was falling as we left the next morning. Chalmers moved ahead with half the artillery to protect our little navy from any gunboats that might come up from Johnsonville. Buford did likewise to the rear. The two boats were ordered to stay between these two guardians.

We started in good spirits, despite the rain and mud. Josh cackled loudly at the awkward movement of the boats on the river, and joined in with several others who jeered at our comrades across the way, struggling to keep their boats from foundering.

As the day progressed, though, the taunts reversed course, and those thrown back at us from the river grew tiresome.

"Hey, boys, how's the mud?"

"Don't get worn out there, fellas, we may need you further down!"

"What's wrong, can't you boys keep up? Yer slowin' us down sompthin' fierce!"

We struggled for breath as we tried to move the artillery and ourselves through the sticky mud. The rain had not slackened, and the road grew worse. But we weren't too tired to throw some insults back at the boats: "Watch out there, fellas! We don't wanta be pickin' yer pieces outta the water when them Yankee gunboats catch up with ya!" Josh yelled out, "I hope them damn Yanks blow yer arses right outta the water!"

By nightfall we were dog-tired. We gratefully set up camp near a ruined railroad trestle that crossed the river near Danville. Because of the rain, we were without fires, but were so grateful for the chance to rest we didn't really care.

The rain continued to fall throughout the night. We were cold, damp and miserable when the march resumed the following morning. The roads were even worse than they had been the day before, but we struggled on. The General was there, offering encouragement to those of us who needed it. He knew we were in poor shape, and he wasn't much better. Despite the signs of tiredness about his eyes, he kept on with the strength of two men.

By late afternoon, we were barely moving in the mire. The *Venus*, having no such impediment, began to feel her oats and ran ahead. The General shook his head and cursed under his breath when he saw her steaming around a bend in the river. His anger was justified when we heard the distant firing of guns.

There was nothing we could do to help her. The *Undine* steamed ahead to give her assistance, but couldn't match the power of the two Yankee gunboats that had attacked *Venus*. Soon enough the *Undine* came back down the river under full steam. As she passed, her men shouted out that the *Venus* had been abandoned and her crew had scattered into the woods.

“Did they fire her?” the General bellowed.

“No, sir!” came the faint reply as the *Undine* moved out of view.

“Damnation!” the General said bitterly. “Well, there's little we can do about it now. The Yankees have got her guns.”

We continued on. Another uncomfortable night was had, but the next day promised a cessation of rain. And at least we still had the *Undine*.

On November 3, we found ourselves about two miles below Johnsonville. While the artillery was being placed, the *Undine* ventured out and tried to lure three Yankee gunboats to us. The bait was not taken, however. They stayed at their posts and seemed to leer at us belligerently.

"I wisht the Genrul would git ta work. This here waitin' around fer them fools in them boats is beginnin' ta git me down."

I looked at Josh in wonder. Most soldiers were happy to have a chance to take things easy for awhile. "What's the hurry?"

"Oh, I ain't in no hurry, exac'ly. Jist ready ta git movin', that's all."

We had hoped the rain would let up, but our luck didn't hold. It began to pour again just as we were ordered to help get the artillery in place for our attack on Johnsonville. Josh, Bradley and I struggled through the thick mud, pushing heavily at what seemed an inordinately stubborn gun, an equal number of men with their shoulders to the opposite wheel. The horses hitched to it strained and sweated. Without our help, they would have made little progress through the bogs and mud holes that comprised the road. Before we had gone fifty feet, we were covered in mud.

"Well, are you satisfied?" I asked Josh angrily as I stumbled alongside him. He didn't bother to answer.

We were luckier than some. Part of the artillery had to be moved across a swamp. A road had to be cut through the dense growth, and the guns carried over fallen timbers that could not be moved. Even though our task was nearly impossible, I felt sorry for the men given that assignment.

We worked all day and into the night of the 3rd. The General placed guns directly across the river from the depot itself, as well as above and below it on the opposite shore to prevent reinforcements from arriving by water.

The scene across the way was a peaceful one. There were 17 or 18 loaded barges and three gunboats tied to the landing before the town. Enemy soldiers loitered about the boats, some of them doing their wash or scrubbing the decks. Drifts of conversation floated across the river to us as they called across the boats and barges to each other. Up at the railhead, there were two freight trains being loaded. No one seemed aware of our presence under the trees across the river.

The landing at Johnsonville was stacked high with all kinds of supplies. The General used his field glasses and announced there was enough there to last us a long while. I rubbed my hands together in anticipation.

Our siege began the next day. Early that morning, six more gunboats came up the river and met with the three already stationed there. The *Undine* was caught and Captain Gracey abandoned and burned her rather than risk his men in a fight. All made it safely to shore, and that was the end of General Forrest's first and only navy.

Our batteries began to boom away at the gunboats. Because the General had placed the lower guns on Reynoldsburg Island, which narrowed the river channel that lead to Johnsonville, the newly arrived gunboats could not get through. They would have had to pass our guns in single file, which would have been suicide. Therefore, they were no help in saving the depot.

In the meantime, the General opened up on Johnsonville itself. The artillery concentrated its fire on the boats and barges at the docks. They burst into flames soon enough, while we watched in sheer pleasure. It was like stirring up an anthill as men emerged from the boats to scamper ashore, and others ran back and forth. Explosions burst from the holds of boats, while others just settled in at a slant. Before long, they all sank to the bottom of the Tennessee River.

With them out of the way, the guns were concentrated on the piles of stores along the bank. Soon these were burning briskly, and the flames spread to the warehouses and sheds close by. I groaned inwardly as I saw the precious supplies going up in flames, but I knew there was no way for us to transport them where they would do any good.

The wind carried sparks, and with them further destruction. Soon the whole landing was on fire. It was quite the sight. The red-orange flames reached a hundred feet into the air, and thick black smoke lazily drifted above us. The tantalizing aroma of those supplies burning across the way wafted over to us and caused our mouths to water.

"Mmm, boy, I shore'd like ta have me some a' that coffee n' bacon that's acookin' over there," Josh sniffed wistfully.

"So do I, but I don't think our wishes will be granted."

As soon as the General ascertained that the destruction was complete, he pulled us out. Although it was dark by that time, the light from the fires still burning behind us made our march much easier.

As we headed south, the General and escort rode along with Thrall's Battery, whose men had done such a fine job half a mile above the town. The boys were from Arkansas and had been named the "Arkansas Rats." When we pulled out, the General offered them his congratulations, and said he would see to it they were renamed the "Arkansas Braves."

One of them piped up with a reply, "That's mighty fine, Genrul, but we'd heap rather have a little sompthin' ta eat. We ain't had nothin' but wind to eat fer days."

Forrest laughed aloud and then turned to one of his aides. "Find my wagon. There are four boxes of hardtack and three hams in it somewhere. Bring them here and give them to Captain Thrall's men."

The rain was still falling and the traveling difficult, but we now had the satisfaction of another success. In truth, it was the most gain for the least loss we'd had during the whole war. That, plus heading back to safer territory with no opposition, helped us rest easier.

When we reached Perryville, thirty miles directly south of Johnsonville, we attempted to cross the river. The General had been directed to move into middle Tennessee and then south to Decatur, Alabama, where he was to join forces with General Hood. We had carried two small boats with us by wagon, and tried to build more out of what planks of wood we could find. None of us were boat builders, but we did the best we could. The General pitched in, like always, and had a good laugh at the puny loads of wood carried to the shore by his staff and the escort. He was as strong as a horse and could carry more than just about anyone else in the whole outfit.

But we finally had to give up. The river was on the rise, loaded with driftwood and debris. The current was so swift the horses could never cross, and we had no means of ferrying them.

"No matter," the General said. "I've gotten word that Hood has moved to Florence, so we'll just move south from here and cross the river at a safer place."

I shook my head as we left the half-finished boats we had worked so hard to construct. They looked forlorn and forgotten as we left them stranded on the churned-up, muddy bank.

It was early November. The weather continued cold, damp and rainy. The road had turned into a morass, with the mud so deep it reached past Goldie's knees. Slowly, the horses that pulled the guns gave out, one by one. The General had as many as sixteen horses to each gun, but they still couldn't pull through the mud.

In the ceaseless rain, the escort was assigned to oxen duty. We impressed teams of oxen from local farmers to pull the artillery, and even these plodding creatures had a time of it. Each evening, the farmers would take their oxen back home while we scoured the countryside for more to use the next day.

We shivered and shook through the nights. Fires could not be kept going, and food was scarce. All of us had dysentery, and the weather seemed to make the condition worse. I heard groans and growls throughout the night as we clutched our bellies and rolled around in our blankets, the pain too fierce to be born.

Fred was in such bad condition that Josh and I were afraid we would lose him. Stubbornly he refused to stay with the wounded, but rode between us, and we helped support him in the saddle whenever a strong attack overtook him.

Josh, too, was hollow-eyed and thin. His rough, weather-beaten hands shook as he held the reins of his horse. But I had long ago discovered that he possessed a well of strength that enabled him to withstand hardships that would have laid low a younger man. His hands might shake, and his shoulders might stoop, but his eyes were steady and his knees unerring as he guided his horse through the mess created by the torrent of rain.

Looking back, it is hard to understand how we managed to survive the ordeal. As our last major campaign with Forrest approached, we still had our spirit, if not our health. God knows we could have used both.

CHAPTER SIXTEEN

It had been a year since we fought as part of the Army of Tennessee. A very successful year for us, overall, but not so for them. They had lost Chattanooga to the enemy at Missionary Ridge under Bragg, and were pushed across Georgia by Sherman while under Johnston. They had lost Atlanta to the Yankees after Hood took command, and Sherman had left northern Georgia to him. We joined with them that winter to attempt to undermine Sherman's base of supply and communications. We were going to launch a full counter-invasion of Tennessee.

It was the middle of November when we joined them in Florence, Alabama, and as we rode in, the men of the Army of Tennessee lined the road through camp and cheered us. Our fame had spread and they looked at us like good luck pieces who would help them beat the Yankees for a change.

The General gave a speech that evening, short and to the point. We were glad to be back home, and we would do whatever was necessary to wring victory out of the enemy. He thanked our comrades for their good wishes and their support. Afterward, the camp took on a carnival air, with bands, singing, fiddle playing and feats of skill.

We had little time to recover from our raid on Johnsonville. We had been forced to send a number of men south to Verona afterward because their horses were too worn, plus some of the Kentuckians dispatched for new mounts hadn't yet returned. On a positive note, we were joined at Florence by Red Jackson's division, which had stayed with the army throughout its struggle for Atlanta. Altogether, even though Forrest was to command three divisions and was in charge of all the cavalry with the Army of Tennessee, the General had but 5,000 men in fighting condition.

Despite our sorry state, we were ready for a fight, especially those who had faced Sherman but a short time ago. They were ready for a chance to attack rather than defend. The Yankee wave that had swept them out of Georgia had defeated them mentally as well as physically. They had seen their comrades wasted on the battlefield and their home folks deprived of the necessities of life. Defeat had stared them in the face and won time after time, and they needed a victory to cure what ailed them.

We started from Florence in three columns on November 21, headed for Columbia. The three divisions of cavalry took the lead.

The weather gave us an ominous beginning. We had awakened in time to witness an early snowstorm, never a welcome sight for a soldier. The Yankees made the day grow worse with their harassment, and forces emerging at intervals on the roads. With cavalry alone they were not strong enough to stop us, but they did what they could to slow us down.

To the west, Chalmers led the first division of cavalry. The General and the escort rode with him, and we moved by way of Mount Pleasant to Columbia. The other two columns led by Jackson and Buford moved first to Lawrenceburg, then east to Pulaski. They had hoped to pen in the large enemy force within the walls of Pulaski and prevent their joining forces with the considerable number of Yankees already protecting the railroad and major turnpike that ran through Columbia, but the Yankees had already gone by the time Jackson and Buford arrived.

Our first big encounter with the enemy occurred near Henryville, before we reached Mount Pleasant. We suddenly came upon a Union brigade, well positioned and ready to dispute our passage. The General sent Rucker and his men ahead to keep them busy in the front, then sent Kelley around to their flank. He led us around to the other flank. The strategy proved so effective, the enemy was forced to withdraw from the field. The General kept us posted at their rear while Rucker drove them backwards later on in the evening. We killed or captured quite a few of them before they could get away. On the other side, Buford and Jackson were executing their own pincer attacks, taking prisoners, horses and supplies.

Despite the cold and the poor condition of the roads, our mission was going well at this point. Fighting and marching had become our way of life, and the hardships that went along with it had become easier to bear. For once, instead of fear of being isolated and surrounded, we had a full army coming up behind us, so it was the Yankees' turn to worry. We had high hopes for success, and these helped to ease the hunger pangs and sore muscles that always accompanied us in those days.

Josh and I shared whatever bits of food we happened upon, as did Fred and Thomas. They had become close in their own way. Fred was a fatherly sort of fellow and much more effective in keeping Thomas in line than Josh and I had been.

Bradley had become a loner. He shared with no one. I thought it would be a pity if any one of the rest of us needed to borrow a bullet from him while in battle, because he would rather have us shot than share. He was reclusive and standoffish during those days. He watched us furtively whenever we came near him, and I remember him scrambling away whenever someone spoke to him.

“Wonder what he's got ta hide?” Josh asked ruminatively. “He acts like he's got sompthin' somebody else might want.”

“I doubt that. He's been the same places we have, and Lord knows we haven't seen much of value.”

“Ain't it kinda strange he didn't try to sneak home lately?”

“Leave him alone, Josh,” I answered sternly. “Can't you see? This war has addled his head. There's nothing we can do to help him but leave him alone.”

We chased after the Yankee detachment that had accosted us near Henryville, while Jackson and Buford pushed others north of Pulaski. The Yankee horsemen on our front numbered about 4,000, but seemed to have lost their determination. We pestered them through Mount Pleasant, and continued until we reached the outskirts of Columbia. When we drew near the town we found ourselves faced with a crack infantry unit, supported by artillery, stretched across the turnpike. There they stayed while the rest of the Yankees filed into Columbia, and there was nothing we could do to dislodge them, since we had gotten ourselves far ahead of our infantry.

We waited impatiently for Hood and the main body to catch up. We knew the longer we had to wait the harder it would be to loosen the Yankee grip on the town. I writhed inside, knowing the danger Clara was in, trapped as she was in a town soon to be assaulted. I also remembered her father in Virginia fighting with Lee, and prayed that if the Yankees learned that information it would not cause her harm.

It had been such a long time since I had seen her. The thought of her so close caused me a great deal of anguish. What if she were hurt, or even killed, during the impending battle?

Josh stayed by my side, and even put up with my childish fits of temper with no comment, an incredible feat of patience for him. One, I might add, that only increased my respect for him, though I would never have admitted it then.

General Hood finally joined us on the morning of the 27th, at which time we were relieved of front line duty. The firing had been slow but regular for two days, and we had lost a few men, who could not be replaced.

We weren't allowed long to rest, but sent out to picket the river. The weather continued cold and wet as we reconnoitered the Duck in search of a safe crossing for our army. That night we lay numb and exhausted about the camp, proud we had managed to keep a few fires going to help ward off the cold. The General made an appearance at our mess fire.

"How's it going, boys?" he asked.

"Well enough, sir, " I answered. "We could be worse, I suppose."

"I guess so! We've seen rougher campaigns, you know. Especially that one to Johnsonville," he replied jovially.

"How 'bout Fort Donelson, 'member? You was jist a colonel then. We ain't never seen cold like we seen then," Josh chuckled.

"That's for sure. But we made it, Josh, although I don't think anyone believed we would. Just like we'll make it through this."

"I shore hope so, Genrul. I don't know what Emma'd do without me."

He slapped Josh on the shoulder. "Hell, nobody could kill off an ornery old cuss like you. Emma doesn't have a thing to worry about!"

"Ya know, that goes both ways, Genrul," Josh cackled in reply. The General laughed heartily as he moved on.

"Son of a bitch," Bradley muttered, venom in his voice, as soon as the General was out of earshot.

Josh leapt to his feet. Despite his limp, he rushed to Bradley, grabbed him by his tattered coat and lifted him into the air.

"I've done had it with you, boy. I ain't gonna repeat myself. Don't you never talk about the Genrul like that where I kin hear ya, or I'll kill ya dead. You understand me?" Bradley nodded his head obediently, fright written across his face. Josh meant every word he had spoken, and Bradley knew it. Josh held him in the air for a few more seconds, then threw him down. He wiped his hands on his trousers as he calmly walked back to his blanket. Bradley glowered at him from across the fire, but said no more.

"Careful, Josh," I said to him while he wrapped himself in his blanket. "Don't get him upset. There's no telling what he's capable of."

"I meant what I said. I ain't afeared a' him. An' I ain't puttin' up with his disrespect. We got enough troubles without havin' ta listen to him badmouth the Genrul. Go ta sleep, boy."

We were awakened early the next morning with news that the Yankee army within the trenches around Columbia had evacuated. They had crossed the Duck River early, before daylight, and had burned the bridges across that troublesome stream.

We were undaunted, for plans had been made the evening before to trap the 23,000-man Yankee army. We rode to the east and forded the river against little opposition from the other side. We were instructed to protect the crossings at any cost so pontoon bridges could be laid down for the infantry. After several hours of skirmishing with disjointed units of Yankee cavalry, we were safely ensconced on the north side.

We continued to protect our position as the pontoon bridges got underway. Meanwhile, the Yankee commander, Schofield, began to realize the danger of his position in town. He started most of his artillery and a portion of his men up the road, headed to Spring Hill.

The General immediately set to work on the rest of the Union cavalry. We hit them both front and flank and forced them north and east. As soon as we had gotten them a reasonable distance away, he left Ross's Texas Brigade to hound them while we turned and pressed to the west, toward Spring Hill.

Hood left two divisions and most of his artillery in Columbia, to keep up a demonstration before the town so that the Yankee commander would not be aware that most of our force had crossed the river. With his other seven divisions Hood headed toward Spring Hill to seize the turnpike and cut off the Yankee retreat.

We hit major resistance a mile or so outside Spring Hill, to the southeast. We met them head on, just as they got dug in. The General had been ordered to hold them at Spring Hill until the rest of our army could catch up. The Yankee column was stretched thinly along the road from Columbia, and afforded us a perfect opportunity for victory.

We rushed their position three times on horseback. Then the General dismounted one brigade and sent it against the Yankees on the left, where their wagon train was lumbering into position behind the line of battle. We fought with vigor, but watched the General's patience grow thin as we waited for the infantry to come up with us.

Hood had his men marching north along the byroads while the Union army marched parallel along the Columbia-Franklin Pike. Hood's troops finally began to filter in about 4 o'clock. We cheered as they came up, confident things would go well for us.

The Yankees had a full division in the field, well supported by artillery, but they also had to protect the whole of their wagon train, a considerable one that had to supply more than 20,000 men. More Yankees were to the south, deployed to prevent an attack on the turnpike while the rest of their troops were still on the outskirts of Columbia, protecting the rest of the blue army from a nonexistent enemy.

The first Confederate division that reached us, headed by Cleburne, deployed to our left. Cleburne and the General led us on horseback, both waving their sabers about their heads. We charged exuberantly, even though our ammunition was much reduced, as the ordnance wagons found it impossible to keep up with us.

We pushed them back, until a battery of at least eight guns, loaded with shrapnel, opened fire on Cleburne's flank. A number of men fell, or ducked into shallows for cover, and we were forced to make an orderly retreat.

Cleburne began to make immediate plans to re-form and attack again, but was prevented by an order from General Cheatham. He was to await further instructions before renewing the assault. Darkness began to fall.

We were withdrawn after the attack to feed and tend to our horses. We wearily set up camp, and most of us fell asleep immediately. There was no food for us that night.

I slept fitfully, my rest frequently interrupted by nightmares. Clara was very much on my mind. I pictured her dead, in the arms of her mother, Eva weeping endlessly in the background. I would wake with a start, only to be bothered by a similar picture when I dropped off to sleep again.

While we slept, confusion reigned. Cheatham's Corps, consisting of three divisions commanded by Cleburne, Bates and Brown, had been stretched along the Columbia-Franklin Pike, with instructions to await the order to attack. This they did impatiently, as they could hear the Yankees moving north along the pike.

Cheatham finally returned to headquarters to learn the reason for the delay, and was told by Hood to wait until morning. Unhappy and dissatisfied, he returned to his men.

General Stewart, commander of another infantry corps, stumbled upon our bivouac sometime during the night and had a brief conference with the General. The contradictory orders they had been given distressed them both, so they rode together to headquarters. There, they discussed the situation with General Hood.

All I know of that meeting is hearsay, but I consider the source reliable. Josh picked up the information while he was hanging around the General's tent the next day, and I have found that he could discover the truth about anything if you gave him enough time. Even though I wasn't present at the gathering that took place between the General, Hood, and the infantry commanders of the Army of Tennessee, I would stake my life on the story Josh told me.

Upon arriving at Hood's headquarters, Stewart was told to let his men rest and not to worry about the contradictory orders floating about. Hood then turned to the General and asked him if he could block the road into Spring Hill and prevent the advance of the enemy. The General replied that his men were without ammunition, which was the truth, and were unable to get any more since all our ordnance was still at Columbia. Hood then turned to the infantry commanders and ordered them to supply us with bullets. Stewart and Cheatham said they had none to spare, but Red Jackson said he had captured some ammunition earlier in the day and would share what he had. The General told Hood "he would do the best he could in the emergency" and returned to camp.

Jackson took Ross's and Armstrong's brigades with him and attacked the enemy wagon train just above Thompson's Station, directly east of Spring Hill. But it was little they could do to halt the stream of thousands of bluecoats heading for Franklin, north of Spring Hill. They destroyed some wagons and managed to block the pike for a few minutes, but the inevitable flow was too much for them and they were forced to withdraw.

So while two entire corps of Confederate infantry slept on their arms, the enemy walked by them, with no one willing to resist except cavalry that had been fighting all day. According to Josh, the language thrown about at Hood's headquarters in the morning was hot enough to burn the ears off a sailor, but the chance had been missed.

Before morning, the full Yankee army had reached Franklin, and as the morning progressed they began to strengthen the old, familiar entrenchments before the town.

The General borrowed more ammunition from Walthall's division of infantry, and we were on the road again before daylight. We moved north, leading the army's advance while throwing out scouts to the east in case there were threats on our flank.

The infantry was grim and quiet that day. Most of them had been posted along the pike the night before and had heard the Yankees moving up the road. Bitterly, they had seen victory march by them, and were under no illusions as to what they would face when they met the enemy anew, safe behind the entrenchments of Franklin.

We moved with the General, directly north on the pike. The road was littered with odds and ends left behind by the Yankees – bent canteens, discarded worn out shoes and clothing, and mainly empty knapsacks. Even though the General kept us at the heels of the Yankee rear guard, we watched these bits of trash carefully, just in case we found something useful.

"I guess them Yanks was in a big hurry. Lookee, I found me a purty good canteen," Josh said with satisfaction as he leaned over in his saddle and tapped me on the shoulder.

"You've already got a canteen. What need do you have for another one?"

"Ya never know when an extra one might come in handy," he replied, nonplussed.

"Well, if you find any food, let me know. The rest of this junk can stay and rot for all I care," I said crossly. "And don't let the General catch you on one of your side trips, or he'll give you hell."

Before we reached Franklin we found a number of Yankees firmly in place near Winstead's Hill. We had a sharp skirmish there as soon as Stewart's infantry caught up, but the Yankees soon gave it up and retreated across the broad, grassy plain and into the entrenchments that fronted the town.

We looked forlornly over at the Yankee position. They were well protected, and I couldn't see a way we could possibly make them give it up. Not only were they fully supplied with artillery, but the only way to reach them was across an empty stretch of ground that had no shelter for an advancing army.

Hood caught up with us about 1 p.m., and went immediately into conference with the General. Forrest did his best to persuade his commander to give him more troops to flank the enemy out of the town, but to no avail.

Still sore about not blocking the Yankees at Spring Hill, Hood was determined to come face to face with them at Franklin, before we had to meet them at the even more impressive fortifications at Nashville. Like most determined men, he was blind to the logic of another man's plan.

The infantry moved up and deployed on the edge of the plain. The General sent Chalmers' division over to the far left to fill the empty space between Cheatham's line of infantry and the river. Buford did the same on the army's right, next to Stewart's corps. Our other division, led by Jackson, was sent north across the river by a ford east of the town, to cut off the enemy's road to Nashville. The General sent Jackson to do what he had wanted to use his entire force for, and would have, but for the refusal of his superior.

The battle started before the cold night air descended. Because we were placed on the flanks of the battle line, we were saved from the brunt of the fight, but the poor men of Cheatham's and Stewart's corps suffered some of their worst casualties of the entire war.

They were sent in a charge against the entrenched Yankees without the benefit of artillery, still on the road from Columbia. They went courageously across the barren plain, hardly wavering when the enemy's cannon carved great holes in their line. They broke an advance line of the enemy and tried to follow them into the works, when suddenly the entire Yankee front exploded in a wall of smoke and fire. Our men fell in front of the breastworks, bloody and crumpled by the hundred, while their comrades snatched up their banners and ammunition and pushed on.

After that first onslaught we had to follow the battle by sound more than sight, as we were busy enough with the Yankees in front of us. For a few minutes the thunder of rifle and cannon fire was the loudest I had ever heard. It was clear, though, that the attack wasn't progressing into the town, and that the enemy was still standing firm.

Across the river we vied with a couple thousand Yankee cavalry until our ammunition ran out, and the General realized there would be no pursuit of a beaten foe to be had. When we re-crossed the Harpeth the true nature of Hood's assault was unveiled.

Curses could be heard among us, violent and sanguine, as we saw the results of the bloody drama to the west of us. The stupidity of the situation disgusted me. I couldn't decide who had the least sense – Hood, who sent his men to be uselessly slaughtered, or the men themselves, who continued to march on despite the death and destruction that awaited them.

Darkness fell suddenly, as it often does in November. Our infantry had reached the enemy's entrenchments and engaged hand-to-hand. The Yankees had counter-charged our penetrations and the battle had stalled along their line of entrenchments. Muzzle flashes burst through the gloom, both sides still trying to kill each from only yards away. Across the field, despite the darkness, survivors of the Confederate charge continued to fire at the Yankee parapets.

The fighting slowed, then petered out near midnight. Schofield, the Yankee commander, stealthily pulled his men out of Franklin and sent them on to Nashville, a fact that wasn't known by Hood until the following morning.

Since we had come through the battle relatively unscathed, we were up and off by daylight the next morning. Before we left, our eyes kept straying over the heaps of dead that lay before the empty parapet. The grisly sight shocked us. With a sense of relief, we moved out, headed north toward Nashville.

"I shore feel sorry fer the fellas that have ta bury all them," Josh said morosely as we rode off.

"I hope that fool Hood has to watch each an' every one of 'em git buried," Fred said grimly.

"Tain't likely. Seems like the fools a' this world never have ta see the sorrows they cause."

While the Army of Tennessee reorganized, the General led us in an attempt to catch the Yankees before they reached the safety of the heavily fortified city of Nashville. He had ordered Morton's guns to be brought up, and they played havoc with the Yankee rear guard. But we weren't able to reach the main army, and by noon of December 1, they were out of our reach, behind the lines around the capital of Tennessee.

The Union commander of Nashville, General George Thomas, had no less than 60,000 men in his command, with more filtering in by the hour. Nashville had been turned into a veritable fortress, more than halfway encircled by the mighty Cumberland River on its north, while Yankee fortifications had been built on the hills that commanded approaches from the south. The Army of Tennessee had been reduced to less than 30,000 men, tired and hungry, their morale sadly chiseled at Franklin.

We camped that afternoon, the state capitol building within our sight. The shining white dome brought tears to my eyes as I gazed upon it, fully aware it was out of our reach. Depression overcame me as I forced myself to accept our defeat.

Without enthusiasm, we watched the infantry come up and camp to the south of us. We were a silent group, each man busy with his own thoughts. Bradley wisely kept his mouth shut. Josh was in no mood to be trifled with.

Forrest spent several moments staring off at the symbol or our state's sovereignty, then shook his head and abruptly went about his duty. He must have been furious at the bumbling efforts of Hood to chase the enemy out of Tennessee, but he did not show it. Briskly and efficiently, he set about doing his duty, with no apparent regrets.

Later, we would be grateful Hood sent us southeast to attack Murfreesboro. We would not have to witness our shameful defeat before the capital of our beloved state.

We left on the afternoon of December 2nd, after the General sent his division under Chalmers to blockade the Cumberland River a few miles west of Nashville. We proceeded at a moderate pace, and destroyed what bridges and blockhouses we came across, taking supplies and prisoners. Bate's division of infantry met us a few miles south of Lavergne and we joined forces.

Murfreesboro had changed considerably since our last visit, not long after David and I had joined up with Forrest. It was now heavily fortified and strongly held by the Yankees.

As soon as we arrived before the town on December 6th, the General took his staff and a handful of us along with him on a reconnaissance of the enemy position. We circled the town slowly and carefully, going in as close to their works as the enemy sharpshooters would allow. The General's staff took notes as he threw tidbits of information over his shoulder, but as far as we could see there wasn't a weak spot anywhere.

The General was calm as he confronted the seemingly hopeless situation before him. He spoke crisply, quickly. We could almost see his brain working on the problem he faced. He had been ordered to attack Murfreesboro, and that is what he aimed to do. But to throw his men needlessly at the formidable obstacle before him was out of the question. Since we were vastly outnumbered, he would simply have to draw the Yankees out.

His luck was still with him. Early the next morning, we spotted a number of Yankees moving out of their fort, with the obvious intention of meeting us on the battlefield. Josh crowed with delight when he saw the Yankees coming.

“We got 'em now, boys! They can't git away from the Genrul!” he cackled.

The Yankee column, over 3,000 strong, moved out and met our infantry, in the center of our position. The General put a division on either side of them, with the intention of flanking them and preventing any attempt to retreat back to the fort. Morton's artillery, along with some of Buford's men, was sent around to the east with instructions to do what damage they could.

Eerily, we moved across the same battlefield that had witnessed the Battle of Stones River, and it was still scattered with mementos of that slaughter. Rusting canteens and other field gear, along with faded, torn pieces of clothing that fluttered drearily in the faint breeze, littered the field. Here and there, I spotted the bleached bones of some poor soul whose body had been thrown into a hastily dug grave, and the sight made me shiver. Two years had passed since Stones River, but I could still hear its echo.

The enemy veered through some woods, and then hit quickly and hard at the center of our position. The infantry held firm for some moments before the left side slowly began to crumble. We could see the General, on King Phillip, ride in among them, alternately cursing and pleading with the men in an attempt to get them to reform their line. He began to wave his saber about, and struck out at the milling mass of bodies with the flat of it. The worthless men that engulfed him simply dodged around him. He grabbed a flag out of the hands of a fleeing color bearer and began to use the sharp end of it on the men outside his saber's reach, but to little avail. Cursing mightily, he finally flung it at the fear-ridden mass.

Abruptly, the Yankees in front of us began to retreat. Quizzically we watched them go a short distance, then we followed them, firing as we went, as close to the fort as we dared. There we heard the firing of Morton's guns as he assaulted the inner works of the town. The artillery fire soon ended. The Yankees had picked off and killed their horses, and the men were forced to withdraw their artillery pieces by hand.

We were all withdrawn to safety, where we rested up for a day or two before we began some foraging. The General sent us far and wide in search of supplies for our hungry numbers, while others destroyed the railroad line that ran from Lavergne to Murfreesboro. Ross's men captured an entire train coming up from the south. The enemy stayed huddled in their fortifications, which suited me just fine. We needed food more than we needed to fight.

Despite the cold, we did our wash in Stones River, and a few brave men even bathed. It had been some time since we had been able to do so. Our horses were given extra fodder, which they sorely needed, and the blacksmiths were kept busy repairing equipment and shoeing horses. In short, we took advantage of our respite to do the things necessary for our continued success.

Hood was still before Nashville, hopelessly waiting for the Yankees to attack him. Bitterly, we discussed his situation. Greatly outnumbered, he faced the growing cold without enough supplies. He refused to retreat, even though his supply line stretched all the way back to the Tennessee River. Yet, he could not go forward because the Cumberland River was heavily patrolled by a fleet of gunboats.

There he sat and waited for reinforcements that would never come. While he wasted time before their fortifications, the Yankees were busy training and preparing for the coming campaign.

A freezing rainstorm interrupted the Yankee plans for a few days, but the weather soon cleared and the enemy marched out of Nashville on December 15. Couriers were sent for us, and we learned of the engagement late that afternoon. Orders were given and we were ready to march the following morning.

But by then, we heard of the terrible defeat of the Army of Tennessee. On the second day of battle, Hood's army had utterly collapsed. Without flinching, Forrest immediately sent word to Buford to move toward Lavergne to protect the rear of our fleeing army.

We moved with 400 prisoners, herds of hogs and cattle, and our own sick and wounded. The weather was bitterly cold and wet, one of the worst winters the state had ever seen. It suited our mood. We knew our defeat before Nashville was a crippling blow. We carried on only because the General expected us to.

We reached the Duck River at Columbia on December 18, and by the next day we were all across it. I looked at the town with dreary, heartsick eyes as we set up camp.

There were thousands of us there, huddled and hungry, but Clara somehow managed to find me. She had already spotted me as I looked up from the campfire and saw her. She hurried toward me with her skirts lifted above the half-frozen mud. I rushed to her and grabbed her to me.

We didn't speak for a moment. I looked into her deep brown eyes, the ones I had remembered so well. She was the same, just like the image I had carried in my mind.

“How, what. . . !” I sputtered.

She laughed happily. “I heard Forrest was here. I just had to find you.”

I dropped my arms and rubbed my dirty hands on my pants. “We can't talk now, Clara. I'll see if I can come see you tonight.”

“But John, I've missed you so,” she pleaded.

"And I you," I whispered fervently. "You don't understand – the Yankees are right behind us. I'll see what I can do, but I can't promise anything." I walked her back toward town, then returned alone.

I waited for what seemed an eternity. After several hours, I saw the General return to his tent. I screwed up my courage and marched boldly to his quarters.

His aides tried to prevent me from seeing him. He was busy, they said, making plans and preparing for a hard march. I loudly demanded to see him, and said it would only take a moment.

"Let him pass, fellas!" the General called loudly from inside his soggy tent.

I took a deep breath and entered. Inside his tent was immaculately clean as always. He sat before a small desk covered with papers. Anderson was there also, seated next to him, a pen in his hand.

The General looked up at me. "What is it, John?" he asked, not without kindness.

"I need your permission to go to town for a few hours, sir," I answered calmly.

"Why are you bothering me with this?"

"Sir, I realize the spot we're in, and I didn't want to put the responsibility of my leaving on someone else."

"Going to see the Brown girl, huh?" I looked at him in surprise. He chuckled and waved his hand at me. "I know all about it. I think we can spare you for two hours."

"Thank you, sir." I rushed out into the freezing night air. I went by the mess fire and told Josh where I was going, then headed off at a fast trot.

My lungs ached from the cold air I gulped on the way to Clara's house. At last I was there, the small sign proclaiming "William Brown, Atty" swinging familiarly at its post. I knocked loudly at the door and it swung open immediately.

Clara reached for my arm and pulled me into the house. Her mother was in the parlor, and she smiled as we entered.

"It's a pleasure to see you again, ma'am," I bowed politely.

"Thank you, John." She rose from the sofa. "I'll leave the two of you alone."

"Sit down by the fire, John. You're cold." Clara sat down on the footstool next to the chair. The firelight lit up her sweet face as she looked at me.

"How long can you stay?"

"The General gave me two hours. Generous of him, considering the position we're in."

"I know. We heard all about the battle." She looked down at her hands, playing with the folds of her dress. "I prayed for you."

I reached down and grabbed her hands. “Clara, you've been in my dreams for so long, it's hard for me to believe I'm here.”

“It's been hard, I know. You look much thinner.” She smiled forlornly. “I wish now you had one of those warm Yankee coats so many of you wore when we first met.”

I looked down at my broken shoes and stockingless feet. “I'm managing. Tell me, what's been happening here?”

She hesitated. “We've had our share of suffering, too. Food has become mighty scarce, what with both armies foraging for it.”

“The Yankees haven't bothered you in any way, have they?”

“No, not directly. They've confiscated everything they could use. And Eva's not been the same since she heard the news about David. Her heart was broken, I guess. She's always been shy. I've never seen her say more than two words to any man, until David.”

“There seems to be something else on your mind.”

She stood up and began to pace about the room. “We've had some news from Virginia. My father is missing in action. My mother is distracted out of her mind.”

"I don't know what to say. I know how much you love him. I'm sorry, Clara."

She ran to me and knelt down beside my chair. "That's why I had to come out and find you today. I had this awful feeling that something had happened to you, too, and I just had to know." Tears trickled down her face and dropped gently onto her mended gown.

I put my arms around her and let her cry. Bitterly, I thought of all the hardships the war had caused and wondered how the wounds would ever heal. "It's all right, Clara. Cry, if it will help you feel any better. But you won't have to worry about me any more. I'll make it through the war. And when I come back, I want you to marry me."

She raised her tear-stained face. "Do you mean it?"

"Yes, I do. I don't see how we can fight much longer. The war is over here in Tennessee, after Nashville. And things are not going any better in Virginia. I'll be surprised if we hold out another six months."

"Then what will we do?"

I sighed deeply. "You and I will be married. The best thing for us to do is to live in Athens, with my father. I know people there, and I think I can find work."

"That sounds fine, John."

Just then her mother rustled into the room. “I've prepared you a little something to eat. Please come on into the kitchen.”

“Ma'am, before I do, I have something important to ask you.”

“Yes, John?”

“Since Clara's father is away, I must ask you. I would like your permission to marry Clara.”

“I see.” She moved to the sofa and sat down. “May I ask what your plans are?”

“Yes, ma'am. As soon as the war is over, I will come back here and we can be married. Clara has agreed to move to Athens with me, where I think my prospects would be better.”

“I'm much relieved. I was afraid you would want to be married immediately. I'm happy to give my permission, if you will wait.”

“Oh, thank you, Mama!” Clara cried. They rushed at each other and hugged while I stood there foolishly and looked on.

I left after gobbling down the warmed-over food Mrs. Brown had prepared for me. Clara and I shared a long kiss on the porch before I left, and I promised to come for her as soon as I was able.

Hood headed south the following morning, after appointing the General and the men under him as permanent rear guard. We had been much reduced in size, thanks to the weather, disease and casualties, and had little more than 3,000 men. The General scraped together another 2,000 infantry from various sources. Many of these had no shoes, and the road ahead, half-frozen mud littered with the remains of a retreating army, would not be easy for them. But I must say it would be hard to find a more earnest group of soldiers. There was hardly a complaint among them, only an honest desire to leave the state with as many men alive as possible.

We had barely gotten out of sight before the Yankees began to shell Columbia from across the swollen Duck River. I watched the shelling in terror, fearful I would lose Clara before she was actually mine. The General watched in trepidation also, and finally called a few of us together and galloped to the edge of the river under a flag of truce. The man in command of the artillery on the opposite shore rode forward and called askance of us.

"What is it, sir?" he called loudly, tersely at the General.

"See here," the General boomed back, his voice well able to be heard above the roaring, rushing water. "I have not stationed any troops in town. You are firing on helpless civilians and the wounded, both yours and ours."

The opposing commander conversed with one of his aides, and then called across to us again and stated the firing would cease. The General inquired if he would agree to an exchange of prisoners, but the Yankee officer declined. Josh cursed at him under his breath, a logical thing since we were burdened with the feeding and care of about 2,000 prisoners taken during the campaign, a nuisance to a retreating army such as ours. We returned, at least satisfied that the shelling had stopped.

We waited for the Yankees to cross over the Duck River and begin the pursuit, but our patience began to wear thin. There is nothing worse than waiting for a catastrophe that takes its time catching up with you. The scouts brought in reports that the Yankees were waiting for their pontoons. For some reason they had been sent to Murfreesboro, and it took a full 48 hours for them to arrive.

The blue horde began to pour across the river the night of the 22nd, and we began to withdraw south to Pulaski. The first day, the Yankees nipped at us and caused us to turn on them several times. But our retreat was orderly, despite the wounded, the prisoners and the livestock we pushed ahead of us.

We were tired, hungry and cold on the 24th, so much so it is hard for me to imagine how we kept going. The Yankee pursuit became more persistent, and we were forced to participate in a constant skirmish until we arrived in Pulaski that night. Our hands, numb and weak from the bitter weather and lack of food, fumbled aimlessly as we tried to prepare our blankets and fires for the night.

The following morning, December 25, 1864, the General had us destroy a large amount of ammunition Hood had left behind, as well as two trains we had captured at Spring Hill and had moved to Pulaski, before we moved out. He ordered the covered bridge across the creek in Pulaski destroyed. A group of civilians watched as we marched south, silent, their eyes showing their bewilderment as we abandoned them for good to the Yankees.

About seven miles south of town, the General laid an ambush along the road to Bainbridge. The hills there were steep and high, and he placed us where we could fire along the entire length of the Yankee column that followed us.

He paced among us, nervously but cheerfully, and offered a cool sort of encouragement. "We'll give them a little something to write home about, boys. Just stay where you are until I give the signal."

We stomped our feet and rubbed our hands together as we waited. While we moved, we could almost forget about the freezing rain that drizzled down on us, but there, waiting for the General's signal, we became all too aware of the pellets of water and ice that turned our bodies numb. As we saw the Yankees approach, we reached for our rifles and pistols, silent, but ready to do our duty.

Suddenly, the General rode forward, tall and straight, his saber in hand. He began to yell at us in excitement, “Charge! Charge!” Without hesitation we moved forward, infused by the General's enthusiasm.

They fell back under our pressure, but before we could make it a complete rout they were reinforced. They flanked us and we were forced back.

Josh was hit during the Yankee counter-charge. An enemy bullet took off the little finger of his left hand. As we moved to the rear, I bandaged it with the remnants of a torn, dirty kerchief I had in my pocket. It still bled profusely, however, and I tried to insist he go to the doctors and get it bandaged.

“Naw,” he replied hoarsely. “Not right now, anyways. We gotta get outta here first.”

As it grew dark and we put some distance between ourselves and the Yankees, Josh agreed to see the doctor. We found the wounded more by smell than anything else in the pitch blackness that surrounded us. With the help of a small lantern, a medico deftly bandaged Josh up, and agreed the wound was a lucky one. At least it was clean, and the freezing weather would prevent any infection from growing. We returned to our places at the back of the column, thankful to be out of earshot of the groaning, dying men being carried south by the wagonload.

I had some hardtack I had been saving, hardly more than a crumb, that I gave to Josh. At first, he refused, but I insisted he have it.

"You've lost a great deal of blood. You have to keep up your strength."

"All right. Jest don't gotta git riled up," he said quietly.

We got word next day that the remnant of the army that marched ahead of us had reached Bainbridge and had begun to cross the Tennessee River. The news brought us a certain amount of satisfaction. If our luck held, perhaps we would be able to cross also, and find the rest, warmth and food we so desperately needed. The Yankees were still hammering at our heels, but at last we had something to look forward to.

Forrest again turned us at Sugar Creek, in what we hoped would be the last fight we would have to endure before reaching safety. We had the ordnance train to protect, left behind while its mules were used to pull the pontoons to the river. A thick fog had settled about us, which lent a nightmarish quality to the scene.

Still in control despite our position, the General hid us in the fog. A few men were set up in front as decoys to draw the Yankees to us. Still able to tote a rifle, Josh lay next to me as we calmly waited for the signal to fire. When the order was given, we all rose and fired at the Yankees simultaneously.

Caught unawares, the enemy turned and ran, their dead and dying left where they fell. We whooped aloud with joy, and ran forward to capture the horses and men left behind. Even those of us without shoes, their feet torn and bloody, joined in the fun before we were called together and ordered to continue the retreat.

It wasn't until we were well on the way again that I noticed Bradley was missing. I asked Josh about him. He looked at me without flinching.

"He fell back there. Got it right through the chest. Never knew what hit him."

I nodded. I wasn't shocked. It was the only fitting end for Bradley. The war had eaten him up like a cancer. If it had continued, his life would have been lived in torment. He would have been a man grown bitter and withdrawn, unable to live a normal life. I didn't mourn his passing. I only felt a certain amount of regret that life had proved too tough for him.

I heard Josh cackling. He was rummaging through a Yankee saddlebag he had found. "Lookee! Real coffee! Boy, are we gonna have a real feast whenever we git the chance!"

"Remember, Josh, we share and share alike . . ."

CHAPTER SEVENTEEN

It was a sorry lot of men who made it across the raging Tennessee River. Half-frozen and starving (we had plenty of cattle and hogs with us, but no time to butcher and cook them) we huddled before the blazing fires we found waiting for us and drew sighs of relief. Our ordeal was over. Once again, notes of cheerfulness could be heard as the first rations we had seen for days were passed out. The pressure of the campaign was off, and we could finally admit to ourselves how great the odds had been against us.

The main army moved off south to Tupelo while the General took us back to Corinth. Even there, the weather was unseasonably cold, and what clothing we possessed was in tatters. We were woefully short of men, horses, guns – everything we needed to carry on our share of the war.

What was left of the Army of Tennessee, a mere remnant, soon left Tupelo for the Carolinas to defend against Sherman. At Corinth, we were the only force of any sizable strength left to defend the western portion of the country. There were dozens of armed and dangerous bands of men roaming the countryside, the population helpless against their outrages. They called themselves cavalry, but had no allegiance to our government. They were, quite simply, thieves and sometimes murderers, and they only added to our overwhelming job of keeping the Yankees out.

We had changed. Those hard, bitter miles south of Nashville had drained something out of us. The hope we had clung to through the hard, weary months had slowly left us. Our eventual defeat loomed ahead, not far down the road. We accepted our circumstances, however, and even began to yearn for the end.

On January 1, 1865, the General issued orders for furloughs for all the men who could reach home. They were told to clothe themselves while there, and if possible, bring back any men or horses they could find.

I helped Josh with his gear and told him to give my regards to his family. I had decided to stay. The

Yankees were swarming all over Tennessee, and now that I had Clara's promise of marriage, I didn't want to risk going home.

The lucky ones who were leaving hustled and bustled about camp in high excitement. Their weariness disappeared as they rode out in different directions, through a snowstorm that surpassed anything we had ever seen.

Those of us who stayed were kept busy with scout and picket duty, but we still found time to get the rest we so desperately needed. We yearned for home, too, and jealously discussed what comforts our comrades were enjoying. At least our food supply was greater than it had been in months, since we had fewer mouths to feed,

The General's wife was there, and her cheerfulness and concern for our welfare helped to ease our pain in having to remain behind while others enjoyed their furloughs. We enjoyed the preachers she encouraged to come worship with us, and we found time for Bible study, something we sorely needed after the ordeals we had recently been through.

By the middle of the month, the men began to filter back to us, better clothed and with a few recruits in tow. We welcomed them back. The war was still with us, and we were ready to get back to it, even though we knew it was a losing proposition.

Josh had made it back, with a new pair of trousers and socks. He still wore the ragged coat and half-broken shoes he had left with, but had managed to exchange his horse for a newer, fresher one. I was happy to see my old friend's face at the mess fire again.

Forrest was promoted to Lieutenant General and given command of all cavalry in the west, as well as the Districts of Mississippi and East Louisiana. He immediately ordered all roving bands of illegal cavalry to be rounded up, and either returned to regular service or run out. He believed that "kindness to a bad soldier does great injustice to those who are faithful and true." He sent his brother Jesse, absent since the wound he had received at Athens but since recovered, into northern Mississippi to arrest and bring back what men he could find.

We had altogether less than 10,000 men, charged with covering the better part of four states, an impossibly large territory. Rumors reached us of a fine Yankee force, headed by General Wilson, confirmed by our scouts. Camped in northern Alabama, it was composed of over 20,000 well-fed, well-equipped men on fine, plump horses. We tried to shrug off the news with reminiscences of our past escapades, when we had evened out odds just as great, but our bragging had a hollow ring to it. We were in better shape then, with finer mounts and decent equipment and food, with men still in their prime. Young boys and half-crippled older fellows filled our ranks in those last days, and we were no match for an army of over twice our number.

Forrest remained cheerful and optimistic right up to the end. As we began the long, slow process of moving south toward Selma in order to protect the vital ironworks and arsenal there, he encouraged us in every way possible, and his calm, reassuring voice brought us the only reassurance we had in those days.

The General had issued orders against horse racing, which would wear out what few animals we had left, and target shooting, which wasted ammunition, but some of the men couldn't resist the temptation. A horse race was scheduled and the track laid out near the General's own headquarters. Bets were heavy as rival companies supported their own animals and catcalled their dislike of each other in the bargain.

Quiet descended on the proceedings when the General stepped out to watch. It became apparent he had no intention of stopping the fun, and even placed a bet on his favorite horse. He smiled as he watched, and graciously accepted his scant winnings when the horse he had chosen won.

But as the ringleaders of the day's entertainment made their way back to their camps, they were arrested by the provost guard. Even the General's son Willie paid his punishment by carrying rails on fatigue duty. Josh and I had a good laugh, since we had not been among those who planned the race.

"By dingy, the Genrul's gotta be the smartest man north a' Mobile," Josh chuckled. "Had a real fine time watchin' the race an' let them fellers think they wuz gettin' away with sumpthin', but he got 'em in the end. Maybe they'll learn better'n try ta pull sumpthin' over on him."

By now Mobile was besieged, and the powerful Yankee force in northern Alabama was on the move. The General ordered Chalmers to head for Selma and Jackson's command in Mississippi to ride east. The escort followed behind them on March 27, 1865.

Spring had touched the air and warmed our long ride. We joked and laughed along the way and pretended the old days were back. But to look at us, it would be hard to imagine that at one time we were the finest fighting unit in the war. Why, we could bring to their knees any unit three times our size, then ride fifty miles in any kind of weather and be none the worse for wear.

But by March 1865 we were bone-weary and without much hope. Despite his bravado, the war had done its share of damage to the General, too. He was terribly thin and his hair considerably more gray. His back was still straight in the saddle, but his shoulders had begun to stoop from the responsibility that rode upon them.

And we had changed, too. We had no decent clothing to speak of, and Fred's flabby skin, once firm and well fed, was a testament to the sorry state of our quartermaster's department. Our horses limped along, their equipment patched with odds and ends, their ribs plainly showing. Poor old Goldie. I was afraid he would never make it home.

Our fighting spirit was also about gone. There was no good news about the war. The only thing that kept us going was our devotion to the General, and we all knew it. Without him, we might have joined the thousands of deserters that had overrun the countryside.

We were well into Alabama when we heard the sounds of battle. A band of militia was trying to make a stand against a brigade of Wilson's cavalry. The General cheerfully charged us to keep up with him as accompanied only by the escort he rode ahead and flew into the enemy.

He provided the impetus as we broke the enemy column in two, then drove each segment off in opposite directions. Without losing a moment, the General learned from the wounded and prisoners that the home guards had been engaged in running battle most of the day. We camped that night, somewhere below Randolph.

Our situation was dark, but the General had not given up. We would attempt to slow the Yankee advance while the rest of our men caught up with us. He sent messages to General Jackson, somewhere near Tuscaloosa, and Chalmers, delayed by the weather but still on his way to Selma.

Our luck had changed. His messages fell into enemy hands. The Yankees increased their pressure and we were forced to turn and face them at Ebenezer Church, six miles from Plantersville.

We didn't have a chance. Including Roddey's men, there were about 1,500 of us, faced with 9,000 Yankees armed with the latest repeating rifles. We fought in desperation and with rage. We had never faced such steep odds before. The General had always seen to that.

We fought alongside General Forrest that day, proud to be with him. Lieutenant Boone led us and we were joined by Captain Tyler and his two companies from Kentucky. We used our pistols at close range at the horde of bluecoats that surrounded us, but what damage we inflicted was swiftly swept away. Boone went down, so seriously wounded we doubted he would make it. In a hand-to-hand duel the General received several saber cuts on his arm before he could kill his Yankee assailant, and his horse was covered with his blood. Retreat was sounded. We rode away from the battlefield as fast as we could.

The Yankees dogged our trail the rest of the day. They picked off more of our men, ones we couldn't spare after our terrible losses at Ebenezer Church. We rested only briefly that night and rode into Selma about midmorning, led by our blood-spattered General.

The town was in an uproar. The civilian population ran about, gathering possessions together for the evacuation of the town. Enemy prisoners had been sent away, as well as the piles of stores owned by the government. There was a train waiting at the depot, ready to head west, and steamers were tied up to the dock on the Alabama River.

Children, dogs and chickens brought pandemonium to the streets, while a few old men and ladies looked at us balefully from the sidewalks. The news of defeats around Mobile and Richmond had just reached them, and they were none too pleased with us.

Without a moment's pause, we fell into the miles of entrenchments that rimmed the town. Armstrong's brigade was there to meet us, but the rest of Chalmers' men were still absent. Jackson's division was held up at the Cahaba River. At Selma, along with a few militia and some of the townsfolk, we had altogether not much more than 3,000 men. Many of them were without guns or ammunition, and most of us hadn't had a respectable meal in days, but the General had ordered us to protect the town, and that is what we would do.

The General had us, the escort, posted behind the center of our position, manned by the militia, to help bolster our weakest point. When the Yankees began their charge shortly before dark, Josh turned to me and said, “Here it is, John.”

Despite our attempt to hold the town, our efforts were useless. The militia crumbled under the heavy onslaught and were pushed back into town. We were caught in the middle of a fleeing mass, but stood firm, huddled together for greater protection.

As the darkness grew, we fumbled and fought our way to the train depot. Desperately, we tried to hold onto it, but the superior numbers and the repeating rifles of the enemy were too much for us. In the darkness we abandoned it. A group of us, including the General, fought our way to the Burnsville Road. We made our escape, while small pockets of firing could be heard continuing in the town.

There were but a few hundred of us. As we fled, my heart pounding, I began to see the hopelessness of our situation. We had little left. Most of our fighting men were but old men and young boys. I knew, then, finally, that our fight could not continue much longer.

After we left Selma we came across some Yankee stragglers and outlying detachments, who were unlucky to catch us in the mood we were then in. We found ourselves in a couple of minor skirmishes, but managed to find our way to Plantersville, then on to Marion, Alabama. There, we met up with Chalmers, Jackson's Division and all of our artillery. We stayed in Marion for about 10 days.

We soon learned that the Yankee commander had left Selma and turned to the east, heading to Montgomery and beyond. They were no longer pursuing us.

On April 15, the General established his headquarters at Gainesville, Alabama. Soon after, rumors began circulating that Robert E. Lee had surrendered in Virginia. Our hearts dropped. Depressed, we as a whole decided to stay loyal, for the General's sake if for nothing else. On the 25th, Forrest addressed us. He could not confirm the news of the surrender, and asked us to stand firm. But five days later he was informed that General Taylor had surrendered to Yankee commander General Canby, and finally, on the 6th of May, Lee's surrender was verified. The war was over.

A proud number of our fellow soldiers refused to accept it. They wanted to keep on fighting, but the General would not allow it. He insisted we must accept our defeat with grace and dignity. We had done our duty, and no man could be expected to give anything more.

On May 9, 1865, Forrest surrendered. His farewell address was moving and included these words:

> I have never, on the field of battle, sent you where I was unwilling to go myself; nor would I now advise you to a course which I felt myself unwilling to pursue. You have been good soldiers, you can be good citizens. Obey the laws, preserve your honor, and the Government to which you have surrendered can afford to be, and will be, magnanimous.

As for Josh and myself, we had formed a deep bond, one I am now proud of, and one that can only be forged in the heat of battle. But for now, we were headed home. Back to our families. And back to Clara.

The End

POSTSCRIPT

I found this journal while going through my grandfather's chest, one in which he stored his mementos from his days fighting under General Nathan Bedford Forrest during the War Between the States. He passed away on August 1, 1903, but we didn't have the heart to go through all his private papers until some years later. I believe he had every intention of publishing it, but for some unknown reason, never did.

As the decades roll along, and the generation of our people who struggled through those war years begin to pass on, memories fade, and I'm unwilling to see the sacrifices made by my grandfather and his comrades forgotten. In an effort to keep their memories alive, I have decided to print his journal for the benefit of the generations to come.

I have fond memories of him and my grandmother, Clara. She was a fine woman, quite pretty even in her advanced years, with soft brown eyes and a pleasing, plump figure. She was a fine cook and seamstress, and always had a kind word for all of her grandchildren. She passed on also, a year after my grandfather.

He was not a big man, being on the thin side, and had gotten slightly stooped as the years passed. He had a fine shock of white hair and beard, and bright blue, piercing eyes that could dance with delight while watching us play and cavort whenever we visited him. He had a military bearing, and was very neat in his habits, I suppose because of his time in the service.

When my grandparents married and started their family at war's end, times were very hard, as they were for all Confederate veterans. As soon as they settled in Athens, his father, a doctor, passed away. He had always encouraged my grandfather to follow in his footsteps, but after the carnage and blood he witnessed while at war, he had no stomach for it. He started his work life at the First State Bank as a clerk here in Athens, a position he gained from Franklin Knox, the father of his childhood friend, David. But it wasn't to his liking. Being confined to four walls after spending years on horseback was too much for him. He determined to use the skills he had learned while out in the field, and began a business repairing harnesses, bridles and saddles. He started the business in his barn, and made a good go of it, despite the lack of leather in those first few years after the war.

After a time, he was able to find a storefront in town and was able to make a decent living providing nicely for his family.

His most trusted employee was Matthew, the young colored boy he found on the wayside as he made his way home after being wounded at Chickamauga. Right after the war, my grandfather saw to it that Matt attended the Freedman's Bureau school in Athens and learned to read, write and do his sums. Matt became a fine workman in leather, and the saddles he made became quite popular in our county. Whenever grandfather was out and about, Matt was left in charge of the shop, and any person who did not feel comfortable dealing with a colored man was welcome to take his business somewhere else.

My grandparents raised three children to adulthood – Nathan (my father), Joshua and Martha. They in turn blessed him with 10 grandchildren.

Grandfather taught me and my siblings and cousins how to ride and to shoot. He would often take us out into the country, along the roads, paths and trails he had ridden himself as a young man. He often spoke of David, his childhood friend who died at Chickamauga, and as we rode captivated us with stories of his days in the saddle, chasing Yankee soldiers and winning victories with General Forrest.

I remember the time I met his old comrade, Josh. He had made his way from Fayetteville to visit. He was quite a character, even then. To a young boy, the most impressive thing about him was his left hand, missing the last digit. He has also passed on now.

I still ride the trails shown me by my grandfather. On a cool, misty morning, if I turn my head just right, I can almost hear the jangle of harnesses and bridles, and the sound of pounding hoofbeats.

Nathan Barrett
January, 1908

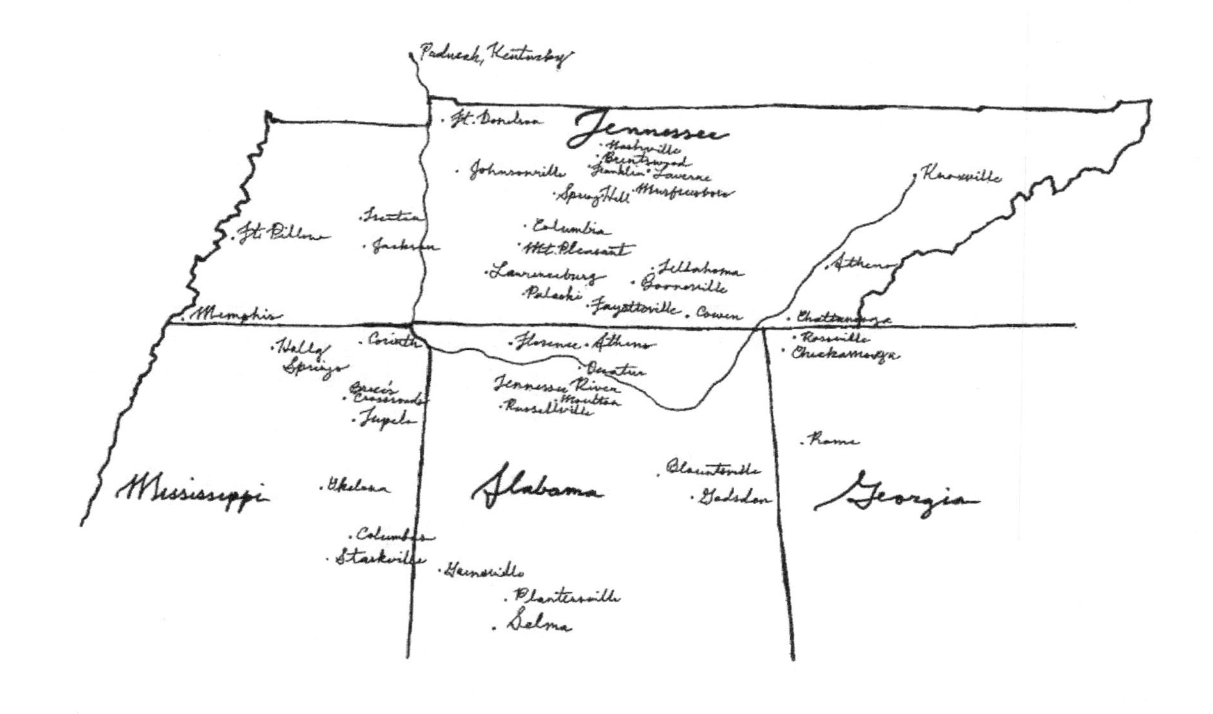
Paducah, Kentucky
Ft. Donelson
Tennessee
Nashville
Brentwood
Franklin
Lavergne
Murfreesboro
Johnsonville
Spring Hill
Knoxville
Ft. Pillow
Jackson
Columbia
Mt. Pleasant
Athens
Lawrenceburg
Tullahoma
Pulaski
Fayetteville
Cowan
Memphis
Chattanooga
Corinth
Florence
Athens
Rossville
Holly Springs
Chickamauga
Decatur
Brice's Crossroads
Tennessee River
Moulton
Russellville
Tupelo
Rome
Blountsville
Mississippi
Okolona
Alabama
Gadsden
Georgia
Columbus
Starkville
Gainesville
Plantersville
Selma